Binding Dante Lovelace

JENNIFER RAINEY

CONTENTS

JENNIFER RAINEY

Binding Dante Lovelace

I.

All of Marlowe, Massachusetts gathered to watch the Hubbins house burn down.

Not all fires are the same. Some are mischievous little brats leaping from branches and parapets. A fire that claims lives has a rich darkness about it. It reaches with long arms to strangle and take anyone who stands in its way. Even the flame dancing upon a candle wick has its own personality, coy as it tempts Man to bless it with the opportunity to grow.

Dante Lovelace knew all about fire.

The Hubbins house blazed, its windows like jack o' lantern eyes in the night. A party guest or two—very important people, to be sure—had perished, and

Frederick Hubbins sputtered through his great beard that it must have been the staff's fault. Alice Hubbins blubbered at her husband's side. Firemen fought. Neighbors gathered to watch and shake their heads and mutter amongst themselves, and had someone possessed the entrepreneurial insight, he would have made quite a profit selling sacks of peanuts.

To the people of Marlowe, a fire maintained a middling rank on the long list of catastrophes over which they were happy to speculate and chatter. Freak accidents were more entertaining, and shipwrecks—well, nautical themes were all the rage that autumn. But a fire was still *something*, and it would give them a reason to pray in church on Sunday.

The flames that raced up the curtains and melted the portraits and claimed two lives were not of the human world. The party had been some frivolous soirée with no purpose other than to put the wealth of the Hubbins family on display, but Hell decreed their house should burn, and Hell decreed that only a catastrophe artist such as Dante Lovelace could set that fire.

Why the Hubbins family? Hell would say, "Why not the Hubbins family? And don't be cheeky. You might be next."

Dante watched from afar. Fire may have seemed the obvious choice for a demon looking to wreak havoc, but it wasn't as simple as tossing a match. All the same, fires were easier to orchestrate than railroad disasters, and they weren't as soggy as shipwrecks (a case in which proper footwear was paramount). And every tragedy, he believed, had about it a unique sadness…

Sadness in which, for his own sake, Dante could not afford to wallow. This was only business, after all, he reassured himself. To indulge sadness meant ruination. Triumph was in the numbers, the newspaper stories, the soul-rotting behavior to come. Tragedy makes a man weak. Weakness makes a man sin. This was Hell's logic, and it suited them just fine.

Amid the crackling roar of the fire and the lamentations of the crowd, Dante heard a quiet *mew*. He turned to the tree to his right and saw a pair of gleaming green eyes and a small pink mouth. He frowned and approached the cat, nestled in the crook of the tree's lowest branch. Her fur was soft, but her eyes were frightened. Could this have been her home?

Dante sighed. He scratched beneath the cat's chin. "I'm sorry," he said, and he meant it.

"A terrible tragedy."

A woman sidled next to him. Dante had drifted unseen around the party, observing the guests before setting the fire, but this red-headed, ruddy young woman was not one he recognized. She wore a modest navy-blue walking dress, not the sort of attire Alice Hubbins would have tolerated at the party. Another nosy neighbor perhaps. Marlowe was full of them.

"Yes," Dante answered. "However, I've always held that God has a reason for everything."

"No. I don't believe that," she said darkly.

Neither did he, but it was just the sort of thing a human would say, he thought. Dante caught the woman's murky green eyes. "And what makes you so rebellious against our Lord?" His skin itched even when he uttered such blasphemy in jest.

She laughed melodically and extended her hand. "Beatrice Dickens."

"Benedick Hurley," he answered as he took her hand.

She didn't believe him, and it showed in her half smile.

Dante attempted to dip into her thoughts, but her mind was a treacherous swamp crafted with the intention of keeping out creatures such as Dante Lovelace. Despite her rosy complexion and sweet smile, there was something dark about this woman. She smelled of fire herself, a distinctly different scent than the Hubbins flames. There were dozens of freckles like ash upon the apples of her cheeks.

"Wait. Beatrice Dickens. You're a spiritualist, correct?" Dante asked. "And a fortune teller?"

"I am."

Lucifer Below, Dante cursed internally. *A witch*. At the very least, Beatrice Dickens was using magic to keep her thoughts under lock and key. She may not have completely given herself over to witchcraft, but in Dante's experience, a little witchcraft went a very, *very* long way.

"I'm quite a skilled… *spiritualist*, if I do say so, and I know that events such as these are not part of some greater plan. Not God's, anyway." She gave a respectful nod before walking away. "Good evening, Mr. Hurley."

The fire progressed nicely. This was another tragedy, small in the eyes of the world, which Dante could add to a long list of masterpieces. Somewhere, just beneath his heart, he felt Hell's tense knot loosen.

Dante bitterly called that knot his melancholia, and the nuisance was satisfied for the evening.

He turned back to consult with his feline friend again, but she was gone. Dante left the Hubbins family to the miserable plight he had caused in the name of Hell and headed toward home.

Marlowe was a lonely city these days. Perhaps it always had been. He missed sharing the gloomy place with Iago Wick. For nearly two years now, Dante had been the only demon in Marlowe. A catastrophe artist such as himself was quite adept at causing everything from mischief to soul-rotting tragedy, but it wasn't enough to satisfy him. A trip to Boston was in order, he thought, and he smiled.

The earliest signs of autumn were creeping in, teasing about what was to come. The world would die again when winter came, Dante thought, but what a long and beautiful death preceded the cold.

"Such melodrama, my dear. You sound like a poet," Iago would say.

Dante supposed that every catastrophe he caused in the name of Hell was something like poetry. Tragic poetry, but poetry, nonetheless. And indeed, Dante looked like a poet, due to a passionate affinity for black clothing. He recalled once—in the name of some party he was to attend—donning a bright green necktie in experimentation.

He shivered violently at the recollection.

Iago had, unsurprisingly, loved the change in wardrobe. *"It adds just enough color! You look lovely. Lovely Mr. Lovelace."*

Dante's home at 13 Darke Street had the sort of address more superstitious humans avoided. He frequently witnessed the postman dart unnecessarily across the street.

If only the poor devil could see the interior.

The home had a sweet, dusty perfume about it—a dead flower scent which Dante found incredibly charming. A bit funerary, perhaps... but charming, nevertheless. He opened the front door to be greeted by glassy-eyed taxidermy, post-mortem photography, and decorations of bone. It was as cozy as a sepulcher on a winter's day.

Dante settled at the writing desk in his parlor as soon as he removed his coat. In an old cigar box on the corner of the desk, he kept a stack of letters between himself and Iago Wick. Dante's letters were short, sweet, and utterly romantic. Iago's letters were pages and pages long, for Iago Wick so loved words. Admittedly, those words occasionally tended toward the bawdy. *Those* letters were kept in a different box upstairs, in Dante's bedroom. A fresh, blank page stretched before him now, a prescription for his solitude.

In another box was a messy collection of newspaper clippings chronicling Dante's recent successes, including a small shipwreck, a collapsed roof, and another fire. There was a time when he would have promptly added them to the black albums on the bookshelf across the room. He was falling behind. The enthusiasm Hell expected was becoming more and more difficult to foster. The false pride and boasting used to come so easily.

He preferred candlelight when writing. Electric and gas lamps just didn't have that same sense of romance. Across the room and over his shoulder loomed Montgomery, a spectacular stuffed vulture with talons outstretched. He was little more than menacing at this point, but he menaced wonderfully for something so utterly dead.

A strange sound reached Dante's ears. It was not unlike the scratching of the pen against paper, but when Dante stopped writing, it continued. A mouse, perhaps? He sought the source and determined that the sound was coming from the front door. It was persistent, like claws against the wood.

Dante was not in the habit of opening the door to just any stranger in the night (strangers are quite a bit stranger when one is a demon), but the curious nature of the noise forced him to investigate.

Upon his doorstep, he found the same black cat he had encountered at the Hubbins home. Dante arched a brow. "Hello. Did you follow me, dear?" he asked, and stooped to scratch behind her soft ears. Her pink mouth was closed awkwardly around something craggy and bony.

She did not greet him in return, as cats are not usually so inclined. Instead, she placed the object at his feet.

Dante picked up the strange gift. "Did you bring me a present?" he asked, but she promptly scurried into the night. It was a pointy and strange thing: the talon of some great bird—not unlike Montgomery. It clutched a glass orb containing a single black hair.

His hair?

His mouth dropped open, and he realized with gut-wrenching certainty that this cat did not belong to the Hubbins family after all. "Oh, no."

The words had barely left his lips when a frigid wind whipped the door shut. He stumbled to the center of the foyer. At once, the candles and the fire went out in the parlor, and Dante's skin prickled with numbing, miserable cold. It seeped from every dark corner of the house. He hurried back to the parlor but stopped in his tracks.

The fireplace flared suddenly, illuminating the parlor in a blossom of light.

Dante was not alone.

On the settee was a man-shaped being with leathery skin pulled tight over its skeleton. It had dark, empty eyes that swallowed the rest of its face, and smooth, gray skin stretched over the space where a mouth should be. It was ghastly in the firelight.

As foul a creature as it was, Dante couldn't forget his manners. "Good evening," he greeted warily. He sidestepped toward the fireplace. His visitor's hollow gaze followed him. "I apologize. I was not expecting company tonight. A drink, perhaps?"

The emaciated creature cocked its head to one side.

It stood, bones creaking like ancient tree branches. It was a head taller than Dante, and it turned the room to ice.

"No?" Dante asked. "I have a very nice scotch—"

The creature took a massive step forward, and Dante reached for one of the iron pokers by the fireplace. He held it at arm's length, and the monster shrank away.

"I suppose I can't really expect you to answer, can I? Or drink, for that matter." Dante crept to the doorway. The creature stood back, rocking on the balls of its feet. "Iron," he added. "Not a spirit's favorite, I know."

This spirit was a skeletal, to be exact. They were quite repugnant, repelled by cold iron, and sported a rather unpleasant odor. This one smelled like mud and earthworms with just a slight hint of manure for character.

"You wouldn't be here if someone weren't looking for me," Dante said uneasily, and backed into the foyer. "You're here to retrieve me for someone. Was it Miss Dickens, the witch?"

The creature flexed its wrists and shoulders, bones cracking loudly in something like affirmation. Dante swallowed, and movement to his left caught his eye. Ah, not one skeletal, but two had come to call. The second leaned against the front door, head twisting as it examined him.

Dante swung the poker wide and watched the creatures tense. It wouldn't do to sit all night with a poker at the ready, but he struggled to conjure another option.

Behind the first skeletal came the rustle of more movement. A third—the tallest and most substantial, by far—crept from the shadows.

Dante was forced to admit to himself that he was miserably outnumbered.

With one final swipe of the poker, Dante turned and sprinted up the stairs. He hurried past a murder of taxidermic crows perched outside his bedroom door. The skeletals charged swiftly after him, their joints clicking and cracking and their long toenails rapping against the floorboards.

Dante ducked into his bedroom, throwing the door shut behind him and pressing his back to the wall. He steadied his breathing and tightened his grip on the poker as he raised it high.

If he could escape the house, then there was a possibility he could lose the skeletals, at least for a while. There wasn't a single place to which he could escape other than Boston, but he feared the foul things might even accompany him on the train. A train car was hardly the place for some supernatural confrontation, and besides, what good would it do to bring a band of repulsive spirits to Iago's door? Still, it wouldn't do him any good to stay at home with the monsters.

The skeletals clicked in tandem just outside the room, and Dante prepared to swing. As though the door were mere gauze, one of the creatures pressed through the wood, seeping into the room like fog.

Dante had always favored aesthetics over athletics, but he took a valiant swing at the creature. It shriveled and stumbled backward through the door again.

It was now or never. Dante rushed to throw open

the window. He felt a blast of cold air and met another empty gaze just below. A fourth skeletal climbed the side of his home and gripped the window sill with bony claws. Some low and inhuman growl came from inside it, rattling in its chest. In shock, Dante let the poker tumble to the ground with a resonant clatter. He spun around.

With a chilling series of cracks, one of the spirits reached its hand into Dante's chest. Penetrating flesh, bone, and muscle, it took his black heart in its grasp. Dante gasped for air and felt his heart throb wildly in its grip before darkness overtook him.

II.

Dante rolled over in bed and buried his face in pillows. With an agonized groan, he reached to his bedside table. A small bottle of restorative hemlock oil was in the top drawer, perfect for mornings such as these.

He limply swatted at the air and endeavored to crack open an eye. He craned his neck to look. There was no drawer. In fact, there was no table. The bedsheets were rough, unfamiliar.

This was not his bed.

Dante forced both eyes open. He was in a dimly lit bedroom, which was not his own, in a bed, which was not his own, in clothes, which were his own but had been decidedly disheveled.

The skeletals, he remembered as he managed to sit. Everything ached, and he slowly unbuttoned his shirt. A dark and unfriendly bruise stained his pale skin. It took quite a lot to bruise a minion of Lucifer, but the grip of one of those terrible spirits was enough.

He righted his shirt. The modest and pleasantly decorated bedroom possessed a light perfume both earthy and floral, like flowers upon a fresh grave. The lights were low, and until he could beat back this headache, Dante was thankful for that.

"Oh, good. You're awake. I was beginning to worry about you."

At the doorway stood Beatrice Dickens in her same neat blue dress, her green eyes sparkling.

"You're a witch," Dante said bitterly.

"And you're a demon. There's no reason to vilify. We are what we are, are we not?" she said bluntly. She walked to a small table and retrieved a teapot. "Your insides must be in knots. The skeletals are horrible things. I don't enjoy using them, but I wouldn't have been able to hold you still on my own."

"Hold me still?" Dante asked. He swallowed back nausea. "For what? What do you require of me?"

Beatrice came to his bedside with a warm, sweet smile and a cup of tea. "I don't think there is a way to tell you this delicately, Mr. Lovelace."

"You know my name?" he asked, cautiously taking the cup. Nothing good ever came from taking strange potions from witches. For all he knew, this was his one-way ticket to becoming a frog.

"Of course. Dante Lovelace," she said. "Drink, please. I know you're in pain."

"Are you trying to poison me?"

"If I wanted to poison you, I could have done it ten times already in ten unique ways. *Drink*. It will soothe your insides."

Carefully, Dante took a sip of the liberally-spiced concoction.

His body instantly calmed. His head was soothed, his stomach settled, and a discreet peek revealed that the bruise on his chest had even disappeared. He wasn't certain what witch's brew this was, but he rather wished he could have bottled it and taken it home.

She continued, "I've been watching you."

As she sat beside him, she reached into her pocket to retrieve a cigarette case. Beatrice placed a cigarette to her lips, then looked in annoyance at a blue glass lighter that had the audacity to be sitting out of reach at the vanity. Dante cleared his throat and snapped his fingers. A flame appeared at the tip of his thumb. "Oh!" she said. "Why, thank you. Much easier than levitating the lighter to draw it near. Very nice, indeed." She drew smoke deep into her lungs.

She possessed a rustic beauty, as though her prim walking dress were a mere costume. This was a woman of dry leaves and red clay, young and ancient at once, the kind of woman who conjured skeletals to do her bidding whether she liked them or not.

"You are the only demon I've found in Marlowe," she said through a smoky haze.

Dante asked, "Are you in the market?" She nodded. "Well, I regret to inform you I am not in the practice of offering my services to anyone. Hell demands enough as it is—fires, shipwrecks, various unpleasantries. There's a lot of work out there for a demon."

She clicked her tongue. "Ah. You see, unfortunately, you have no choice in the matter. I'm afraid I may have performed a bit of magic while you slept. My intent was not only to bring you here, but then, to *keep* you here."

Realization dawned on Dante like a lightning bolt crashing into his skull. If what he feared was true, a little electrocution might have been a far better fate.

"Oh, no," Dante murmured. "I think I might need more of that tea."

"I apologize," she said earnestly, "but I have no choice. After all, you are the only demon in Marlowe."

"No! You... you've placed a binding spell on me!"

"Indeed."

"Why? To what end?" Dante asked breathlessly.

"I need your assistance," Beatrice explained as she leaned comfortably in her chair. "If Lucifer did not wish for His servants to be bound, He wouldn't allow it. But He does. After all, the soul of a witch who binds a demon is a heavy one which whets the appetites of those in Hell. He will have quite a bounty in me when I perish."

She was not incorrect. The affairs of witches were not often good, not in Heaven's eyes, anyway. However, the list of things Heaven didn't like was about three times the length of the list of things it did. Hell, on the other hand, liked a lot of things, including witches. Binding not only assured damnation, but also made the soul extra tasty.

But what tickled Hell's fancy did not always tickle a

demon's.

Dante pushed himself out of bed. The potion may have been potent, but the room still spun around him. He rubbed viciously at his temples. "What drove you to this?" he asked. "To spoil my day, I might add!"

"Business, Mr. Lovelace."

"Business? You are a spiritualist and a fortune teller by trade. You wish to use me so that you might further your business venture? Impress your clients with a little something extra?"

"Hmm. Handsome *and* bright," she said pleasantly, and winked. "I will draw upon your natural demonic power to better my powers. You shall be useful to me, Mr. Lovelace, and I assure you: this house is a beauty. You'll like it here. Would you like to tour the place?"

Dante could hardly believe his ears. He placed his hands on his hips. "Of all the disgustingly selfish things…"

She only smiled, unmoved by his chiding.

"I can't help you," he said bitterly. "I have duties to perform for Hell. I am a catastrophe artist."

"I know," she said, and rose to her feet. "Marlowe is considered quite an unlucky town, and it's all because of you. Catastrophe artists like you know all about drawing from within to create *magic*." She pressed a finger to Dante's chest. "Hell placed their inspiration within you, the force which urges you to commit such catastrophe."

Dante glowered. He didn't need a witch to lecture him on the lot of the catastrophe artist. Inspiration! *Melancholia* was a far better term. "I think of it as an irksome beast which must be fed in order to quiet it. I may excel at my work, even tout my successes, but that does not mean I share its passion."

Beatrice chuckled throatily. "Look at that. A tender-hearted catastrophe artist. That is different."

"Do you talk to many catastrophe artists?" Dante asked.

She drew back her finger. "Hmm. You won't have to worry about those tasks for now. Consider this a holiday. You'll work only for me. The Powers Below will understand." Her face lit up again. "Now, how about that tour?"

~

Beatrice's home was far from the earthen shacks witches inhabited in fairy tales. This was no hut, no cavernous lair where gnarled women danced around cauldrons and committed unsavory acts with eye of newt and toe of frog. Lore certainly did not treat witches kindly, but in light of recent events, Dante believed they probably deserved such slander.

The house was surprisingly warm, cozy, and well-kept. Beatrice's simmering, smoky scent pervaded every room.

"It was not so long ago that I moved to Marlowe," Beatrice explained as she led him into the parlor. "I was told this home once belonged to another witch. That's the story, anyway. I would feel her presence still if truly she had lived here. Most likely a lonely old woman. People like to assume that independent women are witches."

"And in your case, they would be correct," Dante said.

"Yes. I live alone. My brother, Nathaniel, purchased the house for me. It's in his name, though he still lives in Eagleton." She must have noticed Dante's eyes lingering upon the front door, for she added, "You know what happens to demons who attempt to disobey their mistress, don't you?"

Agony that made the rebellious demon long for something a little more pleasant, like disemboweling, perhaps. His melancholia itched to destroy the house, take the witch's life! Dante took a soothing breath to assure it that would not be wise.

The very same feline Dante had already twice encountered occupied the plushest chair in the parlor. She watched him with bright green eyes and a smile that only a cat can give. Belle was her name, Beatrice told him, and she was a terribly unpleasant creature. But Beatrice loved her all the same.

Nearby was a large, leather-bound book—her grimoire, she explained. This was apparently Volume Eight. "A good witch is always learning," Beatrice attested. Dante wanted to throw the damn book into the fireplace, with the other seven volumes close behind!

A stern gentleman in a tweed suit glared at them from the portrait above the fireplace. His great eyebrows knitted in the middle to form one thick caterpillar on his brow. White hair fuzzed in an eccentric halo.

"And who is this?" Dante asked.

"My father. Lionel Dickens," Beatrice answered and then added frankly, "He's dead."

"Oh."

"He was a very private man," Beatrice said. "While I lived with my mother and brother several counties away, he lived in a house all alone ten miles outside of Marlowe. And then, an intruder killed him."

"I'm sorry," Dante said with demonic apathy.

"Did you kill him?" she asked.

"No."

"Then, please don't be sorry, Mr. Lovelace," Beatrice said with a smile. "The very nature of his life's work made him quite a target. He knew the risks he took every day."

"His life's work? And what would that be?"

Beatrice looked curiously upon the portrait of her father. "One step at a time, Mr. Lovelace," she said softly. She shooed Belle away and took her seat beside the fire before pulling another cigarette from the silver case in her pocket. She reached for a lighter. "Please sit."

He promptly obeyed and took the chair across from her. His head ached again already. Where was that blasted tea when you needed it? "Miss Dickens," Dante began.

"Enough with formalities. Call me Beatrice. We are going to be quite intimate, I assure you."

"Beatrice. I am resigned to my lot. I must be," Dante said. "It is a regrettable fate, and I would very much like to take this opportunity to tell you how utterly displeased

I am."

She laughed. "I didn't expect you to be dancing in the streets."

"I will serve you because I must. But first, I have a request. I must go to Boston."

She cocked her head. "Boston?"

"Tomorrow, if possible."

"No. Not tomorrow." Smoke circled her ruddy pink face. "We've a séance tomorrow night, and I wish to see how you perform."

He cringed. Lucifer Below, the idea of *attending* a séance made his skin crawl, let alone acting as an accomplice to so heinous a crime. "The day after, then," he said. "There is someone I must see."

"Someone you must see? A lover?"

"Someone very dear to me," he said delicately.

"Yes, it is a lover," she said with a sage nod. "It shows in your pretty dark eyes. That is peculiar for a demon, yes? I've heard you are solitary creatures. No matter. I'll allow you to go, but know what will happen if you attempt to act against me. I will call you back. I will make you beg for mercy." Her smile was sickeningly syrupy. "I don't think your *lover* would be very happy then."

~

The following morning, a piece of parchment burned into existence in a sizzling flash of fire upon the breakfast table. Dante retrieved it while Beatrice drank a pungent herbal tea that left a cinnamon scent in the air. The letter bore the seal of Brutus Eldritch, Dante's Overseer and a demon whose face Dante wouldn't recognize if the fate of the world depended on it.

"Good news or bad news?" Beatrice asked as Dante broke the seal. "You demons and your bizarre manner of correspondence. You'll burn down another house if you're not careful."

Dante read.

Mr. Dante Lovelace,

*It has come to my attention that you have been called to duty—that is, **bound**—by a witch, one Miss Beatrice Dickens. As is Hell's practice, we will not intervene, and you shall not receive assignments from me until your duties to Miss Dickens are complete and she releases you.*

In Lucifer's name, I wish you luck.

Sincerely,
Brutus Eldritch

"That was quick," Dante said softly.

"You are mine, then?" she asked knowingly, stirring her tea and leaning back in her chair. Belle, who had a cat's blatant disregard for any human boundaries, leapt upon the breakfast table and settled next to her mistress.

"It would seem so," Dante answered. "For the time being."

"Perfect. Tonight's event will be a delight, I

promise." She swallowed the rest of her tea in one gulp and scratched Belle behind the ears. The cat seemed neither pleased nor perturbed but looked to Dante intensely.

In fact, the feline made a point of following Dante, even when Beatrice did not. She was around every corner, always watching. Even as she licked her paws and smoothed her ears, she observed. A human might have thought his overactive imagination was playing tricks on him. She was only a cat, after all. But Dante knew better. A witch's familiar was no ordinary beast.

"Keeping an eye on me, Belle?" Dante asked when he encountered her at the foot of the home's narrow staircase.

Belle cocked her head, eyes unblinking, as if to say, *Well, I'm not merely following you for sport, demon.*

"I'm no fool. I won't disobey," he said, and knelt to pet her. She recoiled with something of a sneer, padded a foot away and settled again, just out of reach.

Beatrice Dickens held her séances, readings, and various other spiritual consultations in the parlor of her home with the portrait of her father looming over the proceedings. Somehow, Dante decided, Montgomery the dead vulture was less unnerving a parlor guest than the dead Mr. Dickens.

Beatrice asked, naturally, that Dante remain invisible to the human eye during the night's event, a simple task for an experienced demon. On the agenda: a family reunion. Beatrice's client badly desired to speak to her cousin who was, as was customary in such cases, thoroughly deceased.

"Who is your client?" Dante asked before the guests were to arrive.

"Edith Donner, née Courtwright," Beatrice said gravely. "She wants to speak to Dylan Courtwright, who murdered his cousin, Edgar, two years ago. Edgar was Edith Donner's brother. I'm sure you recall the debacle, The Fraternal Order of the Scarab? I came to Marlowe shortly after it had all come out. It was all anyone talked about. Not that they spoke to me about it directly. I was an outsider who was 'not fit to speak about that frightful scarab club.'"

How in this wide world and the next could Dante forget the tale of The Fraternal Order of the Scarab? The foul secret organization once had their hands in every affair in Marlowe, and their downfall had been orchestrated by none other than Iago Wick. Dylan Courtwright had been the first member to fall.

Dante couldn't help but smile every time some citizen of Marlowe clucked his tongue and spoke of the scandal of The Order. Decades of wrongdoing had come to light, pillars of society were forever tainted! Iago Wick was ever so proud of the way Marlowe talked of his magnum opus.

Beatrice continued, "Dylan Courtwright was executed, of course, but not before he cut out his own tongue to prevent himself from telling secrets. Mrs. Donner wants the chance to ask him why he killed her brother. She wants to know more about the family's involvement in The Fraternal Order. She is a desperate creature, and we are going to help her, Dante."

The furniture was moved in the parlor to make room for the guests. A round table sat in the center, circled by six chairs.

"You will stand behind me during the séance," Beatrice explained as she sat with Dante in position. "And you must leave your fingers here." She took his hand and placed it to her throat so that he could feel her pulse. "I will draw upon your natural power to better reach Courtwright, who is presumably in Hell. In time, we hopefully will not find it necessary to be physically connected, but for now, I must feel you at all times for this to be a success. Do you understand?"

She turned to look him in the eye. Dante wanted to say *no*, walk out the door, and go home, but he bit his tongue. "Yes, Beatrice."

"Good," she said, and gave his hand a nervous squeeze.

Belle made herself scarce by the time the first guest arrived—nearly an hour early. Ellie Malark arrived alone, for that was the lot of a widow of a certain age: to do everything alone, and to do it with a smile to reassure every young wife that it wouldn't be so bad once her husband dropped dead. Her wild gray hair was pulled back into a disastrous bun, and she cheerfully greeted Beatrice while Dante remained invisible just over her shoulder.

"Beatrice, dear," Mrs. Malark cooed, "it is good to see you again. How have you been?"

"I've been well, Mrs. Malark. Thank you," Beatrice

answered, and ushered her into the parlor.

"And... how *have* you been?" she repeated with strange emphasis and sudden gravity. Her eyes darted briefly to the portrait of Beatrice's father.

"I've been *well*, Mrs. Malark. *Thank you.*"

"It's just that I worry, Beatrice. You ended your mourning so prematurely. It's been mere months!"

Beatrice smiled and placed a hand to Ellie Malark's cheek. "Mrs. Malark, I am well. Better than I have been in some time. I promise."

"Good, good, Beatrice. I am so happy to hear that," she said soothingly. "A good séance always helped me when my husband passed from this world to the next. I do miss acting as a medium... but after that dreadful affair at the Ackle mansion, I simply can't!"

The other guests soon arrived, each extravagantly clothed. Beatrice, however, wore no rouge to color her cheeks, no ostentatious jewelry. With her fiery hair and plain, earthen dress, she looked like the tops of trees in early autumn, a blend of warm rust and mossy green.

Following Ellie Malark came a woman dressed in burgundy, her brown hair piled delicately atop her head like an elaborate dessert. Dante learned her name was Charlotte Cutter, and she had a man on her arm who looked more like an accessory than another human being. He wasn't a husband. He seemed daffy and vaguely unfamiliar with Miss Cutter. A woman of her age and carriage could not attend so macabre and daring an event alone—this Miss Cutter desperately wanted to be there. Her guest, conversation revealed, was called Sterling

Mason, and he was perpetually *delighted*.

"I've never been to such a party before," he told Ellie Malark with a vacant grin better suited for a day at the zoo than a séance. "It should be very fun. I've never seen a spirit before. Once I had quite an encounter in a cemetery, though. I saw something creeping through the shadows."

"Oh?" Ellie Malark asked.

"I heard crackling and creaking, and then, something great emerged from the dark! And me without my pistol. It was a deer! Gave me quite a fright," he said, and jabbed Miss Charlotte Cutter with his elbow. Then, his face turned solemn. "I had nightmares for *weeks*."

Mrs. Malark nodded. "Well… you may be in for quite a shock tonight, then."

"Oh, great!" Mr. Mason exclaimed gleefully.

Edith Donner was the last to arrive, a grim and sour-faced scarecrow of a woman who, though she had long abandoned her black mourning attire for more extravagant dress, still expected the world to ask her how she was coping with her own aging family tragedy. She was accompanied by her husband, Mr. Allen P. Donner, a somber man who had his hands and his money in nearly everything in Marlowe. His vast influence was the only thing that saved Edith Donner from social disgrace after her cousin's involvement in The Order came to light two years prior.

"Dear Mrs. Donner, how *are* you?" Ellie Malark asked with her customary emphasis. It was made obvious by the watery glimmer in her eye that Edith Donner lived to hear that subtle vocal strain.

"Well, Mrs. Malark. My heart will always be heavy," she proclaimed. "But I carry such fond memories of my brother with me wherever I go."

Beatrice busied herself in a cramped closet behind the staircase while her guests took their seats. She retrieved a small bottle and took a brief drink of its contents. Dante endeavored to flicker into sight.

"For courage?" he asked softly.

"To calm my nerves," she answered, "and *you* shouldn't be visible."

"How long ago did your father perish?"

Beatrice took another sip of the murky liquid. "A mere six months ago." She exhaled. "I do not mourn. The greatest tribute to the dead is to continue living. You might not understand that, my dear immortal, but it is true. Now, conceal yourself. We have work to do."

III.

"I was never able to speak to Dylan about the incident before he... before he perished," Edith Donner said, and affected a grandiose sniffle. Her husband gave her a reassuring nod, his stamp of approval for another weepy public lamentation. The role of the blubbering sister-in-mourning was one Mrs. Donner would reprise as many times as society would reasonably allow. "My dear brother! Why would Dylan do such a thing? He went *berserk*. Oh, but maybe that's too passionate a word for normal conversation."

She choked back a sob, and her husband dutifully gave her a handkerchief from his breast pocket. Mrs. Donner could have made a career out of her grief, but Dante imagined she would have simply died if anyone compared her to something so base as an actress. Perish the thought!

"I assure you, Mrs. Donner," Beatrice said, "we will

not partake in *normal* conversation this evening. I ask that you speak freely and hope your cousin, Dylan Courtwright, will do the same."

Unseen, Dante stood behind Beatrice at the table and pressed his fingers to her throat. Her heart raced. He could have broken her neck, his melancholia insisted quite morbidly, but the spell prevented him from acting against her. And what's more, he simply hadn't the constitution to break someone's neck. Crashing airships and playing the role of grave misfortune in Hell's name was one thing. Cold-blooded murder was quite another entirely!

"I shall need everyone to touch, pinkies to pinkies, around the table, please," Beatrice said firmly after Ellie Malark dimmed the lights. "Mrs. Donner, please state the name of the spirit you wish to contact this evening."

"Dylan Courtwright," she said with just the right amount of strife.

"Dylan Courtwright," Beatrice repeated, eyes closed. "Dylan Courtwright, you were a man condemned to death for the murder of your cousin, Edgar." There was something of a forced whimper on Mrs. Donner's part. "And now, Edgar's sister wishes to speak to you. Tell him why, Mrs. Donner."

"I want to know why. He admitted to the crime. He admitted to many things, but his motive remains unclear," she said. "*Why?* Why would he kill my dear brother, Edgar?"

Dante knew well that Courtwright killed her dear brother, Edgar, because he was driven to do so by Iago

Wick. Iago would never kill on his own, no. He merely crafted unpleasant situations—this one involving a puzzle box that drove the owner insane to the point of murder—and watched tragedy unfold. That was simply the duty of a tempter like Iago. Nothing personal.

Dante also knew well that Courtwright's soul was in Hell. The Powers Below weren't fond of humans dragging the damned back to Earth for a quick chat, but it was not impossible with the help of demonic power. Dante closed his eyes and focused on the beating of his own black heart and the parts of him which were still wholly demon. He allowed infernal energy to fill him.

"Mr. Courtwright, you cut out your own tongue prior to your trial. Use mine tonight. Speak to your cousin," Beatrice said.

Beatrice's flesh warmed, and her pulse still quickened. Dante was overcome by a strange sensation, as though she reached inside him and made them one. His hands were hers, her arms were his. Her thoughts, however, remained clouded. She kept those closely guarded by way of magic, and yet, it felt like they were two blurry images on either side of a stereoscope slide suddenly merging in perfect clarity.

"Dylan Courtwright," she continued, "are you here with us?"

Somewhere in the darkness, on the early autumn wind outside, Dante could have sworn he heard Hell's great cacophony, the wailing of bereft demons and damned souls. It was a sound he had not heard in a very long time, and it was not one he necessarily missed.

Beatrice took a sudden gasping breath. "Who calls me?" she said in a mournful voice that was not her own. Sterling Mason yelped in surprise like a startled turkey.

Edith Donner flinched. "D-Dylan?"

"Edith?" the voice croaked, and Dante realized his own lips moved, soundlessly, along with Courtwright's words.

But Beatrice righted herself and spoke in her own voice. "Mr. Courtwright, your cousin wishes to speak with you."

The rasping voice of Dylan Courtwright returned. "Where am I? Am I upon Earth?" he asked frantically.

"Yes," Mrs. Donner said.

"But I am to rot in Hell," he said gravely.

"Tonight, you are on Earth, and we are very thankful for that, Mr. Courtwright. Your cousin wants to know why you murdered Edgar, her loving brother," Beatrice cut in, her voice somewhat weak.

Though he could not read her thoughts, Dante knew one thing for certain: this was no act. More than a few spiritualists were more thespian than conduit to the other side, living on a steady diet of the scenery they chewed and the money of the bereft. Not this time.

And this was no wayward spirit wandering the Earth, a medium's usual contact. This spirit was accustomed to Hell, itching for a human body to inhabit. To allow that misshapen soul into the body of one of the living was downright dangerous. Beatrice had gladly opened herself to him.

Dante placed his free hand upon Beatrice's shoulder

to steady her. She had not only welcomed Courtwright inside her, but welcomed Dante's power, as well. They were, all three of them, an amalgam of witch and demon and spirit, tangling in some dark and dreadful sea.

"It was all his fault," Courtwright said.

"Edgar's?" Mrs. Donner croaked.

"No. The man in gray. He tricked me. He was one of them. He was one of the creatures made of black glass and wickedness and cunning," Courtwright gasped, and Beatrice pitched forward, hands clawing at the table. She snarled like an animal, and Dante kept his touch in place. "A *demon*. The man in gray. He came to me in the night. He gave me a puzzle box, long disappeared now. If I opened it, he said, I would live forever."

The man in gray waited for Dante now in Boston, scotch in hand, and he'd be so terribly delighted to see this melodramatic display all on his account. Of course, Iago Wick, the man in gray, also knew that no one had *ever* opened that puzzle box and that attempts usually ended in glorious, soul-sullying tragedy. See Exhibit A: The Temptation of Dylan Courtwright.

"But I could not open it!" Courtwright exclaimed. "And so, I determined, it must have required something else. A sacrifice!"

"And Edgar happened to be available?" Mrs. Donner whimpered.

"Would you have preferred I came to you for help, Edith?" Courtwright asked darkly.

She didn't respond.

The darkness at the edges of the room now seemed

to swell and shift, as though wicked wraiths lurked in the corners. Shadows threatened to swallow the parlor, and Dante wondered if he was the only one who could see them. Mr. Mason looked on with vacuous glee. Ellie Malark seemed fearful but kept her silence.

Charlotte Cutter, meanwhile, watched Beatrice closely. There was something cat-like about her, her narrow eyes flitting over Beatrice's face, watching her every move with care. Worry creased her forehead.

Dante was not so concerned with this family drama. He'd heard the tale of The Fraternal Order enough to last him a millennium. He concentrated, instead, on the task at hand, his own power rushing within him. He'd never used his demonic power for something like this before. Hellfire simmered in his extremities.

Demons did not often use their power fully in their work for Hell. Lucifer's minions were fierce creatures who had not always served another, but as servants, they were made to know their place. The Powers Below discouraged any unnecessary exhibition of power. It was quite shocking—dare he say, invigorating?—to tap into that primal, demonic fire.

But Dante felt suddenly as though something were slipping through his fingers, like sand, smoke... he was losing *Beatrice*. Her presence waned. Courtwright surged within her. Dante tried to hold Beatrice steady. Being bound by a witch was bad enough. He couldn't imagine being bound by a witch who also happened to be possessed!

Beatrice, stay, Dante thought. *Stay here. Don't let go.* He tried again to hold her fast, to pull her from the abyss. Courtwright seemed to swallow her whole. She was gone, and Dante was strangely lost.

"I was to be one of the immortals," Courtwright groaned. "But I failed, I failed."

Suddenly, Beatrice returned, surging forward as though breaking the surface of a lake for air. Dante reached for her within the strange cocoon of their minds. He felt it in her burning skin, her trembling body; Courtwright was needed elsewhere, and Beatrice could no longer hold him.

Courtwright moaned, milking the role of woeful spirit as much as he could. Such drama obviously ran in the family. "None of it matters! We are all damned. Every single one of us. And here you are, mingling with a witch who has called upon another *demon* to do her foul bidding." Charlotte Cutter's eyebrows peaked at the accusation, and Courtwright roared, "You are all damned, and I shall count you all among my company in Hell."

Beatrice gasped and fell forward as Dylan Courtwright left her body. Her skin cooled, her heart settled, and if it hadn't been for her pulse, Dante would have taken her for dead. Her forehead met the table.

Then, Edith Donner gave a sob worthy of a matinee and cupped her own forehead in a flood of misery.

"Amazing…" Sterling Mason breathed before grinning broadly. "How about another? Abraham Lincoln, maybe?"

Ellie Malark brought her hand to her mouth. "Miss Dickens?" she asked worriedly. "Miss Dickens, are you awake?"

Beatrice drew a limp hand to place upon her throat where Dante's fingers still rested. She slowly raised her head and nodded weakly. There was the smell of sulfur and brimstone on the air, and Dante did not miss the Inferno from which he came.

~

Ellie Malark gave Beatrice a glass of something pungent, perhaps the same concoction she kept in the cabinet beneath the stairs. Edith Donner left the home, sobbing bitterly with her husband in tow. Despite her hyperbolic performance that evening, she had been forced to take second billing to the deceased.

Charlotte Cutter lingered behind with Sterling Mason at her side. There was little to say for Mr. Mason, Dante thought. His mind was as empty as his glassy gaze. Charlotte, however, was a lost woman. Her life leaked out in random and uncontrollable thoughts. Dante was certainly not as adept as a tempter at reaching into the thoughts of humans, and the events of that evening had left him weaker than usual. He could see, however, that Charlotte Cutter was in love. Heartily in love. The object of her deep affection was not Beatrice nor Sterling Mason, but someone else. She kept him in the back of her mind like a locket hung by her heart, though Dante could not see him.

"That was absolutely astounding, Miss Dickens," Mr. Mason twittered.

"A stirring performance," Charlotte Cutter added.

"I'm not certain *performance* is the correct word, Lottie. That implies some sort of masquerade," Beatrice said hoarsely. "But thank you for attending. It has been some time since I last saw you. What brings you to Marlowe, and how did you acquire such a *strapping* companion?"

Charlotte bristled at Beatrice's tone. "Mr. Mason's uncle introduced us. And I am a dear friend of Edith's. I asked if she would allow me to attend."

Mr. Mason interjected, "It was simply amazing. Do you do anything else? Pull a rabbit out of a hat, that sort of thing? That's a real show-stopper."

His comment might have been considered offensive if he hadn't been entirely genuine. Charlotte Cutter was quick to progress the conversation. "How is Harry, by the way?"

Beatrice's face set, and she cleared her throat. "I don't know. I've not seen him in a while."

"I'm sorry to hear that. You were very fond of each other. I know your father didn't approve. But seeing as your father is..." She looked to the floor. "I'm sorry. That was very bold of me."

Beatrice frowned. "Bold, but not untrue."

"Well, send Harry my best if you correspond," Charlotte said with a meek sweetness. She paused before she could turn away and seemed to weigh her next words carefully. "Bea, when you were in the midst of it all, the spirit accused you of having a demon at your side."

"He called her a witch, too, my dear. That's certainly

not true," Sterling Mason said airily. Charlotte Cutter did not seem convinced.

"Empty, angry words," Beatrice insisted. "Spirits try to pit us against each other. I have no demon at my side."

"Good," Charlotte said. "I worry about you sometimes, Bea. I think about you."

Beatrice said, "And I, you, Lottie. Have a good evening."

Sterling Mason followed Charlotte Cutter like an over-ecstatic puppy as they left the parlor. Beatrice deflated in something like relief when finally they left. After Ellie Malark made certain that Beatrice was well (half a dozen times, at least), she departed, and Dante was left alone with the witch.

Dante rid himself of his invisibility and helped Beatrice right her parlor, moving the furniture back to its customary place. Then, they sat before the fireplace. Belle, the cat, wandered pleasantly into the room, demanding attention with her bright green eyes and forcing Dante's hand with a short trill. She couldn't seem to make up her mind whether she liked him or not. Beatrice drank deep from a cup of tea mixed with the same concoction she'd imbibed earlier. It put a spark in her eyes, made her sit up straighter.

"This potion is made with cloves for protection and clarity of thought. It assists in séance work, among other things," she said and added slyly, "It has a few other ingredients, as well, which would make the teetotalers angry."

"Are you feeling better?" Dante asked.

"Mostly," Beatrice answered. "You are *astounding*, Mr. Lovelace. I imagined Courtwright's soul might be in Hell for the severity of his crimes. I could never have spoken to him without the help of a demon. What a grand new experience."

Grand? Being possessed by the tormented and misshapen soul of one of the damned hardly seemed grand, but perhaps they had different definitions of the word. Dante admitted with a shrug, "I am fair to middling in terms of my power. I have known demons far more powerful than I am."

"We work well together, Dante."

He looked briefly to the man above the fireplace. His severe gaze made Dante feel as though he were being thoroughly judged from beyond the grave. "This Charlotte Cutter—"

"Don't concern yourself with her. She is the proverbial wet blanket," Beatrice admitted. "I shouldn't say that. She's an old friend. She's lost, I think. Always has been. Occasionally, she comes to me as though she has something pressing to say… and then, she holds her tongue. I knew she was friends with Mrs. Donner. I wondered if she would use tonight as another opportunity to watch me silently."

Dante asked, "Am I still allowed to visit Boston tomorrow?"

Beatrice crossed her arms over her chest. "Mr. Courtwright proclaimed that a demon had driven him to kill his cousin, here in Marlowe. That wasn't you, was it?"

"No."

"There used to be another demon here, the man in gray." Beatrice smiled. "It shows in your eyes. That is who you are going to visit."

"Indeed."

"And who is he?" Beatrice asked. "Your lover?" Was that the slightest smattering of jealousy Dante detected?

He drew a deep breath. To know a demon's name gave the demon power, but it also gave a human a better chance of gaining power over him. He withheld Iago's name. "Yes. I wish to see him before I commit fully to your service."

She considered him quietly for a moment. "You're quite different than I expected. I did not anticipate binding a demon with so much heart." She paused. "I know love well. My love is very far from me."

"Harry?" Dante asked with a knowing grin.

Beatrice looked into her drink as though she might see her lost love there. "Go to him. But return by Monday. We have much to accomplish." She sipped her tea and looked thoughtfully out the window. "So, The Fraternal Order of the Scarab was foiled through demonic intervention. Interesting. How many demons did it take to commit such an act?"

Dante's smile broadened. "Just one."

IV.

The train depot at Boston's Haymarket Square was a bustling beehive compared to anything Dante saw regularly in Marlowe. The people of Marlowe just didn't *bustle*. They considered it highly undignified to go anywhere at anything more than a moderately brisk pace. Boston constantly moved and hummed like a great machine; every human and every automaton and every creature was a vital cog or spring.

Dante left the train and wandered into the depot, wearing his usual widower's black and looking dreary enough that no one would bother him. No one wanted to make conversation with a mopey widower or, perish the thought, a poet. He carried a small bag, and he surveyed the depot until he saw his partner.

Dante greeted a man more peacock than demon, with bright hazel eyes, brown hair, and a smile that could bring men to ruin. That afternoon, Iago Wick wore his usual gray suit with an emerald waistcoat and pocket square. Not a hair was out of place.

"My dear Dante," Iago said, and drew him into a strong embrace. "Oh, it does this black heart good to see you."

"Does Boston treat Iago Wick well?" Dante asked.

"Boston strongly disagrees with me," he said. "You know that. It has such a foul, pungent scent about it. Almost reminds me of home, at times."

As they left the station at Haymarket, Dante breathed in air heavy with smoke and various chemicals and wished he could find even a trace of the autumnal scent which pervaded provincial cities such as Marlowe this time of year. Still, the city was a wonder. A woman asked one of the android policemen for directions, while an automated carriage careened around the corner, smoke puffing from the back. And towering above them, the extravagant elevated electric line carried citizens from place to place.

The people of Marlowe saw Boston as the stuff of fairy tales; they still balked at the idea of the telephone, while Boston sighed, 'Oh, that old thing?' Dante felt as though he had stumbled into the window display of a toy maker's shop every time he arrived in the city. The purveyors of such gadgetry and machines, however, did not see their work in so frivolous a light. Bostonians were stubbornly proud of the world in which they lived, and it showed. The city put its every achievement on display with a self-aggrandizing cry of, 'Look! Look!'

Marlowe, on the other hand, was trapped in the past

like so many stubborn burgs and towns. Even the simplest automaton (The Mechanical Valet, for example) stunned Marlowe's elite.

"It seems as though every time I'm here, even more advancements have been made," Dante said.

"Yes," Iago said. "Boston must keep up appearances, you know. Wouldn't want New York to gain the upper hand. They're embroiled in such a rivalry."

"Civil?" Dante asked.

"Mostly, if you ignore the 1887 Innovators' Exposition in New York. I hear they still haven't been able to remove the blood from the Athenaeum's carpets."

A woman in a sash thrust a pamphlet into Dante's hand as they walked. She did not bother to meet his gaze. *Votes for Cyborgs*, the pamphlet read. *How Human Must We Be to Vote?* He turned the pamphlet to the other side. *Votes for Women. Half of the Population Cannot Be Ignored!*

An android in a policeman's uniform tipped his hat and greeted them before rattling away. A disconcerting puff of smoke shot from his ear. For now, the automated portion of Boston's police was good for little more than sounding the alarm and assisting with traffic, but all the same, they looked oh-so-smart in their uniforms.

"You'll forgive me, Dante. I require my daily dose of information," Iago said. His eyes darted over Haymarket Square until he spotted another mechanical wonder.

"Ah, there's my dear Harriet!" Iago called as a female-model automaton rolled toward him, her green skirts rustling against the ground. Her face was sweet and doll-like, eyes wide and cheeks rouged. Wild blonde hair was kept in place by a small straw hat. She rattled and shook as she hurried toward them, and for a moment, she convulsed so strongly that Dante feared she might lose a limb.

Harriet, as she was called, was not perfect. She was human-made. The original vampire-made automatons were second to none. But *of course*, the humans stepped in and stole the plans for the bodies and the complex mechanism for the brain that Lord Julius Weiss had worked so long to perfect. And *of course*, Lord Julius Weiss gutted the human who committed such a crime, but it was too late. Mediocre human-made automatons and cyborgs now rattled around the world's metropolitan areas. They were agile... *enough*. Their listening and repetition-response functions were satisfactory—so long as one avoided hyperbole and homophones.

Iago, however, looked upon Harriet with palpable pride.

"Mr. Wick," she greeted in her music box voice, and her mouth pulled until it looked almost like a smile. "How lovely to see you. I trust your supper with Mr. Quinn yesterday evening went well."

"Alas, my dear," Iago answered, "Mr. Quinn was unable to attend. Marital strife, that sort of thing. We are dining together tonight." He motioned to Dante. "Mr. Lovelace will join us. And you remember Dante Lovelace, don't you, Harriet?"

Harriet batted her shoe brush lashes and turned away as though she were blushing. Perhaps that was some inventor's next triumph—a blushing automaton. It was an innovation which would do little but bolster the confidence of men, and so, it was surely at the top of someone's list. "Yes. Hello, Mr. Lovelace. It is very nice to see you again. You are looking quite well."

Dante took her spindly wire hand and placed a gentle kiss to the metal. "If only I looked half as well as you, Harriet."

Harriet cocked her head to one side. Her mouth became a straight line.

"Compliment, Harriet," Iago said. "That's a compliment."

The word triggered something in the automaton's mechanical brain, and she straightened up again. "Oh, yes! Thank you, Mr. Lovelace."

Iago clapped his hands together and led their group to a small outcropping of shrubs and one feeble tree beside the depot, the first plant life Dante had spotted since arriving. "Now! What do you have for me, my dear?"

Harriet made a strange noise as though she were trying to clear her throat. "The sirens have been kept at bay. No further deaths along the coast. Mrs. Atchison's efforts were a success."

"I'm glad to hear it," Iago said. "Anything else?"

"There was an altercation between a goblin and a vampire in Back Bay. It was resolved without attracting human attention," Harriet continued, eyelashes fluttering. Her gaze strayed to Dante again, her lips pursed sweetly. He gave her a playful wink, and her doll eyes widened in mechanical glee.

"Delightful," Iago said. "Is that all, Harriet?"

"No, there is one more story," she said as she pulled her gaze from Dante. "Zero Bancroft has returned to Boston."

Iago's face fell. "What was that?"

"Zero Bancroft has returned to Boston," Harriet repeated in precisely the same tones. "I hear his death toll numbered in the hundreds."

Death toll? Dante wondered. That was a disquieting thing for a man to have, though his melancholia was quick to remind him it was not a foreign concept. "Who is this, Iago?"

His question fell upon unreceptive ears, for Iago Wick looked as though he were preparing to run for the hills. He raked a nervous hand through his hair. "Already? When did he return? From whom did you hear this news?" he asked.

"Why, from Mr. Grimwood, your superior," she answered. "Bancroft returned just yesterday. I thought you should know. You speak ill of him. He is a threat." She paused. "Correct?"

Iago took a deep breath. "Yes, thank you, Harriet. That will be all. We're off to Beacon Street. Enjoy your day."

"Enjoyment is a concept which I cannot grasp, Mr. Wick, but I thank you all the same. Good day, Mr. Wick." She turned and smiled coyly at Dante again. "Good day, Mr. Lovelace."

~

A mere four and a half-minute ride aboard the elevated train would see them straight to Beacon Street.

At the grounded terminal was an ornate sign, painted with figures soaring above the city in a silver bullet. In the background was a smiling Icarus in mid-flight. Dante felt like telling them that Icarus had no reason to be smiling if he were that close to the sun, but he thought the automaton stationed at the terminal would have some trouble seeing the humor.

At Iago's insistence, they assumed invisibility in the shadows behind the terminal. This Mr. Bancroft must have been something frightful. From the moment they crept aboard the elevator which lifted them to the platform above, Iago fidgeted anxiously.

Dante took his place in one of the train car's red velvet seats, hoping no human would think to sit there. As long as he held onto his bag, it wouldn't suddenly appear in plain sight. He looked over the city with wide eyes as they hurried above the bustle below. So much happened in Boston. People were not so entwined as in Marlowe. In this grand city, people passed each other every day and perhaps never spoke.

Then, for a moment, he could only see buildings tumbling to the ground and elevated trains flying off their rails. Dante shook the thoughts from his head and settled his over-zealous melancholia.

Their train car was furnished in dark and regal wood. Gold accents gleamed in the sunlight. Automaton attendants waited at each vestibule, nodding pleasantly as they were taught to do, and there were intricate faces carved into almost every surface. Dante avoided the discomforting gaze of a wooden Dionysus, shrouded in grapes. Behind them, men read newspapers and children urged their mother to look at the buildings, the sky, the people! She calmly told them to take their seats, a noble but futile effort.

Iago, meanwhile, looked glumly out the window. He insisted he was much more comfortable on the ground; flying high was something better suited to the angels.

"Harriet behaves very oddly around me," Dante said, his voice also undetectable to humans.

"How?"

"She always seems embarrassed in my presence."

Iago shrugged. "She finds you attractive. Harriet observes human women behaving that way around handsome gentlemen, and so, she does the same."

"She's an automaton. She cannot understand human concepts of beauty. How can she find me any handsomer than any other gentleman on the street?" Dante asked.

Iago met his gaze and smiled. "I taught her, didn't I?"

When they arrived at the Beacon Street terminal, they boarded one last elevator to take them back to Earth. As the box dropped, Iago released the breath he had been holding the entire journey. An automaton attendant nodded and tried to smile as humans gave him pennies. It looked a bit more like a grimace.

Somewhere, vampire mechanics were cringing in

their coffins.

"Now that you're not shaking like an anxious dog, I'll ask again. Who exactly is this Bancroft?" Dante asked once they set foot on solid ground. "Invisibility, the electric line... he has you scared."

"He's a demon hunter," Iago answered quickly. "If you recall my sudden move from the East Side to Beacon Hill last year? He was the hunter who had discovered where I lived. Zero Bancroft is, in every sense of the word, a problem. But he's my problem, not yours. Let's hope it remains that way."

Dante smiled, but he knew better. In this long partnership, the problems of one always tended to become the problems of both.

In the neighborhood of Beacon Hill, rows of homes neatly lined the streets like sentinels with narrow window eyes. Iago's home was immaculate and stately. It had a spacious parlor, a study, and a bedroom, which was only used when Dante came to visit. That's not to say they felt such passionate affairs of the heart and body should be indulged exclusively behind one's bedroom door—the desk in the study, for example, was quite adequate in Dante's considered opinion—but the bed *was* comfortable.

Across the street, Boston Common and the Public Garden were alight with the hues of early autumn. It did Dante's heart wonders to see such color in this steaming engine of a city.

Just ahead, a diminutive blond man waited outside Iago's home, quite literally twiddling his thumbs. He looked dumbly to the sky, squinting into the sun.

"Lucifer Below, he's here," Iago hissed under his breath. He gripped Dante by the collar and dragged him between two houses to hide. "The foul thing!"

"Who? Is this Bancroft?" Dante asked, and peered around the corner. With his vacant expression and slouching posture, he certainly didn't look like the sort of gentleman who could boast a death toll.

"No! No, it's not Bancroft." Iago took Dante's hand and started to pull him back toward the elevated line terminal. "Invisibility doesn't even *work* on this annoying creature. Trust me. He introduced himself to me a few months ago, and I've been trying to lose him ever since. Let us away. Quickly!"

"Iago, what's the matter—?"

"Mr. Wick? I'd like to speak to you."

The man stood suddenly behind them, placing his hand on Iago's shoulder. He spoke in a marble-mouthed English accent and was the human embodiment of leek soup: pale and slightly lumpy with a vague onion scent.

Iago Wick, minion of Lucifer and thousand-year-old tempter, gave a ludicrous yelp and hid behind Dante. The sudden greeting startled him from his invisibility, and with a quick look around the surrounding area, Dante doffed his, as well. He accepted his newfound role as living shield.

The strange man narrowed his gaze and looked at Dante from head to toe. He didn't appear to like what he saw. Dante didn't give a tig and said, "I'm sorry, may we help you, Mister...?"

"Hawley, sir. Gregor Hawley," the stranger said, and gave a deep and reverent bow.

"Yes, Mr. Hawley," Iago muttered, but failed to emerge from his hiding place. "We were just preparing to leave, sir. If you'll excuse us." He yanked Dante backward by his coat.

Mr. Hawley was not deterred. "I wanted to speak with you, sir, given the return of Mr. Bancroft. You might be in need of some protection."

"Mr. Hawley, the greatest protection you could offer me is to stay away from my home. I've already had to move once! Bancroft would, I feel, be rather suspicious of a man who conjures fire from his fingertips," Iago insisted, but Gregor Hawley only shrugged and flicked his thumb. A blazing flame sprung from his nail. Quite the parlor trick for anyone who wasn't demon. Unless…

Dante raised a brow. "You'll forgive me, sir, but… Iago, who is this?"

"Gregor Hawley," the man repeated slowly, stretching the syllables of his name until one could drive a freight train through them.

"Yes, that much I can gather. Thank you," Dante sighed.

Had Iago Wick the decency to blush, his cheeks might have turned to graphite with his black blood. "Dearest Dante, my life is a long one. I have told you many stories of my time on Earth before we began this long and happy coupling, yes?"

Dante answered slowly, "Yes."

"And do you recall the tale of Lady Heloise? A lovely

woman, if not a bit naughty."

"Yes, I believe you've told me about her. Sixteenth century. The blonde lady with, uh… rather interesting preferences in the bed chamber?"

"Yes, and I was her demon lover, so to speak. You see," Iago began, "when Heloise's life was thoroughly soiled, and the golden scales tipped permanently in Hell's favor, I left her. However, as fate would have it, Lady Heloise was… well, she was with child. *My* child."

"What?" Dante croaked.

"I was well aware of this grave misfortune when I left her, but I was under the impression that this *problem*, as it were, would be eliminated." He looked woefully to Gregor Hawley. "Alas."

A few holes marred Hawley's smile, but that didn't stop him from looking any less cheerful. "My ancestor lived and lived well, sir. Thank Lucifer Below, Lady Heloise kept and raised the half-demonling, and he spawned many more like him."

Dante was still trying to overcome the thought of Iago with a baby on one knee when the pieces clicked into place in his mind. "Wait. You mean to say Mr. Hawley is your great-great-great… great…"

"You may abbreviate," Iago said.

"…great grandson?"

"Yes," Iago admitted. "The multitude of *greats* somewhat assuages the nausea I feel at the idea of paternity. He came across the Atlantic to find me. He is part-demon."

"And a Descendent of Wick," Hawley proclaimed,

and regarded Dante haughtily. Ah, there was that familial pride. At least he took after his distant grandfather in some fashion. Hawley pulled a piece of parchment from his pocket. It bore a crest, crimson and very grave and stamped with a golden W.

"Oh, the prideful fire this must stoke within you, dear Iago," Dante said with a smirk.

"Is that what that is? I thought it was indigestion," Iago groaned.

Hawley explained, "For centuries, my family has refrained from seeking out Iago Wick. Lady Heloise of Locksley insisted upon it, but I could not bear it. Time has passed, after all. Yes, the great Iago Wick might have wronged Lady Heloise, but he is also the source of our power, our direct connection to Lucifer Below!" He might have thumped his chest for all his posturing.

"Ah, yes," Dante said. "And I'm certain Mr. Wick is delighted to be placed upon so lofty a pedestal."

"Shut up, Dante," Iago muttered through his teeth.

"We have you to thank for everything, Mr. Wick," Hawley continued. "My relatives have long honed their skills as demi-demons, and so have I. We take pride in our lineage, and we meet every second Tuesday to discuss such matters and partake in libation." He paused. "Mostly the second part."

Dante furrowed his brow. "And what precisely are your skills, Mr. Hawley?"

Iago guffawed. "He can conjure flame from his thumb, assume invisibility, and is, he tells me, inhumanly talented at card tricks."

Hawley shook his head. "I could do far more than some hocus pocus-ing hack, Mr. Wick. I owe you servitude. To have even a drop of demon's blood in one's veins is a blessing."

"I assure you, that's not the right word," Iago insisted, and hurried to his front door.

"Please, sir! Granddad! Let me help you."

Dante stifled a laugh. The only creature in this wide world and the next less suited to the term "Granddad" than Iago Wick was sitting upon a throne in Hell, reminiscing about the good old days before The Fall.

"Mr. Hawley, your dedication is admirable. But as I've already said, I am not looking for a servant, much less one who is *regrettably* my relation. I assure you that if I require your services, I will call for you immediately. Until then..." Iago bowed. "I am concluding our fourth family reunion this month. Good day."

Gregor Hawley's face contorted in a sour frown. "Lovely to meet you," Dante said politely, and followed Iago into his home.

~

"Granddad?" Dante teased once the door was closed. Iago scowled magnificently.

"I don't wish to speak of it." He ruffled his hair before sweeping it back into place. "He has been a terrible nuisance, and I apologize for not warning you sooner. I was..."

"Embarrassed?" Dante asked as he left his suitcase

on the floor. "I cannot hold your past against you, Iago. It is only natural that some of your early temptations should have... given fruit, we'll say."

Dante followed Iago from the foyer to the study. Iago dropped his jacket upon a brass hook. At his wrists were green scarab cufflinks, a reminder of his final days working in Marlowe.

Watery shafts of sunlight streamed through the window at the front of the room. They were surrounded by books that Dante knew Iago hadn't the time to read. On one cherry bookcase were neat piles of paper, each tied in twine. These were temptations, new and old, a well-curated collection of Iago's centuries of work.

But a different pile of papers caught Dante's eye. "How fares the writing career of Virgil Alighieri?" he asked.

Iago laughed. "Virgil Alighieri is performing quite well!" he answered, and retrieved the bundle of papers from his desk. "My fifth story. Quinn says the last one sold spectacularly. It's so good to have an audience."

Dante rifled through the pages of Iago's latest work. "If Hell knew that one of their finest had walked into a publishing house, proclaimed himself a demon and handed a human several manuscripts based upon centuries of Hellish work, they would have more than a few words for the demon in question."

"Fortunately," Iago said, "they do not know that is precisely what occurred."

And naturally, Mr. Osgood Quinn of Quinn Publishing House could not say *no* to the idea of publishing penny dreadfuls inspired by the work of an actual demon. Filth and naughtiness were Quinn's specialties. It was a match made in Hell.

"You spend more time writing and publishing these licentious tales of sin under an assumed name than you do tending to your Hellish assignments," Dante said.

"And? I am thriving for it," Iago said proudly. "If only I weren't living in Boston!"

"You *are* completing your assignments for the Powers Below, correct?" Dante asked.

Iago quietly collected his latest work and tidied the papers before placing them on his desk, just so. "*Mostly.*"

"Mostly?"

Iago said, "I do what I must. After all, I am demon. But temptation is crafted of words and pictures, of passions. And now, I use these elements to create on my own terms. I feel so much freer for it."

"Oh, Iago…!"

"I am not usually averse to speaking of my work, Dante!" he said with a flourish of the hand, as if to sweep away the topic. "But you are troubled. I can see it in your eyes, my dear. What is the matter?"

Ah, yes. Dante had become so caught up in long lost grandsons and rattling automatons that he almost forgot the manacles around his wrists. He frowned and sat in the plush burgundy armchair by the window. "*Troubled* is putting it lightly. I am accustomed to crafting trouble. This time, it has come barreling toward me at full speed."

"Speak, Dante," Iago said as he retrieved a decanter of scotch and two glasses. It was Iago's customary drink, and while it took an inordinate amount to affect a demon, Dante was willing to accept that challenge given the circumstances. "There's never been a problem Mr. Lovelace and Mr. Wick could not solve by putting their heads together."

"Well, I…" Dante felt like a human speaking of an embarrassing malady. This was an unfortunate boil, an inability to pleasure one's lover, a receding hairline.

"You're being transferred to another city?" Iago guessed.

"No, no."

"You tire of me? A century and a half, and it comes to this?" he cried melodramatically.

"*No!* Not at all. I… This is difficult. I'm not certain what to do, and so, I came to you. Perhaps there's nothing we can do. I only… It's just…" He closed his eyes and took a deep breath. "Iago, I've been bound by a witch."

When he opened his eyes again, Iago looked at him gravely. He added a little more scotch to Dante's glass before handing it to him. "Oh, dear. That is quite a problem, isn't it?"

~

Dante told Iago everything that had happened since the fire at the Hubbins house. Iago listened intently as he sipped his scotch in the wingback chair adjacent to Dante's. His face turned a bit sourer with every detail.

"You mean to say, this Miss Dickens met you and

immediately set her sights on binding you? To better her business?" Iago asked disdainfully. "*Witches*."

"She admitted she had been watching me. She channeled Dylan Courtwright at our first séance."

"*Our?*" Iago laughed. "You're hardly a business partner, dear Dante. I wouldn't be so hasty in throwing around such inclusive determiners."

Dante finished his scotch. "Is there anything at all I can do? I am to be back in Marlowe by Monday, or she will put me through what I can only assume will be grievous pain."

Iago stood and paced in thought. "I have never seen a demon break the spell which binds him to a witch. That doesn't mean it can't be done, but I fear it would be difficult." He turned, arms outstretched and a professorial glint in his eye. Dante knew he was in for a dissertation. "You see, this is why I so distrust the Powers Below. They not only allow debacles such as this, but *encourage* them so that they might fatten the soul of some spell-casting bitch. And all the while, they cheapen the work done by their own agents."

Iago continued, "And here, in Boston! It isn't like Marlowe. The art of demon hunting is becoming modernized, and yet, the Powers Below expect us to walk the streets and take souls as we always have. We are sitting ducks here, Dante, and..." He coughed and looked to the floor. "Not that I wish to worry you. My passion may lead to exaggeration."

Soon, Dante thought, it wouldn't only be in Boston and New York where hunters used new methods to battle minions of Lucifer. Matters were changing. It was a fight Dante was wishing more and more he did not have to join, but Hell expected it just as it expected him to serve Beatrice Dickens. "But what can we do, Iago?"

Iago gave a thoughtful hum. "I've told you. In fact, I've waxed poetic on the topic."

"Not this again."

"Purely hypothetical, my dear! I'm not making plans to run away today. However, there comes a time when one must determine the weight of one's fealty," Iago said. "I feel mine is little more than aluminum at this point." He sat again and took Dante's hand. "Look at us now. We are a mere hour's train ride away from each other, but it is our work, our duties which keep us apart. In theory, we could defect and abandon Hell."

"I really don't wish to speak of this now," Dante groaned.

Iago continued, "I know, despite the pride you force and the quality of your work as a catastrophe artist, that you do not truly enjoy it."

"But as you say, I have no choice," Dante said to calm his indignant melancholia. He thought of the volumes of newspaper clippings at home chronicling every disaster he had ever orchestrated. Tragedy reduced to mere narrative was a bit easier to swallow. Not to mention, he couldn't imagine controlling his melancholia if he defected! The little bastard was quite a handful already, like an unruly child on his birthday shouting, 'Is this all? I want more!'

"It is my duty," Dante said firmly.

"It doesn't have to be. Ever since I left Marlowe, I've been unable to conjure the enthusiasm I once had. Old age, perhaps," Iago muttered. "We have both seen firsthand how little Hell cares about its agents. The world would be ours. We would be free from Hell." He coughed again. "Hypothetically speaking, of course."

Of course.

"And we would be forced to live in hiding," Dante said. "We would still be hunted, simply by our own kind, not by humans." Dante's shoulders slumped. "I understand you, Iago. However, presently, I must consider the problem at hand. Defecting would not assist me now."

~

They were so consumed by their conversation that they did not see the small and softly humming creature that crept beneath the study door. Like a spider, it crawled deftly over the wood before settling upon the wall.

The creature quickly latched its tiny claws into the wallpaper and flattened itself. The back of the device slid open, and mist seeped into the room.

V.

Dante Lovelace was well-versed in the notion that where there's smoke, there's usually fire. This time, however, that was not literally the case.

"Cover your nose and mouth," Iago commanded as smoke spewed into the room. He tucked his face into the crook of his elbow and leapt to investigate. "And open the windows!"

Dante rushed to the front of the study to do as he was told. A young woman stood across the street, her face nestled too deeply in newspaper for Dante to identify her.

"Found it!" Iago announced.

Dante returned to his partner's side to see him pluck a small mechanical bug from the wall. Iago coughed and flipped the creature over to examine its armored underside. Its legs wiggled frantically, cogs whirring. Iago's shoulders slumped, and he uncovered his mouth.

He took a demonstratively deep breath and was none the poorer for it. "I should have known," he muttered at the small insignia stamped into the bug's belly.

"What is it?" Dante asked.

There was one sharp and somehow supercilious knock on the study door.

Iago narrowed his eyes. He answered the door and said, "So, it comes to this? You're letting yourself into my house and attempting to poison me. Ah, this is a marvelous partnership, Atchison."

Viola Atchison didn't smile; she was not in the habit of doing such things, but there was something in her icy blue eyes that vaguely indicated amusement. Dante failed to see how attempted assault was at all amusing. She wore a skirt these days—today, a modest taupe—though she considered such dress a hideous inconvenience. Her blonde hair was a bit longer than the masculine style she'd sported in Marlowe. Not fashionable, but not strange, either. As always, she wore her favorite accessory: an air of untouchable superiority.

"Had that smoke been poisoned, you'd be unconscious already," she bluntly informed them as she entered. Her pale eyebrows jumped toward her hairline. "That's quite the point in my favor."

"Another weapon?" Dante asked, and found himself questioning the company Iago kept. It wasn't the first time.

She peaked her fingers. "My latest creation. Like a spider, it can flatten itself and enter any room. Once inside, it releases a poisonous gas tailored to fit the target.

A compound laced with garlic for vampires, for example. Or lamb's blood, in the case of demons."

"Hmm. Lovely," Iago said, waving a hand through the dissipating mist.

"Oh, never you, Mr. Wick," she insisted dryly. "We have quite an agreement."

"One I trust you honor devoutly, Mrs. Atchison?" Dante asked, unable to keep a chill from his voice.

She scoffed. "Mr. Lovelace, your sweetheart is safe with me. And by the way, Mr. Wick, I thank you for your intelligence on that frightful hobgoblin tribe. I was able to save all three children the monsters had kidnapped."

"Think nothing of it. Harriet gave me the clue," Iago said. "She tells me that your outing with the sirens ended well."

"My outing, you say. You make it sound as though I took them to the opera."

"Perhaps the hags could learn a thing or two about singing if you did," Iago said as he took a seat. He motioned for Viola to do the same, but she wordlessly declined.

"Not a single siren incident since." She had a self-satisfied gleam in her eye as she paced to the bookshelves to examine Iago's selection of literature. She ran long, white fingers along the spines. "While I would be quite content to summarize every gruesome detail of the affair—including the rather messy throat-slitting incident—I sense something else is awry." She turned and grimaced. "What trouble brings Dante Lovelace to Boston?"

"Dante has a bit of a personal problem," Iago said. He reached for another glass of scotch.

"Personal? How so? A physical malady? An embarrassing affliction?" she asked.

Dante narrowed his eyes. "As which of the aforementioned would you qualify being bound by a witch?"

"Ah, a binding spell. Tragic. Name?" Viola asked brusquely.

"Dickens. Beatrice Dickens."

Viola's face twitched in a modicum of surprise. "Dickens? Related to Lionel Dickens, I imagine."

"Yes!" Dante said. "He's her father."

"Was," Viola answered. She approached Iago's desk, eyes darting over the first page of Virgil Alighieri's latest work. "He was murdered earlier this year."

Dante said, "Miss Dickens had mentioned that. An intruder took his life."

"Though I fear I'm not aware of the presumably-unpleasant details, I'm certain this was no garden-variety robbery," Viola said darkly, pausing as she read more of Iago's story. Iago tensed in anticipation. "Mr. Dickens was a demon hunter in his youth, but quickly discovered he hadn't the stomach for it. However, he found his own place. He was an amateur folklorist and historian and realized he could use that to his advantage. Dickens collected cursed and enchanted objects."

"His daughter did not tell me that. Quite the dangerous hobby," Dante said, recalling the witch's hesitance to speak of her father's life's work.

"His goal was to keep those objects out of inexperienced or dangerous hands." Viola tapped her finger upon the page. "Very good, Mr. Wick, but your opening paragraph is still lacking."

"Noted," Iago said. "So, Mr. Dickens made himself a protector of supernatural goods? And all in Marlowe, at that! How had we never heard of him?"

Viola gave a minute shrug. "He lived several miles outside of town and used cloaking spells to hide from anyone who might pay him the wrong sort of attention. That would include a demon such as yourself, Mr. Wick. I met with Dickens once when I'd first arrived in Marlowe. *Strange* man."

It took a unique and extreme sort of eccentricity for Viola Atchison to call a person strange. Lionel Dickens must have been the High Muck-a-Muck of Bizarre.

Dante asked, "All family history aside, do you know of any way to combat a binding spell?"

She barked once in hawkish laughter.

"Thank you kindly for your reassurance, Mrs. Atchison," Dante said wryly.

She hummed. "Sarcasm does not become you, Mr. Lovelace. A binding spell is one of the strongest in a witch's arsenal. It must be, to contain something as powerful as a demon," Viola explained. "You could reason with the creature. I doubt it will do a damned bit of good, but perhaps she'll listen."

"And perhaps she'll set me on fire," Dante said.

"Entirely possible," Viola said, and turned to Iago. "I assume you've heard the news. Bancroft."

Iago swallowed. "Yes."

She regarded Dante with a strange and uneasy gaze. He didn't like it one bit. There were times they spoke in Dante's presence as though they protected all the secrets of the universe, and Dante Lovelace was the first name on the list of creatures not to be told. "Perhaps you should make yourself scarce, Mr. Wick. Bancroft was quite successful in New York, though he returned sooner than I anticipated. Ten targets eliminated," Viola said.

Iago rubbed his temples. "That's not quite as sickening a number. Harriet said a hundred."

"Harriet is made from discarded remnants of my Mechanical Valet," she said. "She's far from perfect. Assist Mr. Lovelace. Return with him to Marlowe. Just for a short while. You won't be missed in Boston."

"Well, you can tell Boston I won't miss it, either," Iago said with a smile. He finished his scotch and stood. "You'll take care, Mrs. Atchison?"

Viola retrieved her ghastly bug, fondly stroking its exoskeleton. "Of course. Mr. Wick, I take nothing but care and the occasional cup of strong coffee. Now, if you gentlemen will excuse me."

Viola Atchison had a way of simply abandoning conversations once she felt they had nothing else to offer her, like a vulture having picked a carcass clean. As quickly as her murderous bug had arrived, she left.

Dante wished he could like Viola Atchison. Well, perhaps not *like* her. Dante wasn't certain anyone *liked* Viola Atchison, but at the very least, he wished he could see her as anything more than a threat-in-waiting. Despite her skirts, he still saw Thomas Atchison when he looked at her, the man she played in Marlowe. The moment Iago did not behave as she pleased, she would have exorcism on her mind again!

Iago said, "Before we depart for Marlowe, I should still like to have dinner with Mr. Quinn."

"This Mr. Bancroft sounds like a serious threat," Dante said. "I gather this was a successful hunting trip from which he's returning. Are you certain going to dinner is wise?"

Iago's lips pursed in thought, and in the end, it appeared temptation conquered fear. "Delrubio's has an exquisite spice cake. Yes, it is *very* wise."

~

On the street below, Sofia Atchison waited for her wife, eyes flitting over the newspaper. There wasn't a thing worth reading, but at least it gave her cause to avoid the gaze of a lustful gentleman who loitered at the edge of the Common behind her. Many boorish men with inflated egos warmed to the task of taking a naïve and pretty Mexican girl under their wing.

Sofia might have been pretty and Mexican, but naïve, she was not.

"Mr. Lovelace is within," Viola said, suddenly at her side. Even after five years of marriage, she could still sneak up on Sofia.

"He is? Has Mr. Wick told him about his *accident?*" Sofia asked as she tucked away the newspaper.

"No. He knows nothing of Bancroft. I encouraged Wick to return to Marlowe with Mr. Lovelace. It seems the latter is having some problems of his own," Viola said. "It would give Mr. Wick some time away from this place. He's becoming quite skittish due to this business with Bancroft. I cannot afford to lose him entirely."

Viola frowned suddenly. Sofia followed her gaze. Beacon Street was pleasantly busy, but most travelers kept moving. The woman a hearty stone's throw away stood still and stared intently at Iago Wick's home.

"Sofia, do you recognize that lady there?" Viola asked.

"No. I do not. She has not been there too long."

"Still, she looks awfully interested in Mr. Wick's location." Viola gave a thoughtful hum. "Our plans for this afternoon?"

"None that I am aware of," Sofia answered begrudgingly.

"Marvelous. We must keep an eye on this little spy," she whispered, "for Mr. Wick's sake."

"Viola," Sofia said. "I know you like Mr. Wick. He is useful, I know. But we cannot continue to put ourselves in danger for him. He is a demon."

"No, he is not only a demon," Viola said, shaking her head. "He is *my* demon."

~

There might as well have been a fee to breathe the air outside Delrubio's restaurant. Its patrons would gladly pay it, simply to show they could.

While there were smaller rooms near the back which allowed a man to dine with his wife and family, most of the restaurant was for the patronage of men only. And so, spirits flowed and some of Boston's grandest men met and dined and happily spent hours away from their wives and families.

The coat rooms were carefully attended to by automatons, but even these proud and modern Bostonians valued the white shirts of their clientele too heartily to allow the machines to act as waiters.

After ducking into the shadows outside to abandon invisibility, Dante and Iago entered and were escorted to their table. Luxurious curtains of red and gold hung from ceiling to floor, and a man who satisfactorily knew his way around a piano provided music, resigned to a fate of always accompanying conversation and clinking glasses, never truly being heard.

Iago watched for Osgood Quinn, insisting that Zero Bancroft was not the sort of man to visit Delrubio's—a fact that seemed to do little for his nerves. Dante, meanwhile, watched everyone around him.

Humans were dumb and brilliant and loving and hateful things, and he was often content to ponder what made them behave as they did. It wasn't always a tragedy crafted by demonic hands or the encouragement of a tempter such as Iago Wick. There was so much that contributed to the making of a man. Dante's eyes settled on one at another table, talking far more than eating, leaving his extravagant meal to grow cold. He would probably send it back, nearly untouched, before the night was over because he could, because he was the master of his own fate and if he didn't wish to eat the expensive meal he paid for, then damn it all, he wouldn't swallow a bite! But he would not go home hungry, Dante noted as he sipped a glass of brandy. This kind of man glutted himself on his own arrogance.

Soon, Osgood Quinn shuffled to their table. He was a thin man with a soft, doughy face like melting wax. He wore unfashionable suits because he didn't know better, and he constantly fiddled with his wedding ring, as though it were a wart he was anxious to remove.

"Mr. Wick, I apologize for last night. Wilhelmina and I… well, I have already told you of our trials," Quinn said as he took his seat. He looked upon the glass waiting for him. "Brandy. How thoughtful. I'll need more than this before the night is through."

"Mr. Quinn, marital bliss is little more than a myth," Iago said. "I've told you before. Perhaps there are greener pastures elsewhere."

"And I have told you, I cannot leave Wilhelmina," Quinn said.

"I never said you had to leave her," Iago said with a grin.

Quinn wrinkled his nose. "Demons. And tonight, I have the good fortune of dining with two of them?"

"It's a pleasure to see you again, Mr. Quinn," Dante said, but he could tell that Mr. Quinn did not count his presence as anything close to pleasurable.

Osgood Quinn grunted, "Mr. Wick, why is Mr.

Lovelace joining us this evening?"

"Because he is in Boston, and I thought it polite to invite him," Iago said.

Dante explained, "I'm afraid I have a problem which requires Mr. Wick's assistance. I had to travel to Boston on rather short notice."

Quinn merely blinked at Dante, as though his words traveled in one ear, were quickly crumpled up somewhere around the temporal lobe, and then, unceremoniously tossed out the other ear. Dante had noticed his words were always mere obstacles to Quinn, something merely to endure. They weren't making him money like Mr. Wick's. "Wick, what in Hell have you done to my automaton?" Quinn demanded. "It's out of control."

"She," Iago corrected. "And anyway, Harriet is only yours in the eyes of the Department of Automaton Licensure. Viola Atchison made her. I've taught her much. She'd be mine entirely, had they not dictated that only businesses and public offices could own automatons. She gives me information, and of course, I thank you for allowing me the publishing house's allotment."

Quinn shook his head and poked a fork in Iago's direction. "If she is caught doing something unsavory, my publishing house's serial number is on the back of her head. When necessary, she charges at my publishing house's assigned dock at the nursery. I'll be the one to pay for it! And I don't need you dillydallying with automatons. I need more stories. Your production is slow."

"I know that," Iago admitted. "Hell has been quite

needy as of late." He opened his menu with gusto. "You know, I haven't truly eaten well in weeks! The oysters here are quite commendable."

"Yes," Quinn groaned. "I seem to recall you ate three plates of the hideous things the last time we dined here."

Dante chuckled inwardly. Most human cuisine appalled Iago. But there were certain dishes he devoured with inhuman vigor, most of them dessert. A supernatural mode of digestion allowed a demon to eat all the cake he wanted without spoiling his waistline.

Mostly. Dante recalled the time Iago discovered he had gained a pound and a half in the decade since he last weighed himself.

Lucifer Below, it was as though the Apocalypse had come early.

Dante ordered guinea fowl and only poked at it. He was entranced by Quinn and Iago's conversation, even though he could contribute little. Iago's writing career was strange to him, terribly human. Dante listened and devoured every word. It might have been nice to have some connection to humanity that was not founded upon destruction. There was a beautiful light in Iago's eyes when he spoke of his writing, and Dante wondered what this brand of pride and excitement felt like.

"I hope this business in Marlowe doesn't keep you away for too long," Quinn mumbled around a mouthful of beef. He ate like the cow he was consuming, Dante thought. "Your latest, the one about the double temptation, as it were... it's captured the minds of my readers."

"The rather foul minds of your readers," Iago said. "Dear Dante, the seal of Mr. Quinn's publishing house is a stamp of *quality.*"

"They sell, don't they?" Quinn asked. "I don't care if it's filthier than two white horses rolling around in the mud. I'm making money and people are reading them, even if they won't admit it. Throw me something to publish, Wick. Anything. I'm not asking for Shakespeare."

"I knew Shakespeare," Iago said proudly. "Quite intimately, I might add, and I can attest that he was an uncommonly bawdy man." Dante clenched his jaw. With Gregor Hawley and Lady Heloise behind them, he'd had quite enough of Iago's past for one day.

Quinn harrumphed. "Thank you for the history lesson I never requested."

Iago ate another oyster before he spoke again, savoring this one's taste. He sucked some residue from his thumb, and his tone was calculated, severe when he continued. "I intend to increase production. I have a plan that will allow me to do so. That is why I wanted to speak with you tonight."

Quinn asked, "Is that so?"

"Yes. All I ask is that you exercise some patience. I foresee myself with quite a lot of empty time in the future."

Dante put down his fork. "Dear Iago, what plan is this?"

Iago drained his glass of brandy.

"Certainly this is not related to the, *ahem,* blasphemy

that left your lips this afternoon," Dante continued. "You would surely find a way to write these fictions and carry out your duties to Hell simultaneously, correct?"

"I can assure you, dear Dante," Iago said with measured thought, "that I will find a way to lead a fulfilling existence."

Dante leaned forward. "No, Iago Wick, your pretty words will not hoodwink me. Speak plainly."

Iago turned to his oysters for comfort again and swallowed two of them before he found the strength to continue. "Quinn, we have spoken of this possibility before. If all goes accordingly, Hell will not occupy my time for much longer."

"*What?*" Dante exclaimed. "When did mere fancy turn into fact?"

"I could no longer live in Boston, but I'd make certain you received your stories by post," Iago continued.

Dante's black blood boiled, and his melancholia casually asked if he wanted to burn the restaurant to the ground. No, he was not quite that infuriated. *Yet.* "Don't ignore me, Mr. Wick," he hissed. "I understand your frustration with the Powers Below, but that does not mean you can completely abandon them. Think of the possible consequences. I—" Dante caught Osgood Quinn's gaze and remembered himself. "I apologize, Mr. Quinn. This is quite a subject of contention between me and my partner."

Osgood Quinn shrugged, still chomping like a lethargic bovine. "Not to worry. I have grown accustomed to—"

"Rest assured, Dante, that I would never take such measures unless you were joining me," Iago said firmly.

This was no whim, no fanciful daydream or hypothetical situation; this was a proposal. Dante balled his fists under the table. "Iago Wick, did you just ask me—in the middle of a crowded restaurant—to desert my kind, render myself an outlaw, and abandon the very work to which I have dedicated my existence for nearly two centuries?"

"Simply put, yes."

"In the middle of Delrubio's?" Dante asked.

Iago surveyed his surroundings. "I may have chosen a poor venue in which to broach the subject, I will admit."

"Do you think so, Mr. Wick?" he said a bit louder than he intended. He lowered his voice. "If you think for one moment that I'm going to agree to this in order to keep up appearances in front of your employer—"

"Doesn't your current predicament make you question the Powers Below?" Iago asked. "Don't they deserve abandonment?"

"Perhaps, but that does not mean I would commit to something so utterly foolish!" Dante growled. Mr. Quinn watched with a bizarre blend of consternation and amusement on his doughy features. Dante cleared his voice. "I'm sorry, Mr. Quinn."

"*Gentlemen.*" Osgood Quinn finished his brandy. "That's enough." He crossed his knife and fork neatly over each other, and he clasped his hands into one pale ball. "Mr. Wick, I don't care if you appeal to Lucifer Himself for your freedom. I don't care if you simply run away from Hell. I don't care if you start wearing dresses and flee to the Orient under the assumed name of dog groomer Madame Alighieri. I don't care. Just write more stories."

And he stood and left.

Dante did not speak as Iago ordered a glass of scotch and a piece of spice cake. He hardly touched the cake, opting instead to moodily drink his scotch.

It wasn't that Dante didn't understand, but he wondered if Iago truly comprehended the gravity of what he suggested. To Iago, everything was a drama, a performance to behold. He believed the spotlight followed him wherever he went. And it would follow him right back to Hell for an eternity of misery if he was caught abandoning his responsibilities.

They managed to assume invisibility in the coat room before leaving. The air was cool and crisp when they left the restaurant, and Iago Wick uttered the words that always troubled him, like sticky taffy clinging to his teeth. "I'm sorry. I put you in quite a nasty spot back there. I let my passions get the better of me tonight."

Dante looked to the night sky, smoggy with the smoke of every mill and factory in the Boston area. This was not the starry blanket he could turn to in Marlowe.

Iago's plan was a dangerous one, but Dante realized with a lump in his throat that his aggravation did not just stem from his partner's recklessness. After all, why *should* Dante be allegiant to the powers which allowed him to be bound in the first place?

He shook that blasphemy from his head. Such thoughts wouldn't do! Lucifer Below, he was supposed to be the sensible one! "Apology accepted," Dante said. "I just wish you would take care when saying such things." He paused and added, "So, you've decided, then? You're dedicated to defecting?"

Iago looked into Dante's eyes. "Never without you. But I can't go back to how I was, Dante, in Marlowe, in Salem, in London nor, indeed, in Hell. I have tried. I am no longer Hell's faithful servant. That fire has been extinguished." He sighed. "I do understand if you are too upset to indulge me tonight. I deserve that snub."

Despite the evening's unpleasant turn, Dante could not deny the desire humming in his bones. It had been too long. They were in the habit of making the very most of their time together these days. Lust was a fine sin and one which had not yet waned in their long partnership. "I wouldn't say that," he said with a grin.

~

The gentleman demons were perhaps so distracted by their own personal dramas that they did not notice the young woman watching Iago's house from Boston Common when they returned. The tall gentleman in black was the man she sought. *Dante.* He was a handsome thing, she thought, and cursed herself. He was a demon, a disgusting creature! Tall, dark, handsome, yes, but disgusting! At any rate, her heart was firmly in the grasp of another.

Compulsively, she pressed her palm to a spot just below her hip. Beneath the fabric of her skirt, she could feel the weapon still strapped to her thigh. She had never killed anything before, not really. Spiders, mice, of course, but nothing so imposing. The thought of killing not one demon, but two made her heart race. And yet, her hands were unsteady. That simply wouldn't do, she thought. He would be so disappointed in her if she failed.

The demons did not see her as they doffed invisibility and entered the home.

~

Fortunately, the young woman in question didn't see Viola Atchison watching her, either.

~

Watching Iago Wick pack for their journey to Marlowe was like watching a one-man relay race. He darted from his closet to his suitcase and back again as he hemmed and hawed over what garments to take. "Dante," he said severely, "which of these waistcoats do you find the most... resplendent?"

It was almost morning now, and Dante dressed in the mirror. The bed had served its singular purpose well. He turned. "The blue one."

"Really? I'm fond of the plum one myself and... oh, I'll just take all three. I'm sure I'll find opportunities to wear them all."

"Perhaps in the same day," Dante said with a smirk as he buttoned his own black waistcoat.

"You know me too well."

A demon could, if he put his mind to it, technically conjure a new wardrobe whenever he wanted, but there was something to be said for a well-worn suit or a familiar waistcoat. Such creature comforts warmed a demon's heart.

Dante readied his necktie and wandered around the neatly-kept bedroom. There was a beautiful copy of *Paradise Lost* on the bedside table, bound in red leather and decorated in gold. Dante had never seen it in Iago's possession before, and he picked it up while his partner deliberated over cravats under his breath.

It felt strange in Dante's grasp, weighted oddly. He opened the book to find it had been neatly hollowed out, and within was an unmarked bottle of clear liquid. "Iago, what is this?"

Iago looked up from his cravat conundrum and made a noise which suggested he did not want Dante to find that bottle. "Oh, it's nothing, Dante. Medicine. It's medicine to... help me... sleep."

"Sleep? You don't usually choose to sleep," Dante said as he uncorked the bottle. He took a whiff of its contents. "Witch hazel." His head swam pleasantly for a moment at its sweet scent, like a beautifully gloomy day intoxicating the senses. It smelled of red leaves on dead, cold ground, the warmth of a fire. It may not have put humans in such a stupor, but demons were heartily affected. "Are you imbibing oil of witch hazel?"

"Diluted," Iago insisted, and snatched the bottle from Dante's hands. "I'm not some miscreant, some degenerate losing my mind to the drug. It's diluted, I promise."

"Why are you taking it?"

"It's quite good for calming one's nerves, Dante."

"You're using this as a nerve tonic? What rattles your nerves?" Dante asked, and why did he have the sinking feeling that the answer began with a Zero and ended with a Bancroft? He had heard of no one else since arriving in Boston. He amended his question. "*Who* rattles your nerves?"

Iago smoothed over his waistcoats, positioning every item in his suitcase just so. "Dante, I—"

A sudden clatter came from beyond the bedroom door. Iago held a finger to his lips. "Invisibility—now," he hissed. Dante did as he was told, and he listened. The sounds of scuffling, of boots on floorboards, came from the hall. There was a muffled curse, a yelp in a different voice.

Iago's hand hovered over the doorknob. Dante crept to his side. "There are two people," Dante said, their voices undetectable to human ears.

"They've decided to have a row in my hallway. I should at least like some compensation for their renting the venue," Iago said as he crouched to peer through the keyhole. "Oh, Lucifer Below."

"What?"

There was a louder thud, then the sound of running.

Iago threw open the door to reveal Viola Atchison, panting heavily on the floor. The window at the end of the hall was open, curtains wafting. Viola spat another curse and leapt to her feet. Dante and Iago made themselves visible to the human eye again as Viola hurried to the open window. She looked from side to side and cursed again for good measure.

"Mrs. Atchison," Iago greeted cheerfully. "How good of you to visit."

"She escaped," Viola growled.

"Who?" Dante asked.

"I don't know her name. Brunette. Hideously pretty. She was a swift lockpick, but she fought like a blind cat. She was also quite hesitant to attack, though she's been watching you since this afternoon."

Iago blinked. "And you, in turn, have been watching her since this afternoon?"

"Indeed. Initially, Sofia and I were both watching, but she left just after suppertime. Pressing matters. A sampler to finish or some such thing. Anyway, I was able to fight the girl on my own."

"Why didn't you just tell us we were being watched?" Dante asked skeptically.

"Where's the fun in that? I had hoped to tear some identifying information from her in our scuffle," Viola said as Iago turned up the lamps. "I did, and though it was not the sort of information I intended to find, it did confirm my fears. She had this on her person."

Viola held up a small vial of shining blue liquid. Such an oddly beautiful thing, Dante thought, like a microcosm of the ocean or some far off galaxy.

"Some pretty potion. What is it?" Dante asked.

Iago looked stricken. "She was carrying *that*?"

"Yes," Viola said. "Which can only mean that this was another attempt on your life, Mr. Wick. She can only be assisting Bancroft. He would never allow someone unaffiliated to use his formula."

Iago tumbled into a chair. "How does he know I'm alive?"

"I haven't the faintest, but if he does know, he'll surely come after me, as well," Viola said, examining the vial. "Can't I do my work in peace without that bald hulk interfering?"

"Alive?" Dante asked. "Why wouldn't you be alive?"

"Lucifer Below," Iago groaned, and placed his palm to his stomach. "Suddenly, those oysters aren't sitting so well. What are we going to do?"

"We? *You're* going to Marlowe. What am *I* going to do?" Viola said, and stalked to close the window. "If anyone asks, I buried you. That is the extent of my involvement. You were dead. You're quite the handsome revenant, Mr. Wick."

Dante asked, "Coming back from the dead? Excuse my ignorance, but what are you talking about?"

Viola looked coldly from Dante to Iago. "You still haven't told him."

"Told me what?" Dante demanded.

"The opportunity hasn't presented itself," Iago muttered.

"Mr. Lovelace deserves to know," said Viola.

"I certainly do deserve to know! …Whatever it is," Dante said. Demon hunters, magic potions, resurrections… Dante was beginning to feel as though Boston was a bit wilder than he thought.

"What good would it have done?" Iago asked, and reached into his pocket for the bottle of witch hazel. He uncorked it and sucked a small amount from the pad of his thumb.

"Are you imbibing that slop again?" Viola said bluntly.

"Sparingly. Mrs. Atchison, I was not aware that you had assumed the role of my mother," Iago quipped.

Dante had had quite enough of this verbal badminton. As they sparred, he reached into his breast pocket to conjure a metal device. It was the size of a house spider, no bigger than Dante's thumbnail. It was a spark. The things came in various sizes, this being the smallest and just enough to make him the center of attention.

He placed the device upon a table and pressed the red crystal at its center.

Viola continued, "By all means, Mr. Wick, drug yourself into a stupor. I'm certain Bancroft will have no trouble catching you unaware then. And one more thing—"

The spark banged like a holiday cracker when it detonated. Iago gripped his heart, eyes wide. Viola turned calmly, silently, to face Dante. A catastrophe artist always knew a thing or two about catching people's attention. Sometimes small—or large—explosions were the best option.

Dante said, "Mr. Wick. Mrs. Atchison. Forgive me, but... what in Hell is happening here?"

VI.

The clock on the parlor mantel proclaimed it six o' clock in the morning, and Iago Wick had already taken two glasses of scotch in approximately ten minutes. A good thing he wasn't easily inebriated, or he'd be unconscious or weepily recalling the Jacobean era by seven o'clock, at this rate. The witch hazel had calmed him somewhat, but it left an uncharacteristic dullness in his eyes. Viola Atchison paced before the fireplace like a caged tiger.

Dante sat beside Iago. "Zero Bancroft is a demon hunter. That much I know. Why has he targeted you in particular? Your partnership with Mrs. Atchison?" he asked resentfully.

"No, no," Iago said. "He doesn't know we work together. I believe now it's because I am proof that his work is not flawless. Also, I may have... *provoked* him once or twice."

Unnecessary provocation came to Dante's partner as easily as breathing. "Why am I not surprised?" he said. "I am reminded of the debacle with the vampires in Marlowe two years ago."

"I'm *still* rather revolted by garlic after that disaster," said Iago. "In this case, I merely taunted Bancroft. Teased him. When I first arrived in Boston, Bancroft was just another over-inflated demon hunter. Admittedly practiced, well-trained. Not the sort of fellow you'd like to meet in a dark alley, but nothing extraordinary. That was before."

"Before what?" Dante asked.

"This." Viola held the vial of blue liquid high. "The Zero Formula: the single greatest development in demon hunting in the last century." There was venom in her voice, and Dante knew she was furious that she had not concocted this formula—whatever it was—herself.

Dante spoke delicately. "Bancroft thought you were dead, you said. He believed that he killed you. But a demon can only be exorcised and sent back to Hell; he cannot die."

"I'm afraid your information is outdated, my dear," Iago said, glaring into his third scotch.

"In essence, the Zero Formula is a demon-killer," Viola explained. "It's a compound of various substances already detrimental to demons. Lamb's blood, holy water, a dash of witch hazel for a sense of mortal euphoria, and about a dozen other ingredients which manipulate the human body the demon inhabits. It puts the demon in a death-like sleep. Since its invention a year ago, no other demon we know of has awoken from that sleep. Even their hearts stop. The demon is trapped inside his human body. Bancroft laces his bullets with the concoction, in addition to using needles and other shooters."

"No one has come back," Dante said, "except for you, Iago? You were…?"

"Dead?" Iago asked. "A little."

"*A little?*" Dante squeaked.

Iago finished his scotch. "It is unwise for a demon to walk Boston's empty streets alone at night. Alas, it is sometimes a necessity. This was nearly six months ago. I was not invisible—stupidity on my part—and Bancroft saw me. I heard him just a second too late."

"A second too late," Viola said gravely, "and you were unconscious for eight days!"

"The bullet grazed just above my left hip."

Dante's chest tightened as he considered the weight of even a second more. He spent his days ending the lives of unsuspecting humans. Death was life and life was death; this was the creed of the catastrophe artist. But applying that concept to a demon—to Iago!—seemed so foreign. "And you were charged with disposing of his body, Mrs. Atchison?" Dante asked weakly.

"I happened to be stalking Bancroft that evening," she said. "Zero Bancroft and I are on *civil* terms. All the same, I make a habit of watching him closely. I appeared, congratulated Bancroft on shooting another demon, and offered to bury the body. He allowed it. Bancroft prefers to bury his victims. The outcome of destroying the human body is unknown. It could very well release the demon. He'd rather leave him trapped inside. Instead of burying Mr. Wick, however, I brought his body home, much to my wife's chagrin."

"At least I was a clean and quiet house guest," Iago said.

"The quietest you've ever been!" Viola said. "I almost miss those days."

"How did you know he would awaken?" Dante asked.

"I didn't. I only knew it was a very shallow wound. It was pure hope," Viola said, "something in which I don't usually put too much stock. But in the case of Mr. Wick, I was willing to make an exception. You see, Mr. Lovelace? I am not so terrible."

Yes, it wouldn't do to lose your pet demon, would it? Dante thought, but held his tongue.

Dante stood and straightened his waistcoat, steadying his hands. A catastrophe artist knew not to let emotion consume him. And yet, he could not help but think of a day over a century ago, prior to the Revolution. Still lounging upon soft linens after a night together, Iago first proclaimed, *"And should any demon hunter break my stride, and I be cast back to Hell, rest assured, dear Dante, that I would come back to find you."*

Hell revels in negotiation. Death, however, is not so easily swayed.

"I believe I've heard enough," Dante said as firmly as he could. "We need to leave for Marlowe. Bancroft knows you're here, and the quicker we get away from him, the better."

"You're not sore with me?" Iago asked.

"I never said that, did I, Mr. Wick? This was not the weather of which you neglected to inform me. You *died*. I should think that would require at least a brief mention in one of your long and loquacious letters, somewhere between the flirting and the recollections of recent cakes you've devoured?" Iago winced. Dante admitted, "However, I also know my nature. I would not have taken such news well, particularly when we were apart."

And for the second time in a period of twenty-four hours, Iago Wick apologized. It was probable that several cultists of varying factions the world over took notice. Two apologies in one day? Surely that was unlikely enough to put a few Apocalyptic prophecies in action.

"It is strange, however," Viola said, "that Bancroft should send an agent after you and not seek you out himself. I should think he would want to be the one to finish the job." She looked curiously over the vial. "Something occurs to me. This may be quite the boon. We now have his weapon in our grasp. It can be examined, analyzed."

Dante said, "You're thinking of finding an antidote."

"Ah," Viola said, "very good, Mr. Lovelace."

"Your fellow hunters would want your head," Dante said.

"That's only if the other hunters know what I'm doing. You gentlemen are different. It would behoove me greatly to protect you. You're an asset," Viola said, her tone positively Saharan.

"Such emotional effusion, Atchison," Iago said. "I

assure you, we are touched."

"When we started on this journey two years ago on that train from Marlowe, I said I would protect you, Mr. Wick, if you assisted me in return. I can craft a suitable antidote," she said, and pocketed the vial once more. "I'm holding up my end of the bargain with the understanding that you will continue to do the same."

Iago was a thousand years old, but never had he looked it. Now, Dante saw a weariness in his eyes. For a moment, he seemed to show every one of his years. Then, he smiled and threw his arms wide. "Away to Marlowe, then?"

Dante nodded. "Away to Marlowe."

~

Charlotte Cutter threw quick glances over her shoulder every fourth or fifth step as she hurried down a South End sidewalk. That frightful woman she encountered in Wick's home was not following her, and still, her nerves were shaken. Not to mention, her legs were wobbly. She'd never leapt from a window before. It was terrifying and invigorating all at once. The landing was, admittedly, less than perfect, but with practice, she might be able to survive even the heartiest attempts at murder by defenestration.

Mr. Bancroft would be furious if he discovered Charlotte had lost a vial of the formula. He was good enough to take her under his wing and test her skills, and this was how she performed, like some incapable child! "I have word Miss Dickens has purchased toadflax and wolfsbane at an apothecary in Boston," he had told Charlotte in confidence. *Close* confidence. "She's planning a binding spell. Get to Marlowe. Watch. And take this, my dear. You'll need it."

And he gave her two vials of the swirling blue concoction which bore his name: The Zero Formula.

The spirit of Dylan Courtwright proclaimed a demon was present at the séance, and while Mr. Mason hailed a cab afterwards, Charlotte even peered through the window to see a man appear from thin air. This was her target! It was all coming together so perfectly...

...and then, she stumbled at the finish line. Or, at least, she was tackled to the ground by another woman at the finish line.

Charlotte stopped at the front door of a rather unpleasant home on the brink of dilapidation, lodged like an unsightly barnacle among other houses in the South End. It suited Sylvester Hacke. He would live in a crate on the side of the road if he wouldn't be arrested for vagrancy.

Charlotte knocked twice. Three knocks came back. She knocked once more. The door opened. Mr. Hacke leered at her lecherously. His moustache was crooked, his hair was oily, and he smelled like raw steak left to sunbathe.

"Thank you," Charlotte said pointedly, and stepped inside.

"I'm not accustomed to having such lovely ladies in my parlor, Miss Cutter," Hacke purred. Charlotte failed to see how the room qualified as a parlor; for one thing, most parlors had furniture. She eyed the peeling wallpaper with a frown. "Perhaps you will stay for breakfast?"

Charlotte sneered. "You greatly overstep your boundaries, Mr. Hacke. I am here to relay information. Nothing more. A breakfast fit for the president himself would not persuade me to dine with you."

"Perhaps not," came a low voice from the adjacent room. A bald and burly man walked from the shadows. His tawny waistcoat barely buttoned over the expanse of his chest. "But perhaps you will dine with *me*?"

The corners of Charlotte's mouth tugged upward without her consent. "Mr. Bancroft. I wasn't aware you were already here." She looked into his eyes and dreaded having to tell him of her failure. "Of course, I'll dine with you." He took her hand and placed a tender kiss to her knuckles. His massive paw dwarfed hers, but he smiled sweetly.

"Come. There's much to eat."

He led her into the dining room. Three plates of eggs and ham waited on the table. The drapes at one narrow window were open, allowing early daylight into the room. Bancroft sat at the head of the table, choosing the plate with the most food. He neatly tucked a napkin into his shirt collar.

"Pretty thing like you doesn't need to eat too much," Hacke said to Charlotte.

"Quiet, Hacke," Bancroft said before he took a mouthful of eggs.

"Ah... your nephew," Charlotte said pleasantly, and poked the food with her fork. "I take it he's well?"

Bancroft swallowed and said, "Sterling is always well. He left to return to Missouri yesterday afternoon. Misses his mother, but couldn't stop talking about you, either, Miss Cutter. He's a fool. Alas, it wouldn't do to have an unmarried young woman attending a séance on her own. He served his purpose. Everything has its purpose in our battle." He smiled. "Eat, Miss Cutter. You must be hungry."

Hacke's home smelled like an unappetizing combination of urine and mud. Still, she took a bite to please her associate. After all, Bancroft was a lovely man. How awful she should encounter him in a place like this. She could think of a few more suitable places, but to consider that too thoroughly made her cheeks turn pink.

"Miss Cutter, I'm surprised at your reservations," Bancroft said. "You've been on such an adventure. I trust Miss Dickens's demon is dead?"

Charlotte swallowed. "Um... I—"

"She hesitates, Bancroft," Hacke spat around a piece of bread and butter. "She's a failure."

"It was not as simple a task as it seemed," she admitted.

Zero Bancroft chewed slowly, thoughtfully. The silence was agonizing.

Charlotte explained, "I initially planned to watch Miss Dickens's home and determine a suitable moment to attack. But then, I overheard the demon bid her farewell the morning following the séance. He was on his way to

Boston."

"Get on with it, girl," Hacke muttered.

"Mr. Hacke," she said disdainfully, "was at Haymarket, and that's when I relayed to you that the demon met another man there. He is also a demon, I later discovered. Shortly after I spoke to Mr. Hacke, I lost them, but not before I overheard them mention Beacon Street. I took a cab, and there, I was able to spot them again. I waited and attempted to attack in the early hours of the morning."

Bancroft urged her to continue with a pleasant raising of the brows, a warm light in his eyes. Charlotte released a shaky breath that proclaimed her failure before she even said a word.

"There was a woman at Beacon Street, protecting them. A human. She was a commendable fighter. I was forced to flee."

"You were attacked by another woman? Fought with her?" Hacke laughed. "There's something I'd like to think about on cold, lonely nights. You've had the formula since you first saw the demon in Marlowe. Why not shoot him there?"

"I thought it was wise to slay the demon in the same city where Mr. Bancroft was waiting, in case I needed help," she answered feebly, but she knew Bancroft saw the truth. She was no killer.

Bancroft took her hand again. "Then, Dickens's demon still walks the streets?"

"Yes. Mr. Bancroft, I am sorry. I overheard some conversation while ducking in the shrubbery outside the depot." An unpleasant and somewhat thorny experience. "They received information from an automaton, and the demons were very frightened by your return. Dickens's demon is called Dante Lovelace, and his companion is Iago Wick," she said hopefully, as though that small bit of information might save her.

"Iago Wick?" Bancroft asked. He boomed in laughter. "That's impossible. I shot him. He's quite dead, dear lady." He looked suddenly thoughtful. "I left his body to..." Bancroft took another mouthful of egg, chewing it thoroughly. He swallowed and dabbed at the corner of his mouth with his napkin before he spoke again. "Were you able to see the face of the woman who fought you?"

"No. It was dark, though I believe she may have been the same woman who visited the home yesterday afternoon. Tall, blonde, short hair."

Bancroft looked troubled. "I see."

"Told you Miss Cutter was a failure," Hacke grunted, and finished his coffee.

"No," Bancroft said softly. "On the whole, women are not as capable as men. This is proven by science. A woman against a woman... well, it's like two apes scrapping for dominance. Miss Cutter just happened to be the weaker of the two. I was wrong to entrust you with this mission, Miss Cutter. I apologize."

She cringed, but the tenderness in his voice spoke to something deep within her. His words were candy-coated bullets.

"You know," Bancroft began, "when I was young

and just starting to learn the ways of this noble craft, my mentor, Ezekiel Faust, would deny me some necessity every time I failed. Food one night, a bed another night. He denied me a roof over my head on the coldest, snowiest Boston nights. I can still recall when I nearly lost my pinkies. They were practically blue when he allowed me back into his home."

He tapped his finger upon the table and continued, "I'm not going to keep you from your breakfast, Miss Cutter. However, Faust's lesson was that everything has its purpose. For everything I neglected, something I saw as having more value was taken from me. Everything in our plan has value. It is all charged with our purpose, for the world and the force of good are on our side."

"Please allow me another chance, Mr. Bancroft. I can be useful," Charlotte said.

"I know you can. You will. Alas, we have allowed this demon to see another day. Dickens knows what we desire. She'll protect it with all of her might." Bancroft stood and looked out the window. "Hunters before us have always persisted. So shall we."

"I know the demon is returning to Miss Dickens, and I'm certain the artifact is no longer in her home," Charlotte said. "We must follow her. I promise my plan for finding the artifact is sound."

"I trust you," Bancroft said gently, turning back to face her. "Please don't give me reason to believe that trust is misplaced. Get to Marlowe, Miss Cutter. I trust you still have the formula." She nodded shallowly. She would have to do with one vial. "And take Mr. Hacke with you."

Charlotte's stomach churned at the very idea.

Bancroft continued, "Keep a watchful eye on Miss Dickens. Do not act. I will join you shortly. There is some *business* I must attend to here in Boston first."

~

Marlowe, Massachusetts was a warm and familiar embrace. Never before had the city felt quite so welcoming. Perhaps it was the lack of wild demon hunters and stalking assassins.

The crisp autumn air and the smell of fire, a beautiful reprieve from the stench of oil and machinery which permeated Boston, rejuvenated Dante. He let the city sweep him off his feet for now. It was good to be home.

All the same, Dante thought, he would need a holiday when all of this was over. Perhaps at a quiet castle in Europe, one with a dungeon. Dante had always been very fond of dungeons, if from a purely aesthetic viewpoint.

With invisibility donned, Dante and Iago walked from the train, through the depot, and onto Marlowe's streets.

"Lucifer Below, I have missed this city!" Iago exclaimed, suitcase in hand.

"This city misses you, Iago," Dante said as they walked down Station Street, the yellow leaves on the trees shimmering in the sunlight.

"Oh, if not for this witch business, it would be so nice to visit The Golden Swine for dinner. Let's go tonight. It would do my heart good."

Dante shook his head. "I doubt Beatrice would even allow me to go out for dinner. It was quite difficult to convince her to allow me to go to Boston. A night of frivolity would infuriate her, I'm sure."

"Now, now, Dante. I shall *require* a few nights of frivolity during my stay," Iago insisted with a devilish smile.

"I'm sure she senses my return. She'll be wondering where I am."

"She sounds like an utter nuisance."

He couldn't deny that. "It is best if you stay at 13 Darke Street," Dante said. "I've never heard of a witch binding two demons, but I'd hate to give her reason to try."

"I would fight her madly if she did! No spell-casting harlot is going to get her foul hands upon me," Iago said. "I'll drag the bitch to Hell, if I must."

"I'm certain there's no need for that, dear," Dante said calmly. "I shall send for you in time. We will confront her *respectfully* when we ask to strike a deal for my release. All steps taken toward this resolution must be completed with the utmost care. She is no fool. Not a single detail is to be ignored, and we mustn't rush matters."

"You make it all sound so simple," Iago laughed. "Witches are *never* simple."

~

"You've returned early. Is your lover well?" Beatrice asked when Dante arrived at her home.

"He is, thank you." *He's also become addicted to witch hazel and is targeted by the most frightening demon hunter in Boston, but really, he takes it in stride. Just be certain not to make any sudden movements or loud noises.*

"Hmm. What is he like?" she asked from her chair by the fireplace. She looked at Dante quizzically.

Dante took a seat and answered, "Would you like to hear how I would describe him or how he would describe himself? He's clever, proud. He loves words almost as much as he loves cake, and trust me, he is *very* fond of cake."

She snorted. "A tempter, I assume. He must be, for his love of words."

"Yes. Not only does he love words, but he adores hearing himself say them," he laughed. Beatrice did not laugh.

"And Boston?" she continued. "How was Boston?"

Dante answered, "A smoky and mechanized wonder, as per usual. Lovely city to visit, but I wouldn't want to live there."

She nodded slowly. "Splendid. I want you to forget about Boston. And your lover. Forget him. Forget anything other than what is between us. Do you understand?"

Dante wanted to tell her, quite vehemently, to go to Hell, but that would certainly not be conducive to securing his release. "I understand," he said instead. "I'm afraid that, given recent circumstances, that will be quite difficult."

Her green eyes grew stormy. "I don't care how difficult it is. I *need* you."

"To better your business, yes," Dante said smartly. "I recall."

Beatrice Dickens looked to her hands, worn and ropy despite her young age. "Yes. Precisely." She softened. "We both must focus. Otherwise, one of us could be hurt. No distractions."

Dante thought of Iago Wick, who most likely lounged at 13 Darke Street as they spoke, devouring petit fours. He resolved to allow Miss Dickens to believe her plan would continue uninterrupted. *For now.* He nodded deeply. "Of course. I am yours. Shall we practice a bit of magic?"

She gave him an earthy, weathered smile that crinkled the corners of her eyes. "Indeed, Dante."

~

Dante's ridiculous address had long amused Iago Wick, but in his foul black heart, 13 Darke Street felt like his home. He had always preferred smaller rooms for himself, places which did not distract him from his work. His home at Beacon Street was an exception, procured for him by his superiors. Meanwhile, Dante's house was a beautiful representation of the demon himself. Despite the austere decoration, it felt so very warm to Iago. Even Montgomery, the dead vulture above the fireplace, reached toward him with sharpened talons as if itching for an embrace.

Iago had just made himself comfortable with a glass of scotch when there came the familiar sound and scent of burning parchment. A piece of paper burned into existence on the tea table. Surely this wasn't Dante attempting to contact him quite yet.

Iago unfurled the letter.

WICK—

YOU ARE NO LONGER IN BOSTON. EXPLAIN.

—GRIMWOOD

Oh, dear, Iago thought, *Greater Powers are upset.*

He walked to Dante's writing desk—which was nothing like the dead raven perched upon it—and was preparing to respond to Boston's elder tempter when yet another parchment materialized. He frowned. He'd been gone for less than a day and the damned city was apparently burning to the ground without him!

Iago snatched it from mid-air and unfurled it. There was a strange aura about the letter, some sort of demonic enchantment. His frown softened. It was charmed to remain untraceable, undetectable to the Powers Below. It could only be from one person.

My dearest Iago Wick,

You have no idea how delighted I was to read your letter. So many times I have thought of you. I have often desired to write you, but it is a cautious life I must lead now. Discretion, something with which I am confident you are unfamiliar, is key.

You seek information. It can only signify one thing. I will come to you, but know that from this moment forward, you creep into dangerous territory. Take care, my friend.

Please remember me to your dear Mr. Lovelace. You two always made such a smart pair—the peacock and the raven.

Lucretia Black

He smiled broadly and looked over his shoulder to Montgomery. The bird reached toward him, but he no longer seemed friendly, more as though he wanted to gouge his eyes. "Don't be sore with me, Montgomery," Iago said. "Your owner will be upset enough, as it is."

~

Viola Atchison had a lot on her mind: possible treason against her fellow hunters, Mr. Lovelace's plight, a need to keep inventing, *Thomas.* Certainly not her brother, no, but the Thomas she knew inside and out. He had started as a tool, and now, he was his own creature, yearning to walk the streets again. He tired of hiding. She longed for him. He was security and walking alone at night and a good mask to wear in the company of men.

But most of all, she thought of Zero Bancroft. Imagine her displeasure when she discovered him standing in her parlor, the hulking beast.

"Mr. Bancroft," Viola greeted blandly. "I had heard of your return to Boston. How fortunate that I should be one of the first people upon whom you call."

"You should teach your maid a little English," Bancroft said. He was too large for the parlor. Everything seemed like doll furniture in his presence. "Sofia, is that her name? If she's going to live in our country, she should be familiar with the language, not stand there like she's deaf and dumb."

Viola hummed severely. "I understand your journey to New York was fruitful. I did not think you would return so quickly."

"Yes," he said with a smile. "Ten of the monstrous Hellspawn tracked and killed in the five months I was gone. But New York is no Boston. I wanted to return home."

"And now, you are in my parlor," Viola said. She did not invite him to sit, nor did she move a muscle herself. There was a pistol concealed in the pocket of her skirt, though she would hate to have a scuffle in Sofia's parlor. "Surely you don't require another weapon already."

He still smiled sweetly. "No, today I require your memory."

"My memory? Is yours faulty?"

His eyes grew cold. "Indulge me. Not long before I left Boston, I burdened you with a task. I apologize. I should have seen to it myself."

"A task, you say?" Viola asked flatly.

"The body of Iago Wick. I asked that you dispose of it." Bancroft laughed bitterly. "How lazy of me not to do so myself, but…" He paused. "Actually, now that I recall… you offered, taking the burden upon yourself. Do you remember that?"

"I do. And I made good on my promise. Wick is six feet underground outside the city," Viola answered.

And still, Bancroft smiled, but Viola had a feeling she would be reaching for that pistol. "Hmm. Where?"

"Why, do you want to put flowers on his grave?"

Bancroft's smile waned, and he reached for his own pistol. Viola did likewise, and in a matter of moments, there was the gleam of firearms amongst the doilies and flowers of Sofia's parlor.

"Atchison, I hate demons," Bancroft growled, "but I hate liars nearly as much, and I know for a fact that you are lying to me."

"Why Wick, Bancroft?" Viola demanded. "He's only one demon. Why such obsession?"

"Wick is a prideful bastard, and I want him dead. Otherwise, I would not have *shot him*," Bancroft yelled, his eyes flaring. He huffed through his nostrils like an enraged bull. "I don't know why you're protecting him, and I don't care. I don't know what you did, you clever bitch, but you'll pay for it now."

"Did it ever occur to you," Viola said, "that perhaps your formula was faulty?"

Bancroft only scowled. *Of course, it's simply unfathomable that there should be something wrong with his formula*, Viola thought.

"Alternatively," Viola continued smartly, "perhaps you need to perfect your aim."

The words had barely left her mouth when Bancroft brought the back of his hand crashing into her cheek. Viola landed on the settee, scrambling to get pistol at the ready again, but Bancroft's was aimed at her face. He kicked her gun to the other side of the parlor with a sneer.

"Maybe it was my aim," Bancroft snarled. "Luckily, at this distance, I can't possibly miss."

This was certainly not the way Viola Atchison would have preferred to perish. For one thing, she was wearing a *skirt*.

Fortunately, before Bancroft could splatter her brains all over the settee, Sofia attacked.

She leapt upon him, yanking him back by his waistcoat. With a grunt, Bancroft reeled backward, and the gun shot with a deafening bang. The bullet broke a floral vase and pierced the far wall, but fortunately, it did not pierce flesh. Viola had some difficulty deciding if Sofia was more concerned for her wife or her parlor.

Bancroft found his balance, and he rounded on Sofia, gun drawn. Sofia, on the other hand, had chosen a far more impractical weapon, though it did have quite the dramatic flair. She aimed a crossbow right at Bancroft's heart. The weapon dwarfed her, but she managed to hold it steady.

"You bastard. Don't you dare touch her," she growled. "And you're paying for that vase!"

Bancroft laughed and lowered his gun. "Well, look there. The mouse can speak English after all. And do you know how to use that weapon, little lady?"

"I assure you, I do," Sofia answered. "And, though I would regret getting bloodstains on the doilies, I would not hesitate to shoot an arrow through your eye."

Bancroft said, "Put it down, my dear. You'll only hurt yourself."

Sofia stood resolute.

Zero Bancroft's smile faded, and after a moment of grappling, he wrestled the crossbow from her hands. He snapped the arrow and tossed the weapon to the ground. "It's not terribly polite to bring a crossbow to a gun fight, at any rate, Miss Sofia."

"Don't touch her," Viola warned.

"Oh, I can't promise that," Bancroft said as he gripped Sofia by the shoulder and held her squirming body close. He kept the gun aimed for Viola. "Once I kill you, I think I'll take her with me. She's a spitfire. I like that in a woman. I need such spirit in the days ahead."

Knock knock.

"Miss Hathaway, is everything all right?"

Thank some higher power for nosy neighbors, Viola thought, as she heard her alias called from the front stoop (one couldn't be too careful after Thomas Atchison made such a fuss in Marlowe).

Bancroft's expression soured. "Who is that?"

"Mrs. Gregory."

"Miss Hathaway, are you there? We heard a frightful noise."

"And Mr. Gregory. Neighbors. Busybodies, to be sure, but it takes all sorts to make the world go 'round, doesn't it?" Viola said, daring to rub the angry spot on her cheek.

The front door creaked open, and Bancroft quickly hid his weapon, stashing the crossbow behind a chair. He released Sofia and turned to the doorway of the parlor just in time to smile at Mr. and Mrs. Gregory, a couple who were made from the boilerplate of over-interested neighbors: Mrs. Gregory with her wide, perceptive eyes and messy hair and Mr. Gregory with his well-meaning tone and a pair of opera glasses by the front window.

"We didn't want to intrude," Mr. Gregory said, "but we heard a bang and feared there had been an accident."

"My own fault, I'm afraid," Bancroft admitted sheepishly. "I shall replace your vase, Miss *Hathaway*. I do apologize."

"Mr. Bancroft was just leaving," Viola said as she rose to her feet.

"Indeed. I apologize for the disturbance," he said. He still smiled, but there was a ferocious glint in his eye as he bowed to Mr. and Mrs. Gregory. The wolf stalked from their home, but Viola knew this was far from over.

It took a few cups of tea to get Mr. and Mrs. Gregory to leave, they were so anxious for tidbits of information about the large gentleman they had discovered in Miss Hathaway's parlor. "It simply wasn't decent for such a man to come to your home in such a way," Mrs. Gregory insisted. "A woman such as yourself must be careful."

When they finally left, Viola walked to the window. No sign of the brute for now. Sofia padded behind her. "What are we going to do, Viola? This is because of Mr. Wick—"

"Yes," Viola said firmly. She reached into her skirt pocket and withdrew the small vial of the Zero Formula. "I know that. We must be on the next train to Northampton. Boston is no longer safe."

VII.

The autumn sky glowed golden and ruby-red at sunset, the light casting pretty patterns on the floor of Beatrice's parlor as it streamed through the window panes. Dante took his place across from her at the round table. Belle watched from the corner, concerned—judging by the slight squint of her feline eyes—that she was not the center of attention at present.

"Place your hand upon mine, Dante," Beatrice said, and he did. "Eventually, I would very much like to draw upon your power without touching."

"Am I so revolting?" Dante asked.

"No, I suppose not."

Dante wondered if that was intended to be a compliment.

A small silver spoon sat in the middle of the table. "There are several kinds of magic in a witch's arsenal," Beatrice said. "Cantrips are the easiest, small utilitarian spells. Levitation, for example." The connection Dante had felt between them at the séance sparked again. It felt more natural now, easier. Then again, levitation wasn't quite as harrowing as channeling the spirits of the damned. Beatrice focused on the spoon, her free hand outstretched. Smoothly, it glided into the air. "Cantrips are easy spells to cast already, but your added power makes them as simple as breathing."

She tossed the spoon into the air and snapped her fingers. It halted in mid-air, hovered until she relaxed her hand, and then fell back to the table.

"Of course, there are also potions and spells which require a lengthy list of ingredients."

"Double, double, toil and trouble?" Dante asked knowingly.

"Ugh, such an awful representation! The Bard ought to be ashamed. Why would tongue of dog hold magical properties? The mutts spend half the time licking their own…" She cleared her throat. "I digress. My clove-laced potion is a better example. It enhances clairvoyant ability. The cloaking spell upon this house requires a page and a half of ingredients to cast!"

"Cloaking spell?" Dante would have to inform Iago when he summoned him, else he'd be wandering blindly up and down the street, looking for a house he'd never see. Amusing, but not productive.

"To ward off supernatural beasties. Doesn't affect you anymore, of course, because you already know where the house is. They're not perfect spells, but they do add an extra layer of protection. I'm never going to come home to a ghoul lounging about my parlor in wait or a rougarou rummaging through the ice box," she explained.

Is she speaking from experience? Dante wondered.

Beatrice sat up straight before continuing, "Now, let's try something a bit more difficult. You must think only of fire. Think as though you are conjuring fire from all thirteen of your demonic conjuring points: fingertips, palms, and heart. Let fire fill you."

When Dante closed his eyes, all he could see was the Hubbins home, ablaze. There were no people, no grieving family members or twittering neighbors. Only the fire. His melancholia swelled suddenly, causing a pang in his chest. *Again*, it cooed. *We must do it again. We can do better. The Powers Below will be so proud.*

And then, on the other side of his eyelids, there was sudden light. Dante opened his eyes. In Beatrice's free hand, an orb of fire hovered just above her palm. It flickered and disappeared.

"Again," she said.

The orb started as a single tiny flame, and then, it grew until it was the size of a billiard ball. She said, "Some of the magic I practice is elemental, drawing on the elements of this world and the next. Skeletals, for example, are of the earth. However, fire is nearly impossible to harness without the aid of a demon."

Experimentally, Beatrice rolled the orb around her palm. It slid smoothly to her finger tips and then back again, like a ship over easy waves. It was of their creation, and so, it could not burn her. With a playful grin, she tossed the orb into the air and caught it again.

Dante knew well this was no toy. Within that orb was the Hubbins fire, the crash of The Lady Liberty two years prior, the Cunningham home. Countless deaths, countless lives ruined in Hell's name.

"It saddens you," she said. "It's the same fire which burns homes, kills the guilty and the innocent alike."

Dante frowned, but did not break his concentration. "You're reading my thoughts."

"No. I am not gifted in telepathy. It's in your eyes. There is a profound sadness in your eyes, Dante Lovelace."

Was it that obvious? "Fire is a beautiful thing. But there are times when I wish..." He swallowed the blasphemy dancing on his tongue. "Just because I am a devout minion of Lucifer does not mean I do not feel the misery and tragedy in what I do."

Beatrice rolled the orb over her knuckles. She was quite dexterous. "How lovely that, with me, you can use this power to help people instead of hurting them."

"I'm not certain this qualifies as helping people. Séances? More like a parlor trick," Dante laughed.

She said nothing, content to gaze into the fire.

Dante said, "I am to help you better your business, am I not?"

"What's that? Oh, yes. That is our goal," Beatrice said, her pupils gleaming.

"It occurs to me now, Beatrice, that this is *not* some medium's parlor trick," Dante said.

"Oh, I don't know," Beatrice chuckled. "I think most parties would benefit from something like this. It beats a rousing game of blind man's bluff, I'd say."

Dante felt an involuntary shiver wrack his bones at the very mention of parlor games. Oh, such torture was surely conjured by one of his Hellish brethren. "While I cannot deny that, it does not change the fact that this magic is a weapon. If this fire were catapulted toward someone, it could do much damage."

Beatrice tossed the orb idly into the air again and again, like a sun constantly rising and setting.

"From what must you protect yourself?" Dante ventured.

A strange intensity grew in Beatrice's gaze. The sun rose and set again, but this time, it settled firmly in her palm. Her fingers cupped around it, and with an animal ferocity, she threw the orb across the parlor. Dante broke their contact and watched Hellish flames race up the heavy green curtains framing the parlor window.

He leapt to his feet. "Why did you do that?" He grabbed the blanket atop Beatrice's favorite chair, pulled the curtain to the ground, and tried to smother the flame.

"It worked," Beatrice said in quiet awe.

"Worked?" Dante asked. "I'm starting to believe my binding has little to do with fattening your profit." He pulled the other curtain down, as well. Hellish fire was not easy to stop. Thank Lucifer Below it had only been a small orb. "Why am I here? Tell me truthfully."

Beatrice blinked. "Dante, I told you. Business."

"No," Dante insisted as he threw the curtains to the ground. "No medium throws orbs of fire. If they did, perhaps I would have a higher opinion of them. You need me for protection."

She narrowed her eyes and looked at her father's portrait.

From the entryway came soft footsteps. Beatrice did not turn to greet their visitor, nor did she appear to hear him at all.

Dante was surprised to see Iago Wick saunter into view. A faulty cloaking spell, perhaps? An ingredient missed somewhere on that long list? He leaned on the doorframe, unable to be seen or heard by Miss Dickens.

"A bit difficult to miss a house that's on fire," Iago said, crossing his arms over his chest.

Dante made a face he hoped would silence his partner. "Beatrice, what aren't you telling me?"

"Ooh, drama, turmoil! I arrived at the ideal moment," Iago said gleefully.

"Shh!"

"What was that?" Beatrice asked.

"That was nothing," Dante said hastily. "That was... that was Belle. She must have seen a mouse." Belle glared in Iago's direction. A cat always knows which person in the room most dislikes cats, even when that person is presently invisible to human eyes.

Beatrice looked skeptically at her familiar. "You wish for me to be honest with you, Dante?"

"Yes. If we are to work together, we must have no secrets."

"Ah. Honesty. No secrets. Of course." Beatrice took three slow steps toward Dante. Then, she swiftly bent down and grabbed a corner of the rug before the parlor door. She yanked it backward, sending Iago Wick tumbling to the ground. His concentration shattered as he landed on the floor, and his invisibility failed him. Dante stifled his laughter.

"Hello," Beatrice greeted. She extended her hand. Pride did not allow Iago Wick to accept her help, and he got to his feet on his own. Beatrice arched a brow. "Honesty, Mr. Lovelace?"

~

"Your little cloaking spell against demons was rather effective, Miss Dickens," Iago said after Dante had properly introduced them. "I grew tired of waiting around Darke Street and thought I might visit. I passed this house four times before I even noticed it was here. If not for the sudden fire in the window, I would never have found it. Well done, though it is quite the elementary spell."

"So, you're the man in gray," Beatrice said dryly.

"They call me that from time to time, but I always thought it made me sound like some wayward spirit," Iago said with a ghostly wave.

"And Dante brought you back to Marlowe with him," Beatrice continued.

"Indeed, he did," Iago said. He approached her like a tiger on the hunt, hazel eyes steely. A shame he was an inch shorter than Beatrice; it somewhat spoiled his ferocity. "You see, I don't appreciate witches interfering in the affairs of demons, particularly when they involve

Dante."

"Ah." She squared her shoulders. "If Lucifer did not wish His demons to serve Man, as well, He would not allow binding. And you are a minion of Lucifer, are you not?"

Iago's mouth turned down sourly. "From birth, it is my lot. But you, witch, you *chose* to engage in such magic, to bind a demon. You *chose* to give your soul to our Lord. I wouldn't speak so loftily, if I were you."

"Iago, please," Dante said.

"It is my choice to make," Beatrice said.

Iago gave a condescending pout. "Yes, of course. Binding a demon to better one's business is quite a folly, if you ask me. Hardly worth the eternity of damnation, but who am I to judge?"

"Correct. Who are you to judge that which you know nothing about?" Beatrice asked. "Some arrogant tempter—"

"*Arrogant?*" Iago started.

Dante stepped between them. So much for careful planning and respect. "That is quite enough. Had I known you two would be at each other's throats this quickly, Iago, I would have chained you to the floor at home. Beatrice, I apologize for this interruption. Now, from what do you need protection?" Dante asked. "Perhaps Iago and I could rid you of this threat. We could assist you without the burden of binding me."

Her forehead creased, and she shook her head. "No, I need you. We are more powerful together." Her eyes flitted to her father's portrait again before she sat by the fireplace.

"Ah, dear daddy," Iago mocked. "The child must pay for the sins of the father."

"You know nothing of my father, tempter."

"I know his name was Lionel Dickens. I know he dealt in supernatural artifacts outside of Marlowe," Iago said. "And I know he's dead as a doornail. I very much wish he hadn't hidden himself so thoroughly in life. I might have liked to... *talk* to him."

Beatrice smirked. "He would never have let you in, Mr. Wick. His entire life was dedicated to protecting others. Yes, he might have dabbled in magic, but only to further his noble cause: to keep the artifacts he watched secure."

"Those thieves broke into his home and killed him," Dante said. "But they left empty-handed, didn't they? You believe the thieves will return for you."

She leaned back in her chair, made herself comfortable. There was a story to tell. "I do not fear for myself. I fear for the world. A very dangerous man has set his sights on a very dangerous artifact," Beatrice said gravely. "I was going to tell you, Dante. Just not yet. I wanted more time to practice with you."

Iago opened his mouth to speak, but Dante knew whatever was going to come out would most likely be unpleasant, foul, and entirely unhelpful at this juncture. "Beatrice," Dante interrupted as he sat across from her, "you must be direct with me. What is this artifact you are protecting, and who is seeking it?"

Beatrice looked sullenly to the empty glass beside her

chair. The liquid courage she kept in the cabinet beneath the stairs had run dry. She was left to face her demons all on her own. "I would assume you gentlemen have some knowledge of cursed and magical artifacts."

"Some, yes."

"My father guarded a variety of them, all tritely named. People seem to tend toward vanity when naming their magical trinkets. The Mask of Oberon, The Scarab of Nefertiti, Merlin's Cross—not as grandiose as it sounds, by the way. It was owned by a second-rate conjurer named Eddie Merlin. However, before Father died, he gave me an item to protect," she said.

"A sort of rite of passage," Dante interjected.

Beatrice shrugged. "I suppose, but I hadn't the faintest idea of the danger that was to come. He gifted me the Orb of Morgana. Have you heard of it?"

Dante nodded. "I have. Demons often share such tales, even in Hell." Dante hadn't the heart to add that they were normally told to mockingly demonstrate the general lack of common sense exhibited by the human race. Most cursed and enchanted objects were the subjects of cautionary tales and, in some cases, the punchlines of jokes.

"The story's just another example of witches meddling in affairs they do not understand," Iago said.

"Morgana was simply misguided," Beatrice attested. "When the monsters beyond her city walls began attacking people, her neighbors came to her for help."

"Their first mistake," Iago muttered.

"They trusted her. She was their midwife, their

healer, and she desperately wanted to help them. So, she conjured a beast to protect the city. How was she to know that beast would be even more threatening than their original foes? She thought she could control it." Beatrice admitted, "Obviously, she could not, but her intentions were good!"

"You know what they say about the road to Hell, Miss Dickens," Iago said.

"Iago, your bitterness grows tiresome," Dante warned in an attempt to prevent their conversation from disintegrating into fisticuffs.

"It's not unwarranted!" Iago said. "Morgana brought into the world a creature cut from the same cloth as the Egyptians' Ammit and the great beasts which lurk beneath the earth. Not even Hell is brave enough to wake them, and she plucked one out of the depths like she was choosing a new puppy out of a shop window. It was a soul-eater, and it *decimated* her city."

Dante knew well the tales of such beasts, the monsters slumbering in the planet's darkest corners. Early humans feared but worshipped the creatures; it was *pray or be prey*. Sometimes the former did not save one from the latter, but it couldn't hurt to try.

A better understanding of the magical arts eventually led to the beasts' containment. Some chose to hibernate on their own at the bottom of oceans or the unexplored caves of the poles. They were a demon's enemy, and yet, Dante could not help but ponder the havoc they would wreak upon the world if released. It was the sort of misery his melancholia would thrive upon, provided the beast did not set its sights on him first.

Beatrice continued, "Devorog is its blasted name. Morgana's texts were incorrect. She didn't know she was conjuring a soul-eater. She eventually found a spell that allowed her to trap it in a crystal orb... but not until it had judged and eaten half of the souls in her city."

And so, an enchanted object was born, and demons had another reason to giggle and joke about the mistakes of humans.

"And now, it's *your* soul-eater," Dante said. "How did the Orb come into your father's possession?"

"He inherited the responsibility from a holy man in Rome. I use the term 'holy' quite loosely here, but he was Father's friend," she chuckled. Holy men were frequently the unholiest. "Father gave me the Orb when he realized someone wanted to take it from him."

"Why did the thieves want the Orb?" Dante asked. "To sell it? Lucifer Below, I hope not to unleash the beast trapped within."

"That is, I'm afraid, precisely why they want it."

"That would be most unwise," Iago said. "A soul-eater stalks the Earth, judging the sins of the living and eating their souls if they do not meet its lofty standards. And it does not give soulless supernatural beings the courtesy of judgment. We are a delicacy to be swallowed whole."

Beatrice nodded. "The man who killed my father knows this. He sees it as the ultimate weapon against supernatural beings."

"Why has your father's killer not been

apprehended?" Dante asked.

"It's not that simple," Beatrice answered. "Have you gentlemen heard of a man by the name of Zero Bancroft?"

Oh, Dante thought, the universe has a terrible sense of humor.

Iago's eyes widened, and his pallor turned a striking shade of green. He reached frantically for the witch hazel in his pocket. "Zero Bancroft?" he squeaked. "That is who wishes to release Devorog?"

Beatrice said, "Yes. He realizes that the souls of humans will be lost, but the idea of a creature on Earth with a voracious appetite for supernatural monsters is attractive to him. The human souls devoured are unworthy, anyway. Bancroft believes it is for the greater good."

In Dante's time on Earth, he had seen far more acts of evil than benevolence committed in the name of The Greater Good.

Beatrice continued, "The fool told me his plans himself! He came to me and asked me to discuss the idea with my father, like a young man asking for permission to marry! He proposed his plan for eradicating the world of supernatural beings. I said no." Her face fell. "A week later, he killed Father looking for the Orb."

"How does he know Devorog would not devour his soul?" Iago asked. "Bancroft is not without sin."

"Perhaps it is a risk he's willing to take," Dante said.

"He's a madman," Beatrice said. "You see, that is why I need your help, Dante. I regret having to bind you, but I am not powerful enough to fight him on my own. Yes, I have damned myself, but I believe it is for a good reason."

Though this was quite an unfortunate turn of events, it was a far nobler cause than adding a few parlor tricks to a medium's repertoire. Catastrophe artists weren't normally familiar with noble causes. And perhaps it would do Dante good to give something new a try.

"You don't need Dante to do this, you unforgivable leech!" Iago said. "I will admit, it is necessary to keep that trinket out of Bancroft's hands, but there is no reason to drag a demon into this fight. It is a death sentence."

"Peace, dear Iago," Dante soothed. "Beatrice, is the Orb with you still?"

"No. It is with a dear friend, far from here. Bancroft does not know this."

"And so, you intend to draw him here and destroy him before he can come close to finding it?"

"Indeed," she answered with a resolute smile. Revenge had a way of tempering murder's bitterness with something a little sweet. "I can teach you, Dante. You can teach me. We'll prepare ourselves for battle."

Well, it was certainly something different from the usual fires and shipwrecks. He had been caught in a never-ending cycle of tragedy for over a century and a half! This was something new; when one is seven-hundred years old, one is not afforded much newness. And since he didn't see what choice he had...

"Miss Dickens, I have changed my mind. I am your willing servant," Dante said, and stood to bow.

"*What?* This broom-straddling hussy has you vexed!" Iago shouted, and stormed to the window.

Dante followed. "Iago, this is a chance to stop Bancroft in his tracks—permanently! The man who tried to kill you, a man set on the destruction of our world as we know it; we could end him. I will admit that a binding spell is heartily inconvenient..." He glared in the witch's direction.

Sorry, she mouthed.

"But this is a worthy cause," Dante said. "We all stand to benefit."

Iago grumbled and sneered. "If Dante so thoroughly supports you, Miss Dickens, why not break the spell? Apparently, we're on your side regardless, though I think a demon would stand a better chance with a cauldron of holy water in a church on Christmas."

"The spell allows me to draw upon his power to better mine," she explained. "Perhaps, in time, he will be able to draw upon my magic, as well. We are stronger together."

"How utterly precious," Iago said bitterly.

"Iago, please. I need you to trust me," Dante said. "Have faith."

Iago's shoulders heaved, and he glared at Beatrice. "I'll have a glass of scotch and a bit of witch hazel. And then, we'll see about faith."

~

Under usual circumstances, Charlotte Cutter

wouldn't dare spend her valuable time with someone like Sylvester Hacke. The very idea that anyone in Marlowe should peer out their window that evening, see them, and mistake them for man and wife profoundly nauseated Charlotte.

"You think they've seen us? We've passed Miss Dickens's house twice," Hacke said.

"They have not," Charlotte said, thankful for the warm autumn scent on the air; it masked Mr. Hacke's foul odor quite nicely. She was not entirely certain the man knew that bathing was an option.

"Bancroft had better hurry into Marlowe," Hacke continued gruffly. "You say she's already sent the Orb away?"

"Trust me," Charlotte said as they walked away from the home. "I'm certain of it."

Hacke snorted. "We're supposed to be man and wife right now, correct? Give me a kiss."

Charlotte tried her hardest not to be ill.

Hacke abandoned the pursuit. "Bancroft will be furious if you're wrong. You'll be heartbroken, missy," he teased.

Heartbroken. They were introduced by a mutual acquaintance at a party in Eagleton. Zero Bancroft had kissed Charlotte's hand. He was very interested in her past, in her various relationships with other families—in her. No one had ever taken an interest in boring Charlotte Cutter, not truly. Her life's compass spun wildly, landing upon a path she'd never even noticed. Charlotte shook her head. "I'm right. I can feel it."

"You *feel* it? Hell, is that all?"

"Quiet!" she hissed before remembering that, though Sylvester Hacke was a disgusting man, he was still a man. "Please. We must follow her, no matter the cost. As I told Mr. Bancroft, I'm certain she's used magic to protect the Orb of Morgana."

Hacke hurled a blot of phlegm to the ground.

Charlotte winced and wished very much that Mr. Bancroft were there.

VIII.

Dante spent the night in thought, looking out the window in the bedroom Beatrice called his and wishing to see the stars. A night sky was a comforting thing, an age-old companion. But a rolling, amorphous quilt of cloud kept the stars hidden from view.

Dante's chest was tight. He may have championed their cause to persuade Iago, but as the evening settled, Dante felt an urge to run. He was no hero. Catastrophe artists were not supposed to protect the world from monsters.

For a spell, Belle leapt to the window sill to join him. She stayed just out of reach, content to be appreciated, but not touched. "We have much to do, don't we?" he asked the cat softly. She gave a feline smirk, licked her paws, and smoothed them over her ears.

While Iago chose to sleep after taking his witch hazel, Dante stayed fast, perched upon the sill and waiting to count even one star.

~

"Breakfast, gentlemen?" Beatrice asked the next morning. She approached the dining table where Dante and Iago sat, carrying a tray of coffee unfettered by sugar, cream, or honey. There was the slightest scent of clove, however, Beatrice's herb of choice.

Iago answered with a false smile, "Given the circumstances, I'm afraid I have little appetite."

Dante closed the copy of *Lyrical Ballads* he'd pilfered from Beatrice's library. 'The Rime of the Ancient Mariner' had never thrilled him, anyway. "This feud grows tiresome already."

"Dante is right," Beatrice begrudgingly admitted. "We should put our differences aside, Mr. Wick."

"Ah," Iago said, "if by differences you mean that I am a demon and you are a spell-casting parasite, then I suppose, *if I must…*"

"You are insufferable!" she cried.

The sound of the mail slot was excuse enough for Beatrice to leave the table again.

"You're being childish," Dante said, taking a cup of coffee. "If she bothers you that much, perhaps you should return to Boston. It seems Bancroft won't be there for long. When we're finished here, I will appeal for my freedom."

Iago glowered. "I don't want to abandon you with the damned witch. She may turn you into a frog." He softened and relented. "I'll behave."

"I don't believe you. You've never been very adept at that," Dante said, and sipped his coffee.

"It's not my forte, no."

Dante added, "Anyway, this will be a nice change from catastrophe. You're a tempter; you spend your days drenched in lust and pride and gluttony. I'm stuck over here with tragedy, and frankly, I tire of it."

Iago paused and ran delicate fingers over the buttons of his waistcoat. "Is the gluttony really that noticeable?"

Dante chuckled, and they settled into comfortable silence. The dining room was cozy enough, and the warm smell of magical herbs and potions and coffee caused the mind to wander. Dante found himself imagining this was *their* home. Oh, the decoration would need a bit of attention, and Montgomery, the vulture, would look stunning in the corner of the parlor. And in this imaginary world, they were oddly unencumbered by Hellish responsibilities.

Even his melancholia was absent in this setting. In reality, he'd grown quite good at controlling it over the decades. Hell's inspiration had a tendency, when unchecked, to sour him. It tormented his thoughts and made him sick of spirit. Though it still chattered away and spoke of catastrophe, Dante was its master. But how fascinating if it were to vanish entirely...

In this imaginary world, Iago still wrote the clever and naughty stories of Virgil Alighieri. He drank scotch at all hours while Dante read voraciously and enjoyed the world that before he had only destroyed. Dante tried his hand at baking (with varying levels of success). They traveled. They attended plays and symphonies without a care, and whenever they felt such an urge, they would retire to the bedroom. Or the parlor. Or perhaps even the dining room.

On this particular beautiful, imaginary day, they sat at the breakfast table, the afternoon's blank slate before them.

Dante shook his head and reminded himself that he was not the sort of demon to shirk his duties to Hell. Such a life could never be so picturesque. He thought of Lucretia Black, a dear friend from a century ago. She had defected, and they had never heard from her again. Such uncertainty made Dante's skin crawl. No, defecting would not do. It was surely the stress of the binding spell and this ordeal with Bancroft toying with his mind.

From the foyer came a sudden commotion. Beatrice charged into the dining room, throwing a single letter on the table. "We're leaving," she said breathlessly before turning to rush upstairs.

Dante picked up the letter.

"Bad news?" Iago asked.

There was no return address, only a postmark from Clarkton, Indiana. Within was a single sheet of paper bearing only a name, written in ink.

Gathany.

Dante puzzled. "Gathany?"

He led Iago to the stairwell, where Beatrice met them with a satchel slung over her shoulder. She slipped her grimoire within, the bag hanging low with the book's weight.

"Dante, we must be on the next train out of Marlowe. We're going to Indiana."

"Not until you give me an explanation, Beatrice. What's startled you?" Dante asked. She had a grave look in her eyes, like a soldier suddenly called to war. But beneath that severity lurked a soldier's apprehension and fear, for battles were not usually the glorious things promised.

"Harry is in trouble. We must leave."

"Your sweetheart, Harry, is the one protecting the Orb, isn't he?" Dante asked.

"How romantic," Iago muttered. "I can't think of a better token of one's love than an ancient beast in a ball."

"Yes, he has it," she said. "Two years ago, Harry left Massachusetts. He lives outside Clarkton, Indiana in the company of a friend."

"And what is the meaning of *Gathany*?" Dante asked.

"It was a secret between us when we were children. Only us. It's a call for help. We had a code," Beatrice explained. "It was made up of the names of streets and businesses in our hometown. We have not even spoken of it in years. *Gathany* was the code word for *help*. He would not do this, taking such care, unless he was truly in danger. It could be Bancroft."

Dante touched her shoulder. "Beatrice, Bancroft was in Boston just yesterday."

"His associates, then! He has many men and women who work with him. I know we have not had much time to practice our magic, but I fear we must go."

Certainly, Dante had not counted on a journey to Indiana in the course of this spell. What, exactly, was in Indiana other than Beatrice's sweetheart and the Orb of Morgana? Corn, Dante expected. There was probably a lot of corn. But when he looked into her eyes, he saw desperation. What choice did he have?

"We cannot be entirely certain that it's Bancroft's men," Dante said. "But if you believe this warrants a journey to Indiana, for the sake of protecting the Orb, we shall go."

He turned to see Iago receiving a piece of parchment by Hellish post. It sizzled until it was fully formed, bearing the seal of Richard Grimwood. Wincing, Iago plucked it from the air.

"Please don't tell me you have bad news, as well," Dante said.

"Dear Dante, does Hell ever have good news?" Iago unfurled the parchment and read it aloud. "*Wick. It is a poor idea to ignore an elder tempter. Where are you? Come back to Boston, or I'll flay your skin...*" Iago cleared his throat. "I probably shouldn't continue. There's a lady present."

"Mr. Wick, I'm a witch," Beatrice said. "I'm not so shabby at flaying skin myself."

Iago's nervous gaze returned to the letter. "*Flay your skin from your bone... disembowel... boil in oil...* You know, your customary demonic chatter." He folded the letter and placed it in his pocket. "Boston does not sound like a happy place right now. The keeper of your Orb is in trouble. Suppose I come with you to Indiana."

"What?" Beatrice croaked. "I'm not in the market for

another demon, Mr. Wick."

Dante grinned. "Beatrice, I'm afraid Mr. Wick and I have seen each other through war, religion, vampires..."

"The trifecta," Iago said dryly.

"You can't be serious," Beatrice said. "You really want to go to Indiana?"

"No," Iago answered bluntly. "But I must. After all, I cannot send my partner waltzing toward danger with only a witch at his side. Lucifer Below, no! I'm coming. But first!" He held up a finger—not the rude one Beatrice surely wanted to extend at present. "I must hastily pen a letter."

"A letter?" Dante asked. "To Grimwood, declining his invitation for a good old-fashioned disemboweling?"

"No. Something important. I won't be long," was all he said.

It left a cold feeling in Dante's chest that he could not entirely explain. Boston had made Iago more secretive. *What are you hiding, Mr. Wick?* he wondered.

~

Somewhere outside Northampton, Viola Atchison was having a crisis of fidelity.

Certainly, this did not concern her fidelity to her wife. Ever since she first saw her at the fair on that sweltering Texas day, there was only Sofia Salas. Miss Salas was on the arm of a former Confederate soldier to whom her father had promised her—an attempt to push his way into American society. She had a fragile smile and a faint bruise under her eye. Viola promptly introduced herself, first as Thomas and then, in a more private setting, as Viola. Two days later, she happily escorted Sofia away.

It all happened so quickly. In recalling the events, Viola thought it a ridiculous thing to do, but she was thankful for their foolishness. Sofia trotted along the path with her large hat, starched blouse and plum walking skirt, a pretty rose in the Massachusetts countryside.

No, Viola's crisis was of a completely different stock. In the distance stood a familiar home. A fire released puffs of smoke through the chimney, and a yellow dog waited by the garden gate. The countryside around them was dotted with trees in the colors of early autumn. A clear blue sky stretched above them.

"What will you tell Mr. Collier?" Sofia asked as they approached the house.

"Not the truth. That is for certain."

"What if he finds out?" Sofia asked.

"He won't." Viola held her head high. She had abandoned the skirts she donned out of necessity in Boston and returned to her trousers. She was not Thomas; he was still sleeping. Trousers, however, were lovely things which one should have the opportunity to wear even if one's name is nothing like Thomas.

Upon their arrival, the yellow dog jumped in a merry symphony of barking. "Down, Archimedes," Viola said sternly, and the front door opened a crack. A weathered sliver of face appeared through the opening before the chain was unlatched.

"Thomas Atchison," the man called. Conrad Collier was a gaunt ghost of a man with cheeks caved in. He waved a hand like a great white spider.

"Not Thomas today," she answered. "Not for a while. Thomas had a bit of bad luck a few years ago, and I don't want to attract the attention of the police."

"Understandable," Mr. Collier said as he opened his door to them. "A pleasure to see you again, Mrs. Atchison and...er... Mrs. Atchison." He placed an entirely chaste kiss to Sofia's hand. "I wasn't expecting company today! What a delight."

"Keeping busy, Mr. Collier?" Viola asked. "The last time I saw you, you tested a bit of brimstone for me. It was a discovery which led to quite an adventure and the reason for Thomas's sudden disappearance."

"Ah, yes. You encountered a demon. No, I am afraid I'm injured. My hip. They were right," Mr. Collier said with a wink. "A man my age shouldn't have a dog. Archimedes has a habit of getting under foot, and my feet are not what they used to be. At any rate, it is difficult to go down the stairs into the cellar. It's dark down there, anyway. Cold. This demon hunting is a young man's game." He paused and corrected himself, "Or woman's."

"Your cellar laboratory is precisely why I wanted to visit you," Viola said. "I wondered if I could use it."

"Of course, you can! It's only collecting dust and cobwebs now! Come in, come in."

Conrad Collier's home was a bit too warm, but pleasant. He and Archimedes lived alone. His wife had perished years before in a manner which was untimely, unpleasant, and in Viola's opinion, Collier's own fault. If he had been more careful in his pursuit of a certain ghoul, then perhaps he wouldn't have buried his wife following a brief funeral with the casket mercifully closed. He was a decent scientist, but a terribly poor hunter, a good friend but an inconsistent resource.

"You replaced that old sofa," Viola said.

"Yes," Mr. Collier said, "Archimedes had quite a taste for it. He tore it to shreds when I was out one afternoon!"

"I recall spending hours laid out upon that thing when I was injured. Damned vampires." And Mr. Collier had received quite a shock that day when he unbuttoned an unconscious Thomas Atchison's shirt to tend to his wounds.

Dozens of cuckoo clocks covered the walls, each unique. One featured small wooden cats, and another featured small wooden dogs; one depicted a carnival scene, and a few certainly wouldn't have graced the walls when Mrs. Collier was alive (Viola had never stopped to consider the market for bawdy cuckoo clocks, but it appeared to be thriving). The newest, pure as snow, depicted half a dozen wooden ice-skaters. "Ah, Mr. Collier! This one is beautiful," Sofia said.

"Yes. I purchased it in Philadelphia earlier this year. It's not actually Swiss. Pretty, though. Sometimes the prettiest specimens are also the falsest," he said philosophically. Viola did not bother to puzzle out why.

"I want to thank you, Mr. Collier. As always, you are an excellent friend. I need a place to work, somewhere far from Boston."

"What's the nature of your work, Mrs. Atchison?" he asked as Viola delicately dropped her large bag to the floor. "You always have something interesting up your sleeve."

Viola gave a secretive grimace. "I have been assisting Zero Bancroft. As I'm sure you know, he has started to use his formula on demons."

"I had heard, yes," Collier answered. "An amazing innovation. He's quite the genius."

"Yes. Unfortunately, we are not seeing eye-to-eye now. We were forced to leave Boston, and it is imperative that you keep my presence here a secret. Bancroft is not only bright, he is frightening," Viola said.

"Is that so? I've never met the man," Collier admitted, and took a ginger seat in a plush chair. Viola couldn't say whether it was the chair or the old man's bones creaking. He motioned for Viola and Sofia to do the same.

"I feared for my safety," Viola admitted. "Our safety."

"He came to our home, Mr. Collier," Sofia said with a passionate pout. "He threatened us, the great brute."

"So, you see, there is a need for quiet, if I am to continue my research," Viola said.

"Your research," Collier said. "Which is?"

Viola answered, "Expanding upon Bancroft's formula, of course. It shall be better. More efficacious. He had a demon walk away, you know. It is not as effective as he says. You might say that demon, Iago

Wick, has inspired my own personal pursuit."

"Ah," Collier said. He grinned broadly. "Intrigue, betrayal. Stealing ideas. Sneaky, sneaky. This is all very exciting—and here in my home! And has he any clue as to where you are?"

"No," Viola answered. "We promptly left Boston by train. Mark my words, Mr. Collier. Bancroft is an intelligent man, but he will cause great destruction in his time. He cannot control himself. He is a bomb, tick-tick-ticking."

And suddenly, every cuckoo clock declared it was ten o' clock, birds chirping, bells ringing, and Archimedes chiming in outside. Mr. Collier showed Viola to the laboratory in the cellar.

In the musty and damp lab, which smelled faintly of rotten vegetables, Mr. Collier suddenly reprimanded himself for not offering his guests coffee. He ambled back up the creaky stairs, and Viola surveyed the impressive laboratory sporting towers of tubes and beakers. An apothecary's chest on the other side of the room contained bottles of various substances, each of which was poisonous to someone, whether they be human, vampire, demon, werewolf, or one of the horrifying creatures which fell into the vast category of *other*.

"He does not suspect," Sofia said softly.

"No. He won't. I do hope Mr. Wick appreciates this."

Sofia looked cautiously up the stairs. "I still don't understand why it is our concern. We should be fleeing the country, moving as far away from Bancroft as possible."

Viola only observed the equipment she had been provided.

"Mr. Wick is a valuable resource, yes," Sofia continued, "but he is not irreplaceable. It is peculiar to me. He distracts you."

"No," Viola said. "Iago Wick betters me. He helps me, forces me to think." She paused and gave a minute shrug of the shoulders. "He's a fine writer, too, that Virgil Alighieri. It would be a shame to see him cut down in his prime."

IX.

"I am not overly fond of trains," Iago Wick said at the Marlowe Depot. He carried a small bag stuffed to the brim with fancy waistcoats and neckties after insisting they return to 13 Darke Street to fetch it. He wore the plum waistcoat today, scarab cufflinks gleaming at his wrists again.

"How else would you suggest we reach Indiana quickly? I fear my broomstick is currently in disrepair," Beatrice said. She wore a burgundy skirt and a mauve blouse, and her red hair had been swept back into a messy crown. It was a good ensemble for traveling, though she was still out-dressed by every Marlowe woman who believed every train ride was an occasion to dress like the wealthy and mysterious lover of some European nobleman.

Iago reached into his breast pocket to retrieve his witch hazel. "Not again," Dante muttered.

"Oh, Dante, it's not so bad. I can stop taking it at any time."

"I didn't say a word about stopping, did I?" Dante said. "I was going to call it bad judgment to impair your senses when we know danger is afoot, but by all means, stop altogether."

Iago sucked a small drop of the liquid from the pad of his forefinger. "I can. I simply don't want to." He pocketed the bottle. "I'll be much more agreeable this way, I assure you. Might we don invisibility upon the train, as well?"

"That would leave Beatrice, more or less, alone," Dante said. "We should agree that invisibility is out of the question so long as we are helping her." Beatrice gave a haughty smirk in Iago's direction. Dante was overcome with the feeling that he would be playing arbiter this entire journey.

Marlowe's skies were a solemn gray, and the leaves were damp from a sudden morning shower. The small locomotive before them would take them back to Boston, where they would board the luxury train, *The Boston-St. Louis Bullet*. Southeast of Indianapolis, they would abandon the train and carry on by foot.

Dante did not find himself traveling often. These days, when he did, it was only to Boston. He did recall a time or two when he and Iago traveled on Hellish business. In 1865, they'd been called to London. Choppy seas and unfamiliar food and peril and werewolves and tea—*so much tea*. And London was nothing compared to the affair with that lizard woman in Paris in 1881, though

Dante did enjoy the way French sounded coming from his mouth.

Both journeys were admittedly dreadful, but he would have taken them again in a heartbeat. There was so much world out there, and none of it looked like Hell. Dante regretted having seen so little of it.

Iago's shoulders slumped as the witch hazel took him in its grasp. Dante ushered him toward the train. "Cake," Mr. Wick said suddenly. "Do you think the *Bullet* will have cake?"

~

From within the depot café, a young man watched and drowned twinges of remorse in a cup of muddy coffee. He fiddled with his moustache. Crooked again! He straightened it, grimacing at how strange it felt upon his upper lip.

"Miss Cutter ain't accustomed to whiskers. She'll give us away," Sylvester Hacke said, and drank from his own cup of sludge.

Zero Bancroft did not reprimand him, nor did he reprimand Charlotte for fiddling with her disguise. Her hair was bobbed at her chin now, the loose tendrils pinned up underneath a man's hat.

Mr. Hacke was disguised as a man who looked as though he could be Methuselah's older brother. Bancroft wore a red wig and gave himself a dusting of freckles. Charlotte was their young associate. They were, respectively, old Mr. Carmichael, Mr. Botts, and young

Mr. Haversham.

Bancroft glared through the window. "There he is," he muttered. Charlotte followed his line of sight. "Iago Wick." Bancroft sipped his coffee. "Mr. Carmichael, take a note."

Hacke blinked and gave a start as he realized he was speaking to him. "Am I your damn secretary? Take your own no—"

"*Take a note.* Kill. Viola. Atchison. I regret letting her get away in Boston. Damned busybody neighbors." His face was set and heavy. Charlotte hated when he looked that way. He could be so handsome if he just didn't focus so heavily on the destruction of others. But suddenly, he smiled. "I'm sorry, Mr. Haversham. I wish you did not have to hear that. You are sensitive, I know."

Charlotte bowed her head and nervously smoothed and straightened the tablecloth under his gaze. He made her feel so small and so grand at once.

"Well, kill the demon now," Hacke grunted. "He's here."

"No. When I was learning my trade, Ezekiel Faust used to preach about the importance of remembering one's ultimate purpose. We must not let passions keep us from that purpose. Would it be invigorating to murder Wick where he stands now? Yes. But this is about the greater good. We cannot be seen yet, not by Miss Dickens or either of the demons," Bancroft said. "We board in five minutes. It will be easy to avoid contact upon the *Bullet* due to its immensity. Here, we must lie low."

Charlotte toyed with her facial hair once more before

resolving to sit on her hands.

Hacke shrugged and spat into his cup. "This coffee tastes like manure."

Zero Bancroft raised a red-tinged brow. "And how would you know what manure tastes like?"

Hacke giggled throatily. "Funny you should ask…"

~

The train to Boston was like half a dozen matchboxes on wheels.

Dante had grown accustomed to the journey, which took, when all was said and done, an hour and a half. He had taken it now in summer and autumn and in the dead of winter and when the first buds appeared in spring. It was easier for him to leave Marlowe and journey to Boston than it was for Iago to escape his duties. Hell's authorities in Boston did not like their demons to be distracted by anything considered frivolous, especially some provincial lover.

He turned to observe the slumbering Iago, whose eyelids occasionally fluttered in his witch hazel-induced stupor. "You've known Harry for a long time?" Dante asked of Beatrice.

Beatrice gave a small and secret smile. "Yes. Harry Foster and I have always been the closest of friends." She smoothed her red hair. "And, of course, when we came of age, our bond only became more profound."

"Why did he leave?"

She turned her gaze to the window. "Harry likes his

solitude. He lives with a friend, Arrow McClellan. Mr. McClellan is a man of few words and even fewer social graces, but he wanted a housemate. Harry jumped at the chance to live in the country. He will always attest that books are better company than people."

"Ah, a reader," Dante said.

"And a writer. Harry studies and writes about the supernatural. He's working on a book currently, which he would be more than happy to discuss with you for at least an hour or two," she chuckled. "His passion is terribly contagious."

She glowed as she spoke of him, a warm lovelight in her usually murky eyes. "A shame you are so far from him," Dante said.

The witch pursed her lips. "In truth, you can also thank Lionel Dickens for that. Harry is a black man. Father, though he claimed open-mindedness in other matters, very vocally didn't approve. So, Harry left with Mr. McClellan. Now, Father's dead," she said frankly, "but it would be difficult to pry my writer from his beloved library. He has made that house his home, his workshop of words."

"The creative mind can be quite particular," Dante said as his own writer dozed beside him.

"Indeed. His knowledge of supernatural affairs made Harry perfect for guarding the Orb. At least, we thought," she said, and frowned. "He volunteered. I've placed a cloaking spell upon his house, but I still should not have let him take it. Such spells are not perfect."

Quickly, she swept away her frown, trying her

hardest to hide her worry. She continued, "At any rate, I found it good to leave Eagleton, too. I was tired of my hometown—such a tremendous bore. Marlowe has been a joy."

Dante was certain no one in the city's long and miserable history had ever categorized Marlowe as a joy.

~

When entrepreneur and railroad man Wilt Walton proposed *The Boston-St. Louis Bullet*, people outside Boston's innovation-obsessed community laughed in his face—and those were the polite ones. But who was laughing now? Walton might have laughed, if he weren't so busy counting his money.

The train was a glorious testament to the upcoming century, to *progress*. Its brass and gilded fixtures were always shiny, and if one of them should tarnish, there were automaton maids to remedy that. It was nearly twice as wide as a typical train, with two levels. The face of the engine proclaimed in gold letters: *THE BOSTON-ST. LOUIS BULLET—AMERICA'S PRIDE AND JOY.*

And, the people of Boston were happy to note, the train did not travel to New York City.

Inside, the cars were lined with plush rugs and electric lamps. As they boarded, an automaton greeted them with a happy song. After that, a suited man, who did not seem half as happy as the machine, came by to stamp their tickets. There is something to be said, Dante thought, for the unwavering morale of a machine.

Shortly after the train left Boston, Dante took a seat in the dining car. He half-listened to the tale of the behemoth as he looked at the car's daily menu.

"It is, to date, the largest train ever built, a bona fide hotel on wheels.

"The Boston-St. Louis Bullet was designed to have two levels, sleeping cars, dining cars, game cars, a ladies' parlor, a gentlemen's parlor, an observation deck, and a ballroom."

For those with impeccable balance and no inclination toward vertigo, Dante thought.

"In 1885, a special track was constructed for the train, due to its unprecedented size. Its construction utilized almost entirely cybernetic and automaton labor. This surely saved the lives of many humans. The train has become an inspiration for others, though the project was not always dealt such praise."

And if one ever forgot the history and amenities of *The Boston-St. Louis Bullet*, there was an automaton on the lower level of the dining car who, when prompted, happily told every detail in her strange music-box voice. One young passenger was fond of turning the machine's crank over and over and over again, and so, after lunch, Dante could have recited the story of the train verbatim.

"But Wilt Walton was a clever man and did not give up. It is because of his bravery and intelligence and perseverance that you are now traveling in comfort from Boston, Massachusetts to St. Louis, Missouri and back again. Let us all thank Wilt Walton."

Dante reckoned Walton wrote the script himself.

"Shall we take a turn around the ballroom later, Mr. Wick?" Dante teased as they took lunch. Soup was a poor choice for a bi-level restaurant on wheels, but so far,

Dante hadn't seen any passengers' suits ruined.

"*Can* you dance, Mr. Wick?" Beatrice asked.

"I'll have you know, dear lady, that I am an impeccable dancer," Iago said. "A desperate man can't very well dance with The Devil if His minions have two left feet."

"He's not lying," Dante said. "Demons are excellent dancers."

Beatrice grinned. "And are you given lessons in your youth?"

"Ugh," Iago snorted, "don't remind me. My partner had quite a smell about her, and trust me, when you're living in a world which amounts to little more than a torturous sulfur pit, that is saying something."

They were nearly finished with lunch when a Hellish letter appeared at Iago's side. He gulped, looking to make sure no humans saw. Then, he unfurled the parchment, read, and turned ashen.

"Is it that terrible?" Dante asked.

"His threats have gotten quite, ah… creative. This goes beyond disemboweling, and quite frankly, I didn't know anyone used the iron maiden anymore." He took a shaky sip of his coffee. "Apparently Richard Grimwood does."

That afternoon, they settled in one of the passenger cars—the lower level, at Iago's request. Beatrice asked that Dante practice connecting with the fire within him, the parts of him most connected to Hell. "It will help us in our spellcasting," she explained. He closed his eyes and thought of that realm from which he came: a landscape of soot and bodies and anguish. *Home sweet home.*

The land outside was giving itself over to autumn in broad strokes of gold. Despite the reason for their journey, Dante felt his wanderlust surging again. The *Bullet* charged through the Appalachian Mountains like a gilded snake, racing alongside the hills and slipping into the massive tunnels crafted especially for the behemoth train. Of course, it could not always maintain top speed as it navigated the land, but it always seemed as steady as Boston's golden path of progress.

Whenever the train plunged into the darkness of the tunnels, and the cabin was illuminated only by orange electric light, Dante found it quite easy to think of Hell. The high hum of the *Bullet* on the tracks conjured to mind the cries of the damned and the giddy wailing of Hell's demons. He focused on tapping into his demonic power then. If he closed his eyes, he could see a familiar face—red eyes, pointed teeth, a faint scar on one cheek. It smiled warmly at him, but Dante opened his eyes. He turned to catch the reflection of his human visage in the window before the train shot into the sunlight again.

When darkness fell that evening, the electric lamps provided a warm, cozy glow within, but they only intensified the night without. Passengers shuffled off to the sleeping cars, and Dante found himself looking to the blanket of stars above.

The roll of the train was accompanied by a constant thrumming of fingers upon wood.

Iago Wick drummed on the arm of his chair anxiously. He had not taken witch hazel since that morning. Occasionally, one hand hovered over his breast pocket, but all Dante had to do was furrow his brows in his partner's direction, and he abandoned his pursuit. Eventually, Iago retrieved neatly folded pages of notes and a gold-plated pencil from his pocket, instead.

"Writing something, Mr. Wick?" Beatrice asked.

"He's not Mr. Wick at present. He's Mr. Alighieri," Dante joked. Beatrice blinked. "Virgil Alighieri. The writer."

Beatrice's eyes widened. "Oh, the hack who writes those terrible tales! The naughty stories that sneaky wives and dirty-minded men read to pass the time. You mean… you're…?"

Iago looked as though he'd snap the pencil in two. "The *hack*, Miss Dickens?"

She shrugged. "The stories seem to be selling well. However, there is no accounting for taste. Are the stories true, then? Are they based on temptations you have orchestrated?"

Iago gave her a withering glance. "Yes, they are, but I'm certain they are *far* beneath your usual level of reading: rotting spell books, *The Necronomicon*, Jane Austen."

"What's the matter with Jane Austen?" Beatrice asked indignantly.

Iago gave a demonstrative roll of the eyes before bidding them a bitter good night. He walked toward the sleeping cars, hand already reaching for his breast pocket.

~

Dante first arrived on Earth at night, nearly two centuries prior. As was customary, he pulled himself from the ground in a spot where the veil between Hell and Earth was thin. As was also customary, he was naked. Pulling oneself from the land, naked and screaming, was so rife with symbolism that Hell just couldn't say *no*.

Hell did not have a sky so beautiful as Earth's. Hell, in fact, did not have much of a sky at all—more an inky, suffocating nothingness, stretching as far as the eye could see. Meanwhile, Earth's sky was a glittering blanket of diamonds the likes of which many demons had never witnessed. Dante spent that first night sitting in a field outside Philadelphia and counting the stars.

By the end of his second day on Earth, he longed heartily for the peace he had known upon arrival, when he was unfettered by worry (or clothes, for that matter). It would be some time before he became a catastrophe artist, but Hell had many unpleasant roles for demons to play.

The *Bullet* felt like some starship now, speeding through the night sky, and Dante wanted a better look. "I think I'll visit the Observation Deck. Care to join me?"

Beatrice nodded and followed.

The Observation Deck was the crown jewel of *The Boston-St. Louis Bullet*, a diamond-cut dome atop the central passenger car. Passengers took the winding, gilded staircase up two levels until they found themselves at the top of the car, shielded by the immense glass structure. The apex of the dome added another eight feet to the train's already gargantuan height.

Alas, they were confronted by one of the train's automaton staff at the second level landing. Heavy, false eyelashes fluttered, and her mouth moved erratically as she spoke. "*I'm sorry*," she sang, "*the Observation Deck is closed for the evening. I'm sorry; the Observation Deck is closed for the evening. I'm sorry…*"

Dante was not accustomed to fiddling with the damned things but boldly reached to turn the machine's head to one side. Her neck cracked like trampled peanut shells.

"*I'm sorry; the Observation Deck is closed for the evening.*"

"Come," he said, beckoning to Beatrice. "We don't need a pile of bolts to tell us what to do." They made certain no one was watching, then swiftly climbed the stairs.

They emerged atop the car, and Dante looked up into the brilliant sea of stars. He let the inky night wash over him as he strode onto the platform. Despite the rumble of the train and the modern, mechanical wonderland beneath his feet, Dante felt swaddled in primal darkness. It was soothing… and a sight prettier to look at than the jerky, bossy automaton below.

Beatrice craned her neck. "Beautiful. If those stars could talk, imagine the tales they might tell."

Great romances, grand victories, tales of terror, Dante thought. He understood the stars, the way they guided and influenced the lives of so many people, then watched from afar as they met their fates. The stars, however, witnessed the good and the bad, the seaman finding his way home and the star-crossed lovers doomed to tragedy.

The dome was illuminated only by a few feeble electric lanterns, allowing the sky itself to take center stage. With a smile, Beatrice hurried to the other side of the deck, managing quite well to keep her balance. In the dim light, she looked like some Puckish fairy seeking mischief. She squared her shoulders and held out her hand in the near-darkness. "Now, think of fire, Dante."

"What? Here?" he asked.

"We must practice. Our great battle may lie just ahead of us."

"No, we'll burn the whole train down. Don't think I've forgotten your little display with the drapes."

"I'm not going to burn anything down!"

A shame, his melancholia lamented. *How splendid it would be to destroy America's Pride and Joy, The Boston-St. Louis Bullet.*

He silenced the bothersome voice, and his thoughts turned to flame. Hellfire burned in his fingertips. "Just be careful."

"Dante, I've never been anything less!" she proclaimed. "Hurry now!" Beatrice closed her eyes as she searched for him deep in her thoughts.

Dante felt a sudden lightheadedness. She reached inside him from afar, slipping her hands into his heart. He stood his ground and continued to think of Hellfire while simultaneously striving to keep his anxious melancholia at bay—not to mention, keep his balance.

A pinprick of light shimmered in Beatrice's hand, as small and twinkling as a star. Then, little by little, it grew until an orb of fire sat above her palm. No longer was she taken aback by his power. She used it calmly, confidently. "Do you see? We needn't even touch. Oh, Zero Bancroft will run for his life when he sees what we can accomplish."

A clever smile tugged at the corners of Dante's lips, and he reached an experimental hand into the air. He imagined that orb in his own hand, flexed his fingers, felt the warmth and power of the fire. The flow between him and Beatrice shifted, tugging in the opposite direction. It was like drinking from a river, cupping his hands and stealing the water for himself.

And the ball of fire moved. It floated smoothly from Beatrice's hand into the space between them. Dante halted it in mid-air, stretching his hands wide and watching the sphere grow at his command. He'd never done such a thing on his own. No demon harbored power quite like this. Even a catastrophe artist didn't have so much control over the element.

It was breathtaking, and if he allowed it to drop to the floor, it could devour the entire train car. His melancholia swelled and ached for Hellfire. This fire, however, was not for Hell or his melancholia. It was under *his* control. The thought pleased him. Was this how Iago felt when he slipped into the guise of Virgil Alighieri?

Beatrice stared into the light, eyes wide and shimmering. Dante clapped his hands, and the orb disappeared in a shower of sparks as multitudinous as the stars above, fizzling to nothing before they could hit the platform. Beatrice laughed in delight. "That was remarkable, Dante! Drawing upon my power already? You have a natural talent for magic."

"That's nicer than what Hell thinks of me," Dante said. "They saw my natural talent for ruining people's lives."

Beatrice's smile faded, and she met him in the middle of the deck. "I fear we'll use this magic soon. Harry is not one to call for help unless he truly needs it."

Dante placed a friendly hand on her shoulder. "Then, we shall face the day arm in arm, Miss Dickens." He offered his elbow and led her back down the stairs before they quietly made their way to sleeping car compartment 315.

Each compartment could house up to four passengers, with two bunks stacked on either side of the room. A porthole provided some light during the day. Dante recalled from the dining car automaton's oration that the design for the sleeping compartments came from Walton's days at sea. They were the plainest feature of the *Bullet*, and Dante imagined it was to encourage passengers to leave their rooms and partake in more *profitable* endeavors on the train.

Beatrice had posed briefly as Dante's wife to make certain they would not raise any Puritanical eyebrows. She insisted she would change her clothes in the washroom across the hall, though she'd brought only a waistcoat and extra blouse in her satchel.

Within their compartment, a single lamp glowed, and Iago Wick snored at the room's small writing desk. Papers dotted with half-finished thoughts and stories surrounded him. Dante examined the open bottle of witch hazel upon the desk. There wasn't much left. He gently shook Iago's shoulder. "If you do choose to sleep, Mr. Alighieri, don't you think it would be wise to use the bed?"

Iago sluggishly raised his head. He blinked and grunted. "Dante. Where did the bird go?"

"The bird?" Dante asked.

He rubbed his eyes and looked in dissatisfaction to the pile of notes he'd written before the witch hazel—a copious amount, it seemed—took hold of his senses. "Lucifer Below, this place is a mess," Iago said.

Dante carefully led Iago to one bed, and the intoxicated author sat on the mattress. "You should sleep." He slipped Iago out of his jacket and removed his necktie.

"Dante," Iago scolded unsteadily, "what are you doing, undressing me like this? There is a lady present." He looked lasciviously to Beatrice. "Unless, of course, Miss Dickens is a willing party."

"Hardly, Mr. Wick," Beatrice said with a sneer.

Dante removed Iago's shoes. "You're going to be miserable in the morning."

"Perhaps," Iago said, "but I am happy to see you now. The bird, my dearest. The bird spoke about you."

"What bird, Iago?"

"In my thoughts, in my dreams. There was a great bird, perched upon the writing desk. One of those birds with the white head and the brown feathers and...?" He trailed off lethargically.

"A bald eagle, Iago," Dante said. "They are only a symbol of this nation."

"Yes, that one. And it said—quite severely, I might add, and I did not appreciate its tone—that you were going to leave me." Dante met Iago's gaze, and for a moment, those hazy hazel eyes seemed clear. "It said a storm was on the horizon. The lights flickered. How could a bird manage that?"

Anything was possible with the power of witch hazel. "Sleep, Iago."

"Then, the room turned dark as pitch. There was fog, smoke. It smelled of Hell," Iago said weakly. He rubbed his forehead. "It opened its mouth and screeched, a nauseating sound, to be sure. I felt it in my bones. And it said a storm was going to take Dante Lovelace."

"Iago—"

"It was rude, I thought. Then, it disappeared. What a rude bird." Iago covered his eyes with one hand and groaned softly, leaning back on the mattress. "Could I have my witch hazel?"

"Absolutely not," Dante said.

"I don't need it, anyway," he muttered. He paused, then slurred, "Dante, tell me something."

"What would you like me to tell you, Iago?"

Iago looked grave. "Tell me the bird is wrong. That ill-mannered avian. Tell me it was wrong."

"*Ill-mannered avian*? Is Virgil Alighieri crafting a thesaurus?" Dante joked, then realized Iago was gripping his lapel.

"Dante, I do not speak in jest. Please."

He glanced over his shoulder to see Beatrice looking away, suddenly very preoccupied with her grimoire. "I am not leaving you, Iago. Never," Dante insisted. "Now, you're going to be in agony in the morning. You need a good, long, restful sleep."

"Pfft! Sleep? I am demon. I need nothing of the sort," he proclaimed with the bald confidence of a drunken man.

Less than two minutes later, Iago snored softly.

Beatrice quietly retreated to her own cot while Dante hung Iago's jacket on the back of the chair. Another stray paper stuck from the coat pocket. Lucifer Below, he'd taken enough notes to write a sequel to *The Divine Comedy*. Dante plucked the paper from the pocket and laid it on the desk with the others.

But he frowned as he caught sight of its contents. This was a letter.

My Dearest Iago Wick, the letter began.

As foolish as it might have been, Dante felt a sick knot in his stomach at the overly-affectionate words until his flittering gaze discovered the writer's signature.

Lucretia Black.

This was no love letter, but something far more dangerous.

X.

"Iago, what is this?"

Iago gave a dissatisfied hum as Dante forced the letter from Lucretia Black into his hand the next morning. The word *morning*, though technically true, might have been a shade generous. It was eleven o' clock. He fell back onto the bed again with a hideous groan.

Mr. Wick already looked a bit green from his indiscretions the night before, and he grimaced further at the idea of discussing this perilous correspondence. "I suppose you wouldn't believe me if I said I wanted to chat with Lucretia about the latest trends in fashion?"

"*No.*"

He cleared his voice, wincing at the sound. "Dante, I can explain."

"Spare me your verbosity. There is only one reason you would dare risk writing a letter to Lucretia Black," Dante hissed. "You want her advice. What better idea than to chat with another defected demon when you're considering the path yourself?"

"Apparently, it was a terrible idea," Iago said.

"To even entertain the thought of defecting can be cause for exorcism, and you might as well have your plans tattooed upon your forehead. If someone intercepted your letter…"

Iago waved his hand dismissively and forced himself to sit. "It's charmed!"

"That doesn't matter! You know as well as I do that if Hell truly wishes to read your letters, a little demonic charm isn't going to stop them," Dante said. "And to carry out such risks when we are already in a dangerous situation—"

"I'm not," Iago said, rubbing his temples. "Before we left Miss Dickens's home, I wrote a letter to Lucretia. I told her to stop writing to me for now. I am taking care, I promise."

Dante scoffed. "Yes, of course. Working with a demon hunter, speaking openly of turning your back on Hell—writing sordid fiction! Yes, you are the very portrait of caution."

Iago cradled his head gingerly in his hand. "Dante, I'm sorry." At this rate, he was going to be quite the expert at apologizing.

Dante softened. "I merely suggest that you exercise a bit more restraint. Please."

"Look at me. I am quite obviously no good at that." Then, he smiled. "But I will try." Iago stumbled to his feet, gripping the cabin's mirror for support. He glared at what he saw and tried to smooth his hair. "I'm going for a walk to clear my head. I'll try not to vomit on any of the automatons, but I can't make any promises." He fixed his collar and necktie before donning his jacket and shoes.

"Before you go," Dante said carefully, "do you remember anything from last night?"

"What did I do? Whatever it was, I deeply apologize. I was not myself."

All night, Iago's premonition of a storm had haunted Dante. He had hoped sleep would give his partner more insight into his strange vision. "It wasn't anything you did, but something you said. You don't recall?"

"I'm afraid not."

Dante might have found solace in the night sky on the Observation Deck, but Iago's ominous words had left him relieved to see the sun rise that morning. "It's nothing. Don't worry. Go ahead. And don't get lost."

Iago arched a brow and gave Dante a short kiss. "Yes, dear."

Dante finished dressing and found Beatrice in a passenger car, reading Jane Austen. "To calm my nerves," she said sheepishly.

They sat in silence, and Dante sought relaxation in the noble sport of human-watching. They were humming all around him like aimless bees. The train had stopped in Columbus, Ohio early that morning to grand fanfare. The *Bullet* ran regularly through the city, but Dante assumed there was little else for Columbus, Ohio to celebrate.

The two women across the aisle from them mentioned boarding at Columbus and now chattered about the Calamine, Indiana Harvest Festival. There were, apparently, gourds and pumpkins there the size of one lady's Great Uncle Otto. Uncle Otto must have been quite a colossal gentleman, for she threw her arms wide to represent his girth. The festival was happening as they spoke, and the two ladies planned to leave the train at Calamine to see it.

Dante was not so interested in giant gourds, but their excitement was somehow infectious. It was a sunny autumn day and they had plans, and in their plans, however frivolous, they had their purpose. And it was a happy one, at that. It brought a smile to his face.

Then, in a sudden flash, Iago appeared. He fell into the seat across from Dante, his eyes bulging in alarm. "We are in trouble, my dear."

"Trouble?" Beatrice asked.

"Profound trouble." Iago looked nervously around the car. "Bancroft is aboard the train. I saw him in the dining car when I went for a cup of coffee. He's disguised, but I'd know that frightening gaze anywhere." He gulped. "He's followed me. Lucifer Below, he wants to finish me."

"Finish *you*?" Beatrice spat. "He must be after me— after Harry!"

"Your fear is based upon mere conjecture. His assassin tried to kill me just two days ago!" Iago exclaimed.

"Leave it to you, Mr. Wick, to allow your pride to go to your head even now," Beatrice grumbled.

Iago reached for his witch hazel, hands trembling

and chest heaving as though he'd run a mile.

"*Ahem.* Might I see that bottle, Iago?" Dante asked, but he did not wait for a response. Rather, he ripped the bottle from his hands, opened the window and gave it a hearty toss outside. He should have done that miles ago!

"Dante, I need that! What is wrong with you?" Iago wheezed.

"I need you to be clear-minded, Mr. Wick," Dante said, "not stumbling around like a drunk."

"We should seek Bancroft out," Beatrice said. "Kill him now. After all, that's why I bound you in the first place. Let us finish him now."

Dante considered such a confrontation, here on *The Boston-St. Louis Bullet.* This was the man who had tried to kill Iago. Wouldn't it feel nice to make him pay for that? But every catastrophe artist knew that passion should never trump common sense. He steadied himself. "No," Dante said. "It's best to lose him. We are surrounded by humans who wouldn't take kindly to a supernatural battle here on the train. Not to mention, he could have more associates with him even now. We don't know what we're up against."

Beatrice pouted. "Then, let's leave the train and lure him to the middle of nowhere! We're ready."

"No, we're not," Dante insisted. "We know Harry is in trouble. Perhaps he can't wait for you to spar with Bancroft."

For a moment, it seemed Beatrice would argue, her eyes blazing. Then, she deflated. "You're right."

"Oh, Mr. Lovelace," Iago said, "I love it when you

take control."

The ladies beside them still twittered of Harvest Festivals. If it was an affair as grand as they proclaimed, it was surely well-attended. Dante bit his thumb in thought. He continued, "We need to lose him, and the best way to get lost, in my experience, is to be surrounded by others. Calamine has a festival. If he leaves the train and follows us, we'll lose him there."

"Excellent. And how about a spin on the carousel while we're there, my dear?" Iago sighed.

"Have you any better ideas?" Dante asked. "We'll create a diversion when we arrive, if we must." He gave a firm nod. "But let's not get ahead of ourselves. We must take this one step at a time, carefully. He doesn't have us in his grasp yet."

And for a moment, Dante surprised himself. His voice sounded so commanding in his own ears. *And why shouldn't it?* If he could control catastrophe, he could take charge of this situation as readily. Dante continued, "We can't be far from the station. When the train stops at Calamine, we'll disappear into the crowd."

~

It felt like an eternity before the train finally began to coast and screech to a halt. The track for *The Boston-St. Louis Bullet* overlapped with the standard rails at the cities and towns where it stopped on its long and luxurious journey. One such stop was Calamine, Indiana. The town sported a small population of people who spent three-hundred and sixty days of the year happily and busily preparing for a five-day festival dedicated to autumn and the almighty pumpkin.

As passengers filed off the train, Dante led his companions to the platform where people greeted each other and kissed and shook hands. Children leapt into the air and waved at the behemoth train, desperate for at least one passenger to wave back.

Iago's hand trembled as it lingered over his empty breast pocket.

"Do you see Bancroft?" Beatrice asked.

"Not yet," Iago said, then cursed under his breath and looked back.

"What?" Dante asked.

"I left my bag behind. My waistcoats," Iago lamented.

"Oh, Lucifer Below! Hush. Let's make our way into town," Dante said. "Quickly, now."

~

"There they are. On the platform. Move," Bancroft growled behind Charlotte as they attempted to leave the train.

Since Mr. Bancroft returned to his seat and proclaimed Iago Wick had seen him, he'd done nothing but growl. Other passengers, far more leisurely in their gait, got off the train ahead of them. The flow of passengers coming down the gilded staircases from the second level was forced to merge with the flow of those on the first, creating a terrible jam. Bancroft placed a heavy hand on Charlotte's back and pressed her forward. They shuffled, and each half-step seemed only to aggravate Bancroft further. She wished he wouldn't push her so.

"Move," he said lowly in Charlotte's ear. "Keep moving. We can't lose them."

They reached the nearest exit, which was mostly occupied by a large man carrying an even larger suitcase.

"My wife always says I bring too much!" he told the porter. "You can never be too prepared, I say." Charlotte could tell his jolliness did not sit well with Zero Bancroft. She fidgeted with her moustache.

The man with the suitcase tried to hop down to the platform, stumbling a bit when he landed. "I brought my swimming suit, just to be safe. You just never know what you'll need!"

"*Go,*" Bancroft said through gritted teeth. Charlotte looked through one of the windows to see the demons and Beatrice Dickens rushing into the depot. They would lose them if they did not hurry.

"I can't," Charlotte insisted, but before she could say another word, Zero Bancroft gave her a solid push through the doorway. She stumbled past the man with the suitcase. Her ankle turned, and she fell to the platform, arms flailing like a mustachioed scarecrow.

"Oh, gracious! Young man, are you all right?" the portly man asked, and bowed on one knee.

"Stay here," Zero Bancroft growled at Sylvester Hacke.

And without another word, he sprinted toward the depot, moving like a wolf on the prowl. There was no semblance of the man Charlotte had thought of so dearly in recent days. This wild animal was not the sort of man a woman would want calling upon her. *Well... maybe*, she thought. There might have been some benefits to such animalistic tendencies, but her ankle hurt too badly for her to consider those now. Charlotte tried to flex it.

"Yes, that's it, young man. Give it a good wiggle," said the man with the suitcase.

"You always were clumsy, boy," Hacke said in an old man voice to match his wig, and he gave Charlotte a toothy smile.

~

Dante, Iago, and Beatrice walked briskly through the depot and emerged in a fairyland. Children with balloons skipped toward the street fair. The sound of hustle and bustle drifted on the crisp autumn air. At the edge of the fair, people cooed over a single automaton that made Harriet look like the Queen of Sheba. Her hair was a frightful ebony wig with a white streak that called to mind a dead skunk. The Amazing Angelica, she was called, and she would happily tell your future if you deposited a penny in a scandalously-placed slot between her breasts. She could only answer 'yes' or 'no' questions, and the people who arrived on the *Bullet* passed her by with haughty glances. They knew they had just seen better examples of automation, and many of them would catch the train again when it returned.

Fairs and carnivals had a tendency to make the troubles of life melt away for a day. All a person needed to lose themselves was a ticket for the carousel or a sugary confection wrapped in white paper.

Dante had ruined such fairs before. Often, the ingredients for a day of wonder need only be slightly perverted to produce a tragedy. Machines and close quarters and anxious animals were easily manipulated, and the thought warmed the grim knot lodged in his chest.

"He's behind us," Iago whispered in Dante's ear. "Outside the depot. He's watching."

Dante looked back over the crowd of eager fairgoers. He could see no one who seemed the slightest bit threatening, save for a man tearing voraciously into candy floss.

"Normally, he's quite devoid of hair, but he's wearing a red wig," Iago continued.

And at that moment, Dante knew he met Zero Bancroft's fierce gaze. His eyes were like burning coals under the copper curls of the wig, and his lips pulled back in a sneer. He ducked out of sight, shoulders hunched.

"Move into the crowd. Hurry," Dante commanded.

The place reeked of animals and food and people, a pungent array of scents that, when combined, mostly just smelled like the back end of a muddy pachyderm. The Calamine Harvest Festival brought in crowds which doubled the small town's population for a mere five days. People walked shoulder to shoulder and, what's more, did not seem to care about the suffocating proximity. They were too busy pointing and smiling and smiling and pointing at everything around them. Dante, Iago, and Beatrice were pulled into the jumble.

"I bet I can guess your weight! Step right this way!"

"Did you see that pumpkin? Even larger than last year, I hear. What will Pitney's Farm think about that?"

"The carousel!! I want to ride the carousel!"

"Invisibility now, Dante?" Iago asked desperately.

"We had an agreement, Iago. We can't."

Dante looked over his shoulder and spotted Zero Bancroft through the crowd. The demon hunter pushed his way through the sea of people, sending one man and his sack of candied nuts tumbling into the dust. Dante thought of the bird in Iago's dream. Was this the storm on the horizon coming to take him?

Not if he could help it. "Faster," Dante said. "Run!"

They took off through the throng with Bancroft on their trail. He kept something in his jacket. The same formula which had nearly felled Iago? Dante could only imagine that it was, and Lucifer Below, he did not want to perish at a festival dedicated to a gourd!

Turning a corner, they charged onto the thoroughfare where farmers could show off their multicolored corns and their bushels of apples. But most of all, there were pumpkins, dozens and dozens of pumpkins in every size and shape a pumpkin might achieve. Tiny ones like pin cushions and large ones as girthy as Great Uncle Otto. It was a cornucopia of goods, the town's bounty laid out for display on long wooden tables. The visitors to the festival seemed positively delighted to view each and every one of them with critical eyes. They slowly shuffled as they commented on every item. Dante squeezed through hulking men and women in giant hats.

He never wanted to see a pumpkin again.

Ahead of them, an observation tower stretched into the sky. Perhaps piles of gourds were even more enthralling when viewed from above. It was a clear and blue day, and though the observation tower was presumably one of the more delightful attractions at the festival, Dante was not in the business of delight.

"I have an idea," he called to Iago. "You two go ahead."

"Don't do anything foolish, Mr. Lovelace!"

"A little faith, please, Mr. Wick!"

Dante stopped when they reached the observation tower. It was not *too* tall, he thought optimistically. There was an excellent chance that no one would perish.

With a deep breath, Dante conjured a spark from the inside of his coat, this one larger than the one he used at Beacon Street. Nerves fluttered in his stomach. The smell of the fair was growing irksome, lingering in his nose and throat. He looked up. Four people stood on the tower above him, issuing banal comments about the festival below. "I'm sorry," Dante muttered under his breath, and secured the spark to one thick leg of the structure.

Dante turned back as the crowd parted. He froze.

Zero Bancroft raised his gun, an animal grin cracking his face in two.

He pulled the trigger.

Dante pivoted as the crowd scattered, obstructing Bancroft's view. Sounds of merriment mingled with fearful cries. Dante blinked, still alive! His heart hammered wildly in his chest. A bullet protruded from the leg of the tower, just above the spark.

He admitted to himself that a bit of witch hazel after this was all over might not be so bad, after all. He pressed the red jewel in the center of the device and ran like a demon out of Hell.

Dante barely made it out of the square before he heard a loud *crack!* Smoke seethed from the spark, and there was an eerie creaking of wood, like a graveyard gate in the wind. The observation tower came tumbling to the ground, quickly crumpling in the cloud of smoke. Survivable, Dante determined, and his melancholia spasmed in disappointment. Dust billowed into the air as visitors cried out, and the rubble of the accident landed right in Zero Bancroft's path.

Dante caught up with Iago and Beatrice. "Bravo, Mr. Lovelace," Iago said with a grin.

"We must keep moving. We haven't necessarily lost him yet," Dante said.

"Were those sparks?" Beatrice asked as they reached the edge of the festival.

"Only a middling one," Dante clarified. "Trust me. Had I used too many, we might have blown the Calamine Harvest Festival sky high."

~

They escaped to the quiet streets beyond the festival. Here, the people of Calamine had rehearsed and preened and prepared all year. The streets were dirt, but the houses were tall, sturdy, and quietly proud. This was the sort of town the people of Marlowe, and certainly Boston, would have mocked, but Dante found it utterly pleasant: quaint, though he might have added a raven or two for character.

The streets appeared to be empty, each and every citizen drawn invariably by the allure of the gourd. Still, they looked occasionally over their shoulders, watching for Bancroft or any other suspicious strangers who might be following.

"How far are we from Clarkton?" Dante asked.

Beatrice chewed her lower lip before she answered, "It's not an impossible trek, but it's going to be a long walk. I hope you gentlemen are outdoorsmen."

Iago grimaced. "You know, if not for the bugs and the dirt, nature might be somewhat bearable."

"Did I overhear you folks correctly? You're looking to get to Clarkton?"

They turned to see a young man in suspenders and a cap. He looked like a newsboy nearing the age for retirement, and his hands and cheeks were smudged with dirt. He turned his gaze bashfully to the ground. "I'm sorry. I didn't mean to eavesdrop. Mama always gets angry about that," he said.

Dante looked to Iago, eyebrows peaked. Iago interpreted the gesture correctly, gazing intently into the young man's eyes before nodding. His intent was good.

This was not one of Bancroft's men.

Dante smiled and shook his head. "Don't worry. Why aren't you at the festival?"

The young man made a grand and unimpressed *pssshh* with his lips. "That old thing? I've lived in Calamine my whole life, and you can only be impressed by giant gourds and carousels so many times." He removed his hat and ruffled a hand through his sandy hair. "Were there gunshots over there?"

"A, uh... an accident, yes," Dante answered.

"Anyone hurt?"

"Not that I know of," Dante said noncommittally.

The young man was satisfied with the answer, and that was good enough for Dante. "Good. By the way, my name is Peter. Peter Blevins. I have something that could help you get to Clarkton."

Iago guffawed. "An airship?"

"No. Something better," the young man chuckled. "Come this way. I live just around the corner."

They followed Peter Blevins to a sturdy brick home with a tall wooden carriage house. He chattered all the way about nothing consequential, just a lot of hot air about the festival, and Dante wondered if Peter Blevins had ever met another human being in his life. Their mere presence had opened the floodgates, and the young man spoke as though he might die if he didn't, a profusion of words tripping from the tip of his tongue.

"I just can't understand the fascination with gourds. My daddy's friend won the big pumpkin contest last year." His eyes bugged preciously. "That pumpkin...

Well, if you would've set that pumpkin on a hill and rolled it toward town, we would've been in trouble, but thankfully, there ain't no hills around here," Blevins explained. "Those pumpkins are nothin'! Wait until you see what *I* have to show you."

Peter Blevins approached the carriage house, chest puffed in pride, and opened the large double doors. He threw his arms wide. "Tah-dah!" he sang with theatrical bravado.

The building housed nothing less than an automated carriage, finished in jet black with brassy details. Those of a more provincial mindset were usually hesitant to accept the machines, but Blevins beamed, looking upon his with the warm glow of a proud father. The people of Boston, New York, and London were utterly tickled with Herr Benz's and Herr Daimler's creations. Dante wondered how they would respond if they knew the truth about these pioneers.

The autos were just the latest in a long line of machines crafted by rogue German werewolves. Their more advanced models far outshone those used by the common human population. Most notably, they crafted an auto with the capability to transform. After all, transformation was something they knew all about. In a matter of moments, their latest autos could don armor, a protective shield folding out of the back like an accordion before covering the entire machine. Perfect defense against silver bullets. Dante had heard that European military forces were quite interested in these models, though one officer disappeared after stopping by unexpectedly to examine the autos.

Humans thought the officer simply fled, a hasty story about a love affair slopped together. The supernatural sect knew the truth; he had caught Herr Daimler at an appallingly bad time of month.

All the same, the autos were beginning to proliferate. One can accomplish a lot when handed immortality.

"You see? I made it!" Blevins proclaimed, motioning to the vehicle.

Immortality... or a lot of spare time in Calamine, Indiana.

"You made this?" Beatrice asked. "On your own?"

"Of course," he said, and fondly patted the front end of the machine. "Modeled it after Daimler's standard auto. However, I made some adjustments. Come in, come in. Gather 'round!"

He made a show of spitting on his palms, and he turned a crank on the side of the automated carriage until it began to rumble and hum. "It's a little loud," he yelled, and a puff of dark and noxious smoke shot from the back of the machine. "Don't worry—that's normal. Hop in!"

Dante asked, "You're going to...?"

"Take you to Clarkton, of course! It's not too far from here, and I've taken Gertrude all over the countryside."

"Gertrude?" Iago asked. "You named it?"

"Of course. She's my pride and joy!" Blevins said with a broad smile. "People always name ships. I imagined I should name my auto. It gives something a lot of personality when you give it a name. Gertie's a real spitfire."

With some hesitation, they piled into Gertrude. The machine rattled unnervingly, as though it wouldn't get to the end of the street, let alone Clarkton. Blevins passed around a few mismatched pairs of goggles and added, "To protect you from bugs!"

This young man was so wholesome, Dante thought, that God Himself was probably taking notes.

The auto lurched forward, rolled onto the street, and stopped. "Here we go!" Blevins flipped a few switches and turned a knob or two. Then, he sat back and smiled. The auto jolted and bucked like an angry bull. Iago gripped the seat and gave an undignified squeak, while Dante endeavored to look outside the vehicle. Was the ground always that far away?

No. No, it wasn't.

Blevins yelled, "We are currently six inches off the ground. This auto can hover! I took the train to Columbus, Ohio, just so I could purchase a hover engine from a man who traveled all the way from London, England. He talked real funny, but you can't argue with the product. I installed it all on my own."

He flipped the switch again, and the auto settled heavily on the ground. Blevins continued, "We're not going to hover to Clarkton. I can't move very quickly when I'm hovering. Impractical. Maybe some day. But between you and me... I'm working on a really nice flying machine. Keep that under your hat!"

He made them all swear to secrecy before they departed.

Peter Blevins turned onto the street and began to drive toward the edge of town. It wasn't nearly as fast as a train, but it was better than walking, and Zero Bancroft would not think to look for them in the care of some young Calamine citizen with a hovering automated carriage. The auto was loud, but Blevins was louder.

The roads beyond Calamine were rocky, and admittedly, they were not easy on the bones or the stomach. Dante looked into the distance, the vibrant blue sky and the empty fields, and he wondered what sort of catastrophes a world saturated with automated carriages would bring.

~

No one perished in the Great Harvest Festival Disaster, but there were a few broken limbs and a badly bent thumb which might never recover. The dust and the people, however, were enough so that Zero Bancroft lost sight of his target.

With a snarl, he turned back and walked to the train station, shoving his way through the people running toward the observation tower. Outside the depot waited young Mr. Haversham and old Mr. Carmichael (or Charlotte Cutter and Sylvester Hacke, depending upon whom you asked).

"I'm guessing they escaped," Hacke said out of the corner of his mouth.

"Quiet," Bancroft grunted, and drew a deep breath. It was a poor idea to try to shoot Lovelace, but once he sought his prey, he could hardly help himself. Such brash behavior would not help him in his cause. He could hear Ezekiel Faust himself berating him, his coarse voice rattling in his skull. Faust was like that right until the end... before the blood choked him, anyway. "Yes, I've lost them." Quietly, he added, "Miss Cutter, I apologize. My passion got the better of me. That's not how I was taught. I am sorry."

And he saw that light in her eyes. She forgave him. Of course, she did. She was enamored. The poor girl was embarrassingly in love with him. Still, she was useful. And when people were useful, Bancroft found he was forced to be a gentleman.

"Where did they go?" Charlotte asked, and pressed a nervous hand to her false moustache again. She looked ridiculous, but Bancroft wouldn't tell her so.

"I'm not certain," he said. "However, we will find them before they reach the Orb. We must. If Foster's home is under a cloaking spell, it will be infinitely more difficult to find if we lose them completely. Come. We can't let them get too far away. Can you walk?"

Charlotte nodded meekly.

"Good. We'll ask for directions," Bancroft said, and turned just as he saw a machine rattling down the uneven street, away from the festival. He spotted Beatrice Dickens's flaming red hair in the back of the automated carriage. For a moment, he wanted to sprint after them, but he held back. Such impulse had not benefited him earlier.

All would be well. Fate smiled upon Zero Bancroft

and his noble cause.

XI.

It was as though someone had made a carbon copy of Calamine, dropped it several miles down the road, and declared it the City of Clarkton. The same simple, proud buildings sprung from the ground. There were the same worn faces and the same dusty roads. Dante was surprised there wasn't an identical Harvest Festival, but there probably weren't enough gourds in the entire country to accommodate two at once.

The citizens of Clarkton looked less than thrilled to see Gertie rattling down their streets. Gertie meant progress, and progress of any kind gave citizens of places like Clarkton a reason to dust off their soapboxes. The auto came to a grinding, laborious halt just outside a small dining room, where two men in threadbare suits approached them. Discretion was tossed aside, and they made quite the show of examining the auto.

"Young man, what is this?" one man asked

suspiciously. "One of those automated carriages?"

"This, gentlemen, is the future," Peter Blevins proclaimed. The two men shook their heads and ambled away, certain to pen letters to the local newspaper about the evils of innovation as soon as they returned home.

"We can't thank you enough for helping us, Mr. Blevins," Beatrice said, and removed her goggles. They left pink rings around her eyes.

Dante added, "Your kindness will not soon be forgotten."

They said their goodbyes, and as he returned his goggles, Iago said, "You're quite talented, young man. Don't let that pride go to your head."

Peter Blevins gave one last boyish grin. "Oh, I won't."

And Dante believed him.

"We'll walk out of Clarkton, heading west," Beatrice said as Blevins prepared Gertie for his journey home. "When we reach the eight-mile marker, look for his house. You shall see it if you know it's there. It's hidden in plain sight."

They walked briskly through Clarkton, garnering more than a few odd looks from the residents. There was nothing more exciting in a small town than seeing a new face, and Dante could only imagine how rarely someone from Clarkton caught a glimpse of three strangers all at once. It was surely like seeing a unicorn, a leprechaun, and the yeti strolling down the street together.

Eventually, the town tapered off into a dirt road, lonely and stretching west.

"How often have you been here to visit Harry?" Dante asked.

"A handful of times. I cast the cloaking spell as soon as I gave him the Orb about six months ago. Those passing from town to town might only wonder if they once saw a house there, but the thought will leave them in an instant. It takes conviction and a knowledge of the precise location to finally see his house," she explained. "The spell upon my home is cast only with supernatural beings in mind. Harry's cloaking spell affects all creatures."

She continued bleakly, "All the same, no spell is perfect. Bancroft's presence on the train does not inspire confidence."

~

"If you ask me, people are crazy for riding in one of those things," Sylvester Hacke said as they followed the dirt road toward Clarkton. "A horse can see. A horse can stop. One of those buckets of bolts will run right into a tree." Hacke spit something yellowish on the ground in disgust.

Charlotte winced, in part because of the yellow glob in her path and in part because her ankle was not quite as unscathed as she had thought.

A sudden rattling came from up ahead of them, a roar of a machine, and Zero Bancroft turned and grinned to his companions. Oh, Charlotte thought it was so lovely to see him smile again.

"Perhaps this young man in his automated carriage can assist us," he said.

The gentleman wore goggles and jumped up and down in the machine. This was not, Charlotte presumed, of his own accord. She couldn't imagine riding in one of those terrible metal beasts.

He saw them, and the machine slowed and came to a stop. The driver removed his goggles, his face smudgy and his eyes bright. "Well, hello there, folks! Where are you headed?"

"The next town over. What is it called?"

"Well, heck, that's Clarkton. I just came from there. Transported a few folks I saw in Calamine. They were looking to help a friend out there," the young man explained.

"Yes, the people you helped—two men and a woman? A red-headed lady?" Bancroft asked.

"Why, yes! That's them. Do you know them?"

"Dear friends," Bancroft said with a sheepish smile of regret. "We were separated. Tell me, is it a long walk? The young whelp traveling with us, Mr. Haversham, has injured his ankle."

Peter Blevins had a softness in his eyes when he looked at Charlotte, and he clicked his tongue. "Look here. I'm expected back at Calamine soon, I reckon, but I'll help you. If it pleases you, you can ride in my auto to Clarkton. The name's Peter Blevins, by the way!"

"Oh, bless you, young man!" Bancroft said sweetly. Charlotte gulped as she stepped into the back seat of the automated carriage. She drew a deep breath, and Sylvester

Hacke sat beside her, snorting deeply before spitting to the ground again. It was an uncomfortably tight squeeze.

"We're all going to die in this thing," Hacke muttered under his breath, then in a creaking, elderly voice, he asked, "Did our friends happen to say exactly where they were going out there?"

"I didn't hear much, old-timer. Or rather, they didn't tell me. Now, my mama says that I eavesdrop too much, but in this case, it looks like I'll be able to help you out. Before they left, they talked about going to the eight-mile marker west of Clarkton," Peter Blevins explained, and he passed around goggles for them to wear. Charlotte fought with the straps. The lenses were dusty and cracked, and she anxiously hoped this auto was in better condition than the goggles.

"The eight-mile marker?" Bancroft asked.

"Yes. I guess there's a house there, though I can't remember ever seeing one. The lady said, 'You shall see it if you know it's there. It's hidden in plain sight,'" Blevins said. "Whatever that means. Seems awful mysterious to me." He fiddled with a few knobs and levers, and the machine rattled to life again, jolting upward. "Now, do you want to see something amazing?"

Bancroft nodded patiently. Charlotte did not wish to see anything this backwards young man might have considered amazing. Imagine her displeasure when she looked down to realize they were floating! She gripped the side of the automated carriage. "How far?" she gasped in a reedy, hopefully-male voice.

"Not too far," Blevins reassured her. The auto

plopped onto the ground again. "Now, hold on!"

~

The walk from Clarkton to Harry's house was not a short one, but Dante supposed it was fine to get a bit of exercise. Some demons indulged too heavily in the sin of sloth. Fresh air did a minion of Lucifer good, he thought.

Iago, however, spent the journey brushing away dust and flicking the occasional over-friendly bug from his jacket in disgust. Never had a fish been more indubitably out of water.

The road before them meandered from side to side like a long river. Dante could not help but think of Styx: a fine myth, though impractical and not a method of transport Hell would ever actually use. Were they now wandering down the river toward Hell? If ever Hell were on Earth, would it be in Indiana?

Quite possibly.

Between snacks of dried meat drawn from her satchel, Beatrice practiced conjuring fire in her hands, the spheres small enough that they would not be noticed by any sudden passersby. Proper young ladies simply didn't conjure fire from their palms. Then again, proper young ladies did not bind demons or hold séances, either.

They planned. They practiced. Beatrice insisted Dante and Iago use invisibility in any confrontation that awaited, much to Iago's delight.

"I assume," she said, rolling a ball of fire over her knuckles, "we are still ahead of Bancroft himself. After we secure Harry's home, we shall pursue him."

But there were too many variables at play. Who or what had frightened Harry Foster? Was it Bancroft? Was there even a threat at all? Perhaps he was ill or merely anticipated an attack. Dante was not accustomed to such variability. His work for Hell required meticulous planning. Iago Wick had his neatly kept temptations upon his bookcase, and Dante Lovelace could wrap the world in the renderings and blue-prints of disasters he had planned.

Meanwhile, Dante's plan with Beatrice was hardly a plan at all! You can't plan for what you can't anticipate, and frankly, they hadn't the faintest idea what awaited them. They discussed possibilities, of course, but that was all they had: wisps of theory and possibility with a dash of probability and a generous helping of maybes.

However, despite any peril ahead of them and Iago's grim premonition of a storm lurking in the back of his mind, Dante could not deny the thrill of adventure. There was something to be said for the unknown. Its sweet siren song rang in his ears.

The sky was perfectly blue, empty, save for a large bird drifting high above.

A tree line emerged on their left, and Dante watched for any movement, signs they were being followed. They appeared to be alone, but it was far from quiet. Somewhere beyond the trees, a river burbled. Birds squawked, bugs clipped, and rodents scampered in the grass. One insect provided a relentless grinding whine that was not unlike the sounds heard in Hell.

Eventually, Beatrice guided them beyond the tree line, crouching and creeping in the brambles. She hiked her skirt up with no trouble, and her boots were sturdy. "We're nearly there. Someone may be watching even now," she said. "We won't do Harry any good if we're captured."

The wooded area brought another biota altogether, mere feet from the domain of the screeching insects. Handfuls of spiders hurried across the ground, ducking into blossoms of web. Beatrice plucked a dead arachnid from an old web and placed it in her satchel. "For later use," she said.

Before long, they stopped, parallel to a chunky mile-marker jutting from the ground on the right side of the road. Beatrice looked across what appeared to be nothing more than an empty field. She could not hide a fond smile. "There it is," she said softly, ducking behind low-hanging branches. "Know that it is there, and you shall see it."

Dante looked intently. A grasshopper shuddered into the air, and a pair of birds settled to dust-bathe. And then, as though fog dissipated before Dante's eyes, windows appeared, the panes of glass streaked with sunlight. A door followed. A well-kept house faded into view, perhaps thirty yards from the road. Its brick was worn and sturdy, accented with deep green shutters, a comfortable porch, and a rocking chair.

"Oh, how quaint," Iago said dryly when he saw it.

"Mr. Wick, would you mind assuming invisibility and scouting the area?" Beatrice asked. "See if anyone is lurking in the trees or around the house."

Iago narrowed his eyes and indignantly plucked a spider by one leg from his shoulder before tossing it eight feet away. "I'll do it because it's wise, not because you asked me." He assumed invisibility and stalked away.

Beatrice looked over the home, the land, and said, "Not a thing seems out of place."

"Still, we must keep fire at the ready as we approach," Dante said. That awful knot in his chest fluttered in delight. Finally, it would see a bit of action, more than some piddling spark spoiling a day at the fair.

His melancholia had been so bothersome lately. When he was forced to tap into it for his Hellish work, day in and day out, Dante became numb to its presence. It was an annoyance, but so were a lot of things: sudden rain at a picnic, salesmen, shoes that were too tight. He would quiet it and move on. Now, he was being reminded of just how much he hated the hungry and anxious thing.

After half an hour, Iago returned from his mission. "I saw no one, nothing which indicates a threat. What are the chances Harry merely needs help opening a particularly obstinate jar?"

Beatrice, it seemed, could not even bring herself to comment. "Come. Let's approach. Remember invisibility." She paused a moment longer. "We haven't practiced nearly enough."

"Perhaps not," Dante admitted.

Iago exhaled. "Let's get this over with. The anticipation is killing me."

Dante and Iago assumed invisibility, allowing

Beatrice to get about ten feet ahead of them. They crept across the field and the road, ducking into the tall weeds. Grasses scratched their cheeks and clung to their clothes. Dante moved carefully as to not disturb the grass too much, in case Iago had missed a scout in his investigation.

Dante's palms itched, ready to conjure Hellfire should the need arise. Fire already simmered in Beatrice's right palm, a disc of flame covering the expanse of her hand.

The trio came upon the porch, where the rocking chair creaked in the stiff breeze. Beatrice knocked twice on the sturdy wooden door and waited. Dante held back, and fire warmed his hands.

The door opened. Dante and Iago tensed.

A single man with an intent gaze peered out at her. He wore a tweed waistcoat and a hesitant smile. "Bea?" he asked.

"Harry," she greeted, and Dante felt her relief in his own heart. The fire waned, and she took Harry's hands in hers. Sneaking silently around them, Dante peered into the foyer. So far, the coast was clear. "It's so good to see you. How are you?"

"I suppose I am well," Harry Foster chuckled as they cautiously entered, Dante and Iago slipping in swiftly before the door closed.

Iago signaled to Dante and left to investigate the house, searching for any hidden threats. Dante stayed by Beatrice's side and examined their surroundings.

A small table by the door was stacked high with books, and an old umbrella stand messily overflowed with rolled maps. Harry straightened his waistcoat and tidied the books with an embarrassed cough. "This house is a mess. I wasn't expecting anyone to call. Then again, I'm never really expecting anyone to call. Not even the most determined solicitor can find this house."

Beatrice quirked a brow. "You mean—?"

"Honey Bea, of course, I'm happy to see you. I always am," Harry said warmly, and ushered her into the study. "Come. Have a seat, rest your bones. I assume you came all the way from Clarkton."

They followed him past the staircase but had barely taken two steps into the study before Dante found himself and Beatrice looking down the barrel of a gun!

At the other end of the weapon stood a remarkably fuzzy man in long johns, tattered so that nothing too indecent was showing. He gripped the rifle in one hand and a bowl of stew in the other. Wild eyes peered from over ruddy pink cheeks. Was this one of Bancroft's men? Dante might have thought Bancroft would associate with someone better composed than this. A massive beard swallowed the man's face, and he gave an angry grunt. "Hmmph!"

Dante braced himself for battle. Beatrice, however, dismissed the assailant with a wave of her hand.

"Arrow," Harry scolded. "It's only Bea. Put the gun away."

The fuzzy man inspected her from head to toe before dropping the gun to his side and settling in a battered old chair with his bowl of stew. Rabbit stew, Dante determined. Long ears flopped over the side of the bowl like two pinkish-gray banana peels. He slurped one like a noodle.

Beatrice cringed. "Good to see you again, Mr. McClellan."

"Hah," he grunted amicably, the positive counterpart to the negative *hmmph*, it seemed. Dante recalled Beatrice telling him about Harry's housemate on the train to Boston. A man of few words and fewer social graces, she had said. Not an inaccurate description.

The study was dominated by large and over-stuffed bookcases. Dozens of papers stuck out of desk drawers, and newspaper articles covered any walls to be seen. *STRANGE DISAPPEARANCE*, one article read. *THE BELMONT MONSTER STRIKES AGAIN*, said another. The place was lit by several lanterns and smelled of tobacco and old books, a rich and welcoming scent.

Some tables were completely covered in books. Other tables were merely piles of books masquerading as tables. The place exuded a sense of enchantment, one which went beyond any charm of Beatrice's creation.

One thing was certain: nothing about the house felt threatening at all. There was no sense of trouble, no tension. Dante was beginning to wonder if Iago's Obstinate Jar Hypothesis could be correct.

Iago returned a moment later and assumed his position at Dante's side. "Books. This house is positively brimming with books, and unless they're a threat, the coast seems to be clear. Although, I can't speak as to whether or not *that* could be a threat." He motioned to the furry old man gulping down mouthfuls of stew.

"That's Mr. Foster's housemate, Arrow McClellan," Dante explained.

"That's a human?" Iago asked, aghast.

Beatrice looked carefully around the study, apparently hoping she would see something, *anything* that would cause Harry to contact her. "Didn't you send me a letter?" she asked warily. She had not completely sheathed her power, Dante noted.

"No reason to. It's been perfectly quiet here," Harry said with a smile.

Iago nodded. "He's telling the truth."

"Oh, dear," Dante said.

Beatrice shook her head in confusion. "Harry, forgive me. Gentlemen, you can show yourselves."

Harry Foster was surprisingly unsurprised when two men suddenly appeared out of thin air in his study. His eyebrows jumped, and he looked at Beatrice in vague amusement. "Working with wizards, Miss Dickens? I never thought you the type."

She sneered. "Harry, I would never throw myself in with that daffy crowd. All that ridiculous wand-waving. This is Dante Lovelace and Iago Wick. They are my companions for the time being. Demons."

Apparently, keeping the company of demons far outweighed associating with wizards. However, at the mention of the d-word, Arrow McClellan half-raised his rifle again, beard dancing as he chewed endlessly on a particularly fatty piece of bunny.

"Put the gun down, Arrow," Harry said. "Demons, Bea?"

"I have my reasons," she said.

"We don't mean you any harm," Dante said, hoping Mr. Foster would not immediately run for the holy water.

To his surprise, Harry Foster motioned genially for them to take a seat in the study's mismatched chairs. "No, of course. I trust Bea. Please, sit. I'm a scholar, not a hunter. I study the supernatural, and I can tell you from experience that not all demons are the monsters we make them out to be," he said fondly. "I'm actually planning to write an essay on the nature of demonhood once I complete my book."

Iago's face lit up. "Ah, you're a writer."

"Yes," he said eagerly, eyes bright. "Do you recall The Belmont Monster? I'm writing a book about it. Disappearances, cattle deaths… dozens over the last fifty years in the same county in Indiana. Locals say wolves, supernatural experts say werewolves. I don't think so." And here, Arrow McClellan nodded as though Harry preached the gospel. "There is precision in the deaths, surgical in nature. No blood spilt unnecessarily. Vampires? Perhaps. Fairies? That would account for the disappearances. I made a chart." Harry enthusiastically pulled a large rolled paper from behind the desk. Then, he grabbed another. "And this is appendix A… this is appendix B… this is—"

"Harry, please! You mean to say you didn't send me a note that said *Gathany*?" Beatrice asked helplessly.

Harry looked puzzled, his arms full of enough appendices and charts to wallpaper the room twice over. "*Gathany*? No, I haven't thought of that old code in years," he said. He replaced the papers. "Why do you ask?"

Beatrice rushed to the window. She cursed under her breath and pulled her cigarette case from her pocket before using a candle on the desk to light one. "How did he know? I might have led him right to your door."

"Who?" Harry asked, and took an intricately carved pipe for himself. The bowl featured the face of an old man, and smoke puffed from his sawn head.

"Zero Bancroft," Dante answered. "Though I would love to hear your theories on The Belmont Monster, I fear we did not simply come for tea and chat."

Or rabbit stew and animal grunting, for that matter.

"That's why Mr. Lovelace and Mr. Wick were invisible. We were poised to attack. Oh, how could I be so stupid?" Beatrice said through clenched teeth. "We saw Bancroft back at Calamine, on the train. He must be the one who sent the letter. How did he know? We are the only two souls on the planet to know that code! It looked like your handwriting, bore Clarkton's postmark. I thought you needed help."

"Calm down, Bea," Harry said soothingly. "The Orb is hidden. Your cloaking spell works well. And if anything goes wrong, Arrow's not afraid to use that rifle."

Beatrice looked less than confident in furry Mr. McClellan's abilities. "I was afraid," she said. "I could not sleep after leaving the Orb with you. I needed another weapon against Bancroft. That is why I bound Mr. Lovelace. I—"

"What? No," Harry said. His face fell into a frown.

"Beatrice, please tell me you didn't."

"I had to," she said sternly. "Harry, I had no choice."

"Binding is *never* a choice!" Smoke puffed from Harry's pipe like a steam engine. His face contorted in shock as he tried to digest the news. Dante could tell it wasn't going very well. "Bea, I love you with all my heart, but what in Hell were you thinking?"

"I did this for you," Beatrice said, and took a long pull from her cigarette. "I needed more protection. My plan was to battle Bancroft in Marlowe, to keep him from ever finding you." She gave an anguished groan. "We can see how well that worked."

"We could have found a better solution. Anything is better than binding, and what's more, you'll have damned yourself for these actions."

"I thought it for the greater good," Beatrice said.

"The greater good?" Harry asked. "Isn't that what Zero Bancroft preached when he came to your door asking for the Orb in the first place?"

The words stung Beatrice, and she recoiled. Dante and Iago exchanged uncomfortable glances. Dante had never been the subject of another couple's quarrel before. Not directly, anyway. Surely a few shipwrecks and carriage accidents had dissolved happy marriages, but that didn't count. While Dante would be happy to defeat Bancroft, he could not disagree with Mr. Foster. If anything, he felt a hearty *hear, hear!* was in order, but he held his tongue.

"I find that the greater good often devalues the

individual," Harry said delicately. "How great, then, can it possibly be?" He relented. "We will discuss this later. In the meantime, make yourselves comfortable. Bancroft is out there. It is best to stay put for now."

"Two bedr'ms d'nstairs. One up," Arrow offered. Lucifer Below, he speaks! "Stay outta th' one upstairs. S'for friends."

"Are we not friends, Mr. McClellan?" Beatrice asked.

"S'for lady friends. Bessie. Gotter room ha sh'likes it." He gave a gravelly laugh that, Dante could attest, sounded as though it came from the depths of Hell.

"Good ol' Bessie," Harry said. "She treats you well, Arrow."

"Hah," he grunted knowingly with a wink, and ambled to his feet. After expertly using his rifle to scratch his posterior, Mr. McClellan shuffled off with his empty bowl.

"Who is Bessie? Where does she live?" Dante asked softly of Harry.

"All in Arrow's mind," Harry whispered, and held a finger to his lips. "He's like a somnambulist. Just let him dream."

Stupendous. A delusional man with an invisible lover and a penchant for firearms. Just what they needed.

XII.

Most demons are, by their nature, not fond of frolicking in the fields and picking daisies. Their general distaste for the pastoral, in addition to sparse human populations, meant there weren't too many demons in the Massachusetts countryside simply wandering about for the taking.

So, Viola Atchison was forced to travel to a nearby town to find one.

In the town of Gingham, Massachusetts, there was but one demon, a wily thing who hadn't been away from Hell for long. He was easy to track and even easier to catch. The demon in question, Boris Nightshade, never saw Viola coming. He fell like a pile of bricks into her arms after she stuck him artfully with a syringe of lamb's blood.

He was the second she had stolen. The first hailed from the town of Owsley and... well, he had quite an unfortunate reaction to her new formula. That took some time to clean up. Modifications were made. Hopefully, Mr. Nightshade would not react in kind.

Sofia helped her conceal Nightshade's body on a rickety wooden cart, and they took him back to Mr. Collier's house. Archimedes, the dog, growled at their bounty. Mr. Collier watched closely as the Atchisons carried the demon through his parlor and down the stairs, Sofia at the head and Viola at the feet. Their shoes were damp and muddy from the autumn rain.

"Reminds me of that book!" Mr. Collier called down the stairwell. "Sneaking around with bodies. *Frankenstein.*"

These circumstances had more in common with Mary Shelley's creation than Collier knew, but Viola liked to think she was a bit more skilled than that egotistical oaf, Victor Frankenstein.

Now, Viola Atchison was not one to bow to aesthetics, but the tiny part of her that could be considered Romantic would have loved a booming storm to provide the atmosphere for her daring demonic experiments. Alas, it was only a soggy day. Not quite as dramatic as she would have liked, but Viola had, *regrettably*, not yet invented a device to control the weather. Next year, perhaps.

And so, with the constant chatter of rain to accompany them, the Atchisons laid out Boris Nightshade and tied him down in Mr. Collier's basement. As they waited for him to wake, Sofia nursed a cup of coffee.

At first, only Nightshade's fingers flexed. He

moaned softly and snored. Viola rolled her eyes and gave him a sharp smack across the face.

"Mr. Nightshade?"

The demon croaked, "Ugh, what is this? Where am I? Did you just hit me?"

"Excellent powers of observation, Mr. Nightshade," Viola said dryly, wearing a thick apron to protect her clothes. She'd learned her lesson after the last demon. She was happy to give Nightshade a brief description of her intent, one which did not elaborate beyond, "You are to be my subject of experimentation, Mr. Nightshade. Your cooperation is appreciated, and if you don't oblige..." She reached for the gun she had crafted two years prior. "...I invented this. I know how to use it."

The demon blinked. "The Atchison Gun? You're Atchison?" He puzzled. "Funny. I always assumed Atchison was a man."

"Many did," Viola said. "Now, hold still." She swiftly injected him with a measured amount of the Zero Formula. Boris Nightshade died in less than five full seconds, his dark eyes rolling back into his head like marbles.

Viola pressed her fingertips to his pulse points, listened carefully for breath. "By all means, dead. Perfect," she proclaimed. "He's as utterly lifeless as Mr. Wick when I found him that night."

"This is dangerous, Viola," Sofia said. "If this succeeds..."

"Then, I won't lose Mr. Wick's partnership," she said, and reached for another syringe. "We'll allow Mr.

Nightshade to stew for a moment."

Sofia fiddled with a stray stethoscope. "And Mr. Bancroft...? If he discovers what you've done—"

"Oh, he'll whine and moan, but he'll recover," Viola said sternly. They both knew it was a vast understatement, but they said nothing of the horrific and potentially-deadly tantrum they knew was to come.

Eventually, the battalion of cuckoo clocks upstairs heralded that over half an hour had passed.

"Notebook at the ready, my dear," Viola said. "I want excellent detail. Times, please. I trust you have your pocket watch."

Sofia reached into the folds of her skirt to retrieve the old watch. "And what if this does not work, either? If he is just like the last demon?"

Viola said nothing for a moment. She crafted her compound of willow's bark and brimstone, ingredients which were known to stimulate a demon's senses, along with stimulants that typically affected the human body. "We keep trying."

Archimedes barked somewhere upstairs. The rain drummed on. Viola stood over the demon. "I am injecting one thimbleful of the Atchison formula into the demon."

Sofia nodded and wrote quickly. Viola stood back.

"Ten seconds," Sofia said as she watched the hands of the clock.

Viola observed the pointed face of the creature before her, monitored his hands, his fingers, his feet for any sign of movement. He was perfectly still.

"Fifteen seconds."

Viola crossed her arms over her chest.

"Twenty-five seconds."

She breathed through her nose. Mr. Wick would put on such a performance if she could not return to him with a solution to his problem.

"Thirty sec—"

At once, Nightshade's eyes flew open, and his body shuddered with a deep and gasping breath. His back arched off the table, though his wrists and ankles were restrained. Viola Atchison grinned, and her wife scrawled short notes in her book.

"A-ha! Welcome back to the waking world, Mr. Nightshade," Viola proclaimed.

"What did you do to me?" the demon gasped. "Oh, I am unwell."

Viola asked, "Tell me, do you remember anything at all from the last half hour?"

"What?" Nightshade moaned. "Oh, I don't know. I can't be certain. I'm ill."

"Deep breaths, Mr. Nightshade." Viola pulled a chair beside the table and looked intently into the suffering demon's eyes. "You are awake. You are well. I need you to relax."

"That's not a simple task, hunter," he growled. "I am pinned to a table!" He leant forward as much as he could, his dark eyes narrowing. His breath came in short, pungent gasps. "I'll boil you in oil, you foul bitch."

"They aren't all as eloquent as Mr. Wick, are they?" Viola asked of Sofia.

"Wick? Iago Wick?" Nightshade asked. He craned his neck to spit on the ground. "He's in a lot of trouble, I've heard."

Viola asked, "Trouble? What kind of trouble?"

"He's disappeared. He left Boston, and Richard Grimwood is angrier than a fallen angel on Christmas. Wick won't respond to him, and he won't return to Boston. Some think he's defected," Nightshade said like a gossipy hen at church. "Wouldn't surprise me. He's no demon. He cares more about himself than the cause of Hell."

Viola had heard Iago spout wishes of abandoning Hell for over a year now. He spoke of independence and discovering his own worth, free from Hell's grasp as long as he could evade it. It meant solitude, living quietly… and it meant abandoning his partnership with Viola, as well.

She frowned. "Well, Mr. Nightshade, I am sorry to hear that you have so low an opinion of Mr. Wick. He is a dear friend of mine."

Nightshade quirked his face unattractively. "A friend? He's a demon. You are a demon hunter."

"We work well together, I assure you," Viola said. "How are you feeling?"

"Miserable," Nightshade groaned, and lay limply on the table.

"Miserable, but very much alive. Sofia, we have some of the Zero Formula left. Could you please prepare a second syringe?"

"What?" Nightshade squeaked. "You're going to kill

me again? What in Hell is the matter with you? This is your hobby, killing and resurrecting demons over and over? My dear, knitting, cooking, and cleaning may suit you better."

"Yes," Viola said, "I have heard that before." She took the syringe from Sofia. "Thank you, my dear." She quickly stuck him in the throat and watched him die again. He flopped to the table like a dead fish.

"Beastly creature. How long shall we leave him now?" Sofia asked.

"Two hours or more," Viola said, keeping a watchful eye on the stairwell. Nightshade's screeching had not disturbed Mr. Collier, at least. "We must take the freshness of specimens into account, the length of time they have been dead. It may be difficult to bring them out of their slumber if they are too far gone."

"You'll be quite the expert in resurrection before we're through," Sofia said.

Viola thought of Nightshade's words, his speculation that Mr. Wick had already cast off the manacles of Hell. "That is my hope, Sofia."

~

Iago's assessment after his initial tour of the house was correct: Harry and Arrow's home had the trappings of ten libraries crammed into the space of approximately one and a half. Every room was covered in books and pamphlets and newspapers, haphazardly stacked from floor to ceiling. The mess, it appeared, made perfect sense to Harry, as organized in his eyes as the most intricate card catalogue.

Arrow McClellan was, unsurprisingly, not much of a reader. He was much fonder of shooting things. Conversation revealed that Mr. McClellan had spent his youth hunting monsters, the beasts which lurked in forests and could not be categorized by zoologists. He had once, he claimed, almost nabbed the Leeds Devil in New Jersey.

As they showed off their home, Arrow carried his beloved rifle, cradling it as though it were a child. With a series of grunts, he showed them several more: two rifles in the pantry, one over the bed he shared with Bessie, another in the parlor. The one carried lovingly in his arms, however, was his favorite.

"Don't tell the others," Harry joked.

Still, despite the profusion of firearms, Dante found the house warm, friendly. Perhaps it was the way Harry enthusiastically showed off his collection of books and paranormal papers. Beatrice was correct. His passion was utterly palpable and entirely infectious.

The house also gave off an almost musical creaking wherever one walked. It told its own story through uneven floorboards, a comfortably vocal pantry door, and several portraits of McClellans on the wall. Each man pictured (and perhaps one woman) sported an immense beard. It added to the house's strange charm, and Dante wondered what tales 13 Darke Street might have to tell.

At the end of the tour, Harry stopped in the parlor at a bookcase not dissimilar to every other one crammed to capacity in the home. He kicked aside a rug to reveal a trap door. "I haven't so much as looked at this thing since you brought it to me, Bea."

He opened the door and retrieved a bundle from within.

The worn cloth fell away, revealing a black sphere, polished and smooth. It was perfectly round, about the size of an orange. It seemed somewhat unassuming, Dante supposed, like any number of mildly cursed objects a witch would covet for her own uses. This, however, was not the sort of object one wanted to hand to any old butterfingered buffoon. Within, Devorog slept. The Orb of Morgana sat heavy in Harry's hand, and Dante's melancholia stirred at the sight of it.

They settled into the place. Iago and Harry chatted idly about the art of the written word before briefly exchanging theories on the mystery of The Belmont Monster. After those who required food had a steaming supper of—*surprise*—rabbit stew, Harry asked to speak to Beatrice in one of the bedrooms. They spoke in hushed tones within.

Dante let them be and returned to the study. The pungent smell of Hellfire lingered in the air.

"Iago, did you just send a letter?"

"What's that?" Iago asked distractedly.

"A letter, my dear. I smell burning parchment," Dante said. "Sulfur."

Iago peered through the foyer and into the parlor, where Arrow McClellan sat and whittled away at a block of wood. "Yes, but I'd rather not proclaim it to the world.

Not yet."

"To whom?" Dante asked. "Viola Atchison?"

"I fear we'll need help in the coming days," Iago said, "help which your witch and her scholar and this…" He motioned toward Arrow. "…fuzzy madman cannot provide." He groaned. "What I wouldn't do for a glass— no, *bottle* of scotch."

Dante chuckled. "Mr. McClellan appears to have a bottle of something tucked under his arm in there. Perhaps if you ask nicely…"

Iago shuddered. "I'd rather drink lye."

~

Charlotte Cutter was, as much as a polite and well-bred lady could be, perturbed.

The goal had been to track Beatrice and her demons closely. Their misstep at Calamine had cost them, but who should give them the greatest clue to finding their targets again but that daffy young man in his automated carriage! And since leaving him at Clarkton, all Zero Bancroft could talk about was how Peter Blevins, though he didn't know it, was like an angel sent from God Himself to guide them on their journey.

And, quite frankly, Charlotte was positively squirming in the grasp of the green-eyed monster.

She was happy to bid farewell to the young man at Clarkton. Bancroft declared it would be unwise to involve an outsider too thoroughly, and an eight-mile walk was good for a man.

Good for a man, perhaps, but Charlotte's ankle was still sore.

"Hell, it's getting dark out here," Hacke grunted as twilight descended.

"Darkness will help us," Bancroft said. "We won't be able to see them at first, but they will be able to see us if they are looking."

Did Mr. Bancroft forget, Charlotte wondered, that they would not even have known the Orb was with Harry Foster if not for her intelligence? They would not have had the secret code—*Gathany*—to use if she had not read Bea's diary behind her back when they were children. Neither would they have had Clarkton's postmark if not for her sneaking through Bea's home just after the séance, while Ellie Malark tended to her. Charlotte always had been quite adept at forgery. And she hadn't even cringed or cried out when Bancroft told her he had killed Lionel Dickens. Quite frankly, she wanted a little more recognition!

And perhaps, a kiss. A kiss from Mr. Bancroft would be nice.

Once they were seven miles outside Clarkton, Bancroft insisted they creep in the outcropping of trees which had appeared alongside the road. This only added to Charlotte's foul mood. Who knew what creepy and crawly nasties lurked in the mounting darkness? Charlotte suppressed a chill.

Soon, they spotted the eight-mile marker, a thick chunk of white stone. Bancroft smiled. "Perfect," he said. "Hacke, look to your right. I'll take the left. Miss Cutter, look straight forward. Now, believe there is a house before you. You know there's a house there. *Think.* There are windows, a door, perhaps a porch or a garden. Know there is a house there, and you will see it."

Crouching, Charlotte pushed branches aside and concentrated. She thought of Harry greeting Bea at the front door with a warm embrace. Was that guilt tightening her throat? Dreadful emotion! She shook it away and focused on believing a house stood before her. It simply wouldn't do to let the past keep her from her future.

In the haze of twilight, suddenly, she spotted windows, the glow of light within. It emerged like a spirit, a ghost of a chance to make Zero Bancroft value her again.

"There," she whispered. "Mr. Bancroft, there! Straight ahead."

Zero Bancroft turned and narrowed his animal gaze.

"It's brick. The windows are alight. There's movement within, upstairs. There is a porch," Charlotte described. She seized, as a spider scurried over her shoe, but did not cry out. Mr. Bancroft would not like such foolishness.

He smiled. "Oh, well done, dear lady. Well done, indeed. I can see it. We shall wait. Collect ourselves. I've quite the task for you, Miss Cutter," Bancroft said, and Charlotte's heart fluttered like a caged bird beating its wings against the bars. "I think you'll do very well."

Pride swelled in her chest, swiftly devouring any guilt she felt. Take that, Peter Blevins.

~

In a bedroom that was not Bessie's, Dante Lovelace took time to do little more than breathe. It seemed like he had not been able to catch his breath for days. He sat at a small writing desk and basked in a moment of glorious solitude.

There was something different about the house that evening, compared to when they had first arrived, a feeling of impermanence. Dante had felt this before, in places on Earth where the veil between the human world and Hell was thin. It was a naturally occurring phenomenon, but now, it caused a sense of dread to grow in Dante's chest. His thoughts kept returning to the storm on the horizon. He'd pushed Iago's premonition from his mind all day. Why did it return so forcefully now?

The door flew open, and solitude packed its bags.

"Fairies! *Fairies,* of all things!" Iago proclaimed as he entered and shut the door behind him. "I respect Mr. Foster's opinions and his processes as a writer, but there is no way in this world or the next that *fairies* are responsible for The Belmont Monster cases!"

"And what is your theory, my dear?" Dante asked, putting his worries aside.

"A werecat," he said definitively.

"Excuse me?"

"They're cleanly," Iago explained, "like their animal counterparts. More particular and finicky than werewolves. It would account for the cleanliness of the

209

deaths, the precise incisions."

"Have you ever seen a cat with a scalpel?" Dante asked.

"Have you ever seen a fairy with a scalpel?" he retorted. "At any rate, I'm glad I found you. I was beginning to worry that creature, McClellan, had done something to you."

Dante waggled his eyebrows. "He's in the upstairs bedroom. I wonder if he believes Bessie is with him."

"I don't even want to entertain what that entails," Iago said, and sat on the edge of the bed.

Though it had only been a day, it felt as though they hadn't been alone together in ages. Despite the perilous situation at hand, a familiar need warmed Dante's heart. He breathed a sigh. Humans certainly weren't the only creatures tempted by Mr. Wick's hazel eyes and clever mouth. The bedroom was quiet, cozy, and the door locked from the inside.

Alas, this was not the time to be *cozy*. They were not all as fortunate as Arrow McClellan and his imaginary companion. "Beatrice says she wishes to go to London," Dante said. "She wants to relocate the Orb. She has someone new in mind to guard it. It will be safer there."

"And will you go with her?" Iago asked.

"If Bancroft has not yet been defeated, then yes, I must," Dante said.

No one Dante had ever met arched a skeptical eyebrow with quite the dramatic poise and incredulity mustered by Iago Wick. "Dante, are you really going to fight him?"

"Do you question my abilities, Mr. Wick?"

"I don't question if you can, rather if you should. He's more animal than man," Iago said. "I've no doubt he lists a zoo as his birthplace."

Dante smirked. "And what am I underneath this human mask?"

Iago allowed a naughty chuckle. "A fearsome Hellbeast with sharp claws and an admittedly pleasing physique." He sobered again. "I'm only nervous. I've witnessed firsthand what he is capable of. Your witch is naïve. I understand she wants revenge, but this will be magic versus weaponry. I don't like those odds."

Dante sighed. He wasn't wrong. "This business has stirred my melancholia. Perhaps that will work to our benefit. All it wants is destruction." Dante wasn't certain he desired to indulge his melancholia or his more demonic parts. Both felt like an ill-fitting suit.

Iago placed his hands to his knees and leaned forward. "And you, Dante Lovelace? What do you want?"

Dante paused. This adventure had been oddly invigorating, to be sure. And yet, he was reminded of his daydream back in Marlowe: a world where Iago Wick and Dante Lovelace could do as they pleased, whenever they pleased, whether it be another grand quest into the unknown or an afternoon of lounging about and doing nothing at all. It would be new and exciting, but warm and familiar at once. He saw that future in Iago's eyes now.

It came at a hefty cost. "It is hard to say," he said

Iago hummed in disappointment and looked to the

floor. "Well, Mr. Lovelace, any trip to London would be better than our last. Hopefully, there will be no werewolves to worry about."

"Rogue werewolves aside, the food was frightful, and the weather was wretched," Dante said.

"And the other demons were insufferable. The British all have that *way* about them," Iago said, his nose scrunched. "That spot-of-tea-cheerio sort of thing. They're all like that these days! All plus-fours and snifters of brandy."

"But at least we were together," Dante said. "It might have been much worse."

Iago stood and bowed. "And should Miss Dickens drag you to merry old England, my dearest Dante, I shall follow."

Guilt blossomed in Dante's belly. "You don't have to do that."

"I didn't have to brave the wilds of Indiana, either," Iago said with a smile. "We should return to them. If she's making plans to leave the country, I feel you should at least be present."

Dante followed him back to the study, where the lamps glowed dimly, and a haze of smoke filled the air.

"I agree that it is a worthy endeavor to take the Orb to London," Harry said as Dante and Iago approached. He puffed thoughtfully on his pipe. "The Earl is one of the greatest protectors of supernatural artifacts."

"When we distributed Father's collection to other protectors, he received a handful of items already. What's one more?" Beatrice said, and scoffed. "I should have given him the Orb of Morgana to begin with, but I felt it was my burden."

"*Ours*, Bea. I just wish The Earl weren't so far away," Harry lamented.

Beatrice avoided Dante's gaze. In his mind, he rooted for their bond, but it was hazy, weak.

Harry continued, "Give this some thought, Honey Bea. We're safe in this house. Let's just lie low for a while, and really think this through. You need a plan, something more than simply binding a demon. Defeating Bancroft won't be that simple."

Iago settled into a chair and plucked *Julius Caesar* from the top of one of the book piles. He thumbed through the pages fondly. "There are many opportunities to lose Bancroft between here and London."

"What about fighting him?" Dante asked. "That's why you bound me. You've wanted your grand confrontation. I wouldn't mind it myself. After all, he did try to kill Mr. Wick." Though admittedly, if Dante used *Violent Adversary to Iago Wick* as the only criterion in determining whom he should battle, he'd have a list as long as his arm with which to contend.

Harry and Beatrice exchanged glances. The tension between them grew thick. "That's another matter altogether," she said sheepishly. "Harry and I have been speaking, and—"

An explosion of wood and glass interrupted her. Everyone jumped to their feet. Hellfire simmered in Dante's palms as he leapt back, and he felt Beatrice anxiously scrambling to strengthen their connection again. The door in the foyer hung open, creaking eerily in the darkened room while the night wind whistled.

Then came the sound of heavy boots on noisy floorboards.

Smiling a wolf's smile, Zero Bancroft stepped from the shadows.

There was something almost demon about him, Dante thought. He was tall with a bestial curve to his back. He no longer wore the ridiculous red wig he had sported in Calamine, and instead brandished two pistols, both presumably prepared with killing demons in mind.

"Why, Miss Dickens," Bancroft said, his voice deep but oddly tender. "My condolences for the death of your father." He turned and considered Iago. "Wick. You're supposed to be dead."

He aimed his pistol at Iago's heart and pulled the trigger.

XIII.

The first time Dante ever committed a catastrophe in Hell's name, he spent the following two days in some strange state of grief. It was a fire, like so many others. Hell told him to start with fire. It's familiar, they said. You can expand your repertoire from there, they proclaimed eagerly.

He did not know a single person upon whom he visited that tragedy, but he wept for them. He was bedridden with grief for a day, until Hell insisted he do it again.

However, there was a spark within Dante that could not be ignored. It was a byproduct, perhaps, of his melancholia. It was the faintest glimmer of pride, not because he had killed people, but due to his own power. Many catastrophe artists reveled in such pride. Dante quickly snuffed it out before it went to his head.

But now, with Zero Bancroft's pistol aimed for

Iago's heart, Dante felt it again.

He had reached deep within Beatrice to draw upon her power, crashing into her very heart to save his. Like the ball of fire on the Observation Deck and the silver spoon in Beatrice's parlor, the bullet halted in mid-air, less than an inch from Iago's chest.

In the annals of close calls, this one deserved to be underlined. Twice.

Dante realized his hands were locked in claws. He relaxed them. The bullet fell to the ground, and Iago released a shuddering breath.

Bancroft scoffed, guns drawn. "Miss Dickens, you not only found a demon, but you taught him magic tricks, too. I'm quite impressed. Perhaps I want Morgana's beast to have you, anyway, Wick." Iago shrunk back, and Dante feared his partner would faint. Utterly undignified, but entirely understandable. "Oh, and no invisibility, demons. Things will not end well for Miss Dickens or Mr. Foster if you don't behave."

"How did you find this house?" Dante asked.

"I'll tell you, Hellspawn, it was quite an adventure," Bancroft explained pleasantly. "A kindly young man in an automated carriage assisted me. He said he always had a tendency to eavesdrop. Thank God for that. Everything for a reason, yes? He told me where you would be. It's not so hard to overcome a cloaking spell when you know precisely where to look."

An orb of fire blossomed in Beatrice's hand, and she growled, "You bastard."

"Such disrespect in light of my philanthropy. There

is evil in this world, Miss Dickens. I'm trying to stop it," he said. His voice was sensitive, but something about the pistols aimed at Dante and Harry made it seem a tad disingenuous. "I only wish you could see that."

Dante's mind raced. To indulge his eager melancholia would be reckless. One miscalculated attack, and they could burn the entire house to the ground! All of Harry's books, his work would be gone. There were no objects directly beside Bancroft to hurl by telekinesis. He'd surely detect the projected movement if they threw something from across the room. He had the sharp, perceptive gaze of a wolf. Not to mention, the element of surprise had weighted the fight heavily in Bancroft's favor.

The fire in Beatrice's hand swelled, though she still hesitated.

"Ah, don't do something you'll regret," Bancroft said calmly, like a parent soothing their child. Then, he called, "Mr. Hacke!"

At his beckoning, a greasy man emerged from the shadows. Also armed, he dragged a young woman into the fray. Her chestnut hair was cropped to her shoulders, and she was wearing trousers. Blindfolded and gagged, she squirmed in the man's grasp, whimpering like a frightened puppy.

Her face may have been partially hidden, but Dante recognized her. Where was the vacant Sterling Ambrose to save her now?

"Miss Cutter?" he asked.

"Lottie?" Beatrice croaked. "Where did you find her,

you brute? Let her go. This does not concern her."

"It concerns all of us," Bancroft said warmly. "Now, I don't know of Miss Cutter's transgressions. Perhaps she will survive Devorog's feast, and perhaps she will not. All the same, I will not hesitate to sacrifice her now."

"He's not bluffing," Iago said.

"Correct, demon," Bancroft said. "I don't wish to shoot any of you, really. Morgana's beast will judge the souls of all humans and rid us of all supernatural slime. Now, put the fire away, Miss Dickens. See reason."

Dante felt the current between them wane again. The fire shrank in her palm, but she did not extinguish it entirely.

"Now, where is the Orb?" Bancroft asked patiently, and pulled Charlotte Cutter in front of him. One pistol remained extended, the other's barrel pressed to her throat. The young woman mewled behind the gag stuffed in her mouth, tears staining her pale cheeks.

From all angles, no matter how one looked at it, it seemed they found themselves in quite the dire situation.

However, let it be said that timing is an art, and it is, indeed, everything.

At that moment, Arrow McClellan gallantly charged into the study, dressed in his long johns and brandishing his best rifle. The cavalry had arrived! With a mighty grunt and a steely gaze, he aimed the weapon at Zero Bancroft and bravely pulled the trigger.

The rifle, however, was not moved to act.

He blinked, shook the rifle, and tried again. And again. Let it also be said that the third time is not always the charm, and the art of timing means nothing if your weapon is faulty. A crestfallen look shimmered in his beady eyes as he limply held the gun in front of him, betrayed by his favorite child.

Bancroft peaked his brows. "Are you through?"

Satisfied with the furry man's silence, he calmly shot Arrow McClellan.

Arrow fell backwards into the foyer, grunting in pain. He squirmed on the floor and gripped his shoulder.

In actuality, the next sequence of events happened very quickly, but they were the perfect storm of distraction and destruction, a flawless dance of misfortune.

Harry made to rush to his friend's side. At the sudden movement, greasy Mr. Hacke anxiously turned his gun on Harry. Dante felt Beatrice's intent surge, and in a flourish of fiery magic, she pulled back to hurl flame in Hacke's direction.

Hacke quickly pivoted and pulled Harry into the line of fire. Beatrice's power waned, but not quickly enough. A small sphere of flame struck Mr. Foster.

"Harry!" Beatrice yelled.

With a growl, Mr. Hacke shoved Harry to the ground. Harry rolled to smother the flames, and Hacke, apparently unhappy with the idea of having fire thrown at him at all, turned his gun on another. He pulled the trigger.

Dante wasn't entirely certain what had happened, at first. There was a loud bang. A sharp coldness started just below his ribs and spread throughout his body. He heard

Iago shout his name as he fell to the ground.

Dante realized, for a fraction of a second, that he was dying.

And then, there was darkness.

~

Heat can drive men mad. It makes a man's skin sticky and his mind sore. It steals his reason and his heart, turns him wild and drives him to commit crimes against his fellow man: theft, murder… some even say light opera was crafted on a particularly sticky island in the tropics.

The exact temperature differs from continent to continent. What burns a man to madness in one land may be pleasant to another across the globe.

They were, all these various temperatures, like the finest summer day compared to the heat of Hell.

Dante was under a leaden blanket of thick, oppressive air when he woke. Demons were accustomed to heat, but Hell's unique and stifling warmth stuck in his lungs after he'd been away for so long.

He opened his eyes to rock, black with soot. Soft firelight seemed to come from everywhere and nowhere at once, flickering upon the cave walls. He blinked and beheld long, spidery hands made of black glass. These obsidian claws were the hands of a demon in true Hellish form, unfettered by a human body. Dante flexed his fingers and felt sick.

Hell was full of numerous caves and nooks and crannies where one might stay and suffer alone for all eternity. After all, suffering was their specialty down here. Who knew what level he found himself upon? In truth, it all looked the same after a while. *A bit like traveling through Ohio and Indiana*, he mused deliriously.

"Don't worry. You needn't be alone."

He heard the high and piercing voice of another demon in true form, simultaneously strange and sickeningly familiar. Dante turned to see a tall demon, crafted of shadows and sporting a clever mouth and burning red eyes. He leaned against the black rock and crossed his arms over his broad, bare chest. "Oh, my Dante," the demon sighed.

"Iago?" Dante asked, and his own screeching voice was shocking in his ears. The true voices of demons made nails on a chalkboard sound like a little light music. "Are we in Hell?"

"In a way," Iago answered, and approached him. He was taller than Dante when they assumed their true forms. It felt a bit strange to look up at him.

"How—" Some unseen wretch's distant screams interrupted him. Everyone was always screaming in Hell. Even when someone found the rare reason to be happy in Hell, they screamed. Force of habit, Dante imagined. "We've been sent back to the Inferno? Bancroft—"

"Actually," Iago began frankly, "you're *dead*. Sorry to be the bearer of bad news."

"Only me? Then, what are you?"

"A mere figment of your mind, crafted of memories of the few precious and intimate times Iago Wick allowed you to see his true form." He stroked Dante's face where

Dante knew there was a faint scar traveling along his cheekbone. Insubordination in his youth had gained him that scar. He did not act out again.

"And I suppose, you're not truly dead. It isn't death, more eternal sleep. It is death to everyone but you," Iago explained. He smiled, showing his sharp and multitudinous teeth. "I see you are uneasy."

Dante blinked. "*Uneasy?* That might be a bit of an understatement!"

Iago snapped his fingers, and the cave changed. It swelled and receded around them, like an ocean at high tide, before it disappeared entirely. Suddenly, Dante was standing in the parlor of 13 Darke Street. A soothing fire simmered in the fireplace. There were familiar sights and smells, a glass of scotch and a box of petit fours.

"Is this better?"

And now, here was Iago in his human form, proud and handsome in a royal blue suit and gold waistcoat. His cufflinks were black and silver moths, gleaming at his wrists. Dante looked to his own hands and saw the pale human ones that had been his for nearly two centuries now.

"A little better," he admitted. "I was shot with the Zero Formula."

"Indeed. Surely my counterpart weeps. Such melodrama. He's nothing but a thespian at heart. But the world had best beware," the false Iago sang. "Mr. Wick will never be the same."

Dante shook his head. "This is foolish. I need to wake up."

"No, you don't. You can stay here with me. This place might be paradise, if you just allow it," Iago explained, and reclined on the settee. He placed a petit four delicately in his mouth.

"Paradise?" Dante laughed bitterly.

"Of course! You choose what happens here. It's your mind, after all. This place can be perfect. Every day is an adventure, unless, of course, you don't want adventure. We can lounge around the house, spend the day in bed. We can visit The Golden Swine. We could travel across the globe! This world is anything you want and nothing you don't. No vampires, no demon hunters, no squeaking door hinges or shoes that are too tight— none of it!" Iago proclaimed. "A perfect world of your design."

"I can't," Dante said.

Iago smiled slyly before sucking cakey residue from his thumb. "Why? Because Hell needs you? That is a farce if ever I heard one. And Miss Dickens, the witch?" He tisked. "I will grant her one thing. She gave you a purpose that wasn't Hell's wicked plan. You have realized you need such a purpose, but not hers. Not anyone's but yours."

"And what is my purpose? To spend the rest of my days in some dream world with an imaginary Iago Wick?"

"To live, Dante Lovelace. Simply to live for yourself. That is what you truly desire, is it not?" Iago laughed. "And now, you have it. How strange that death has afforded you life. It's almost poetic. You always did look like a poet, my lovely Mr. Lovelace."

A rustling came from behind Iago, and with a sudden throaty snort, a beast crawled over the back of the settee. It looked like a gargoyle, infernal and angry, as it perched over Iago's shoulder. It panted, its flat pink tongue flopping out of its mouth.

"And look!" Iago exclaimed as he turned to scratch beneath the beast's chin. "We have a pet."

"What is he?"

"Oh, surely you recognize him."

Dante realized this was no pet. It cocked its large, craggy head. Far away, Dante saw himself, stripped to his waist on a bare, wooden table. A man in a black apron hovered over him. Everything smelled of sulfur. The man held a pinprick of light between thumb and forefinger, the glow reflecting off the blade in his other hand. He assured Dante it would be over soon, and it wouldn't hurt, not too badly.

He took the blade to Dante's skin, wiping away black blood. That did not hurt. It was when the surgeon shoved the light into that small incision in Dante's chest that he cried out, spine arching off the table. For a moment, he was blind with pain. There was silence, then the man spoke.

"All finished, Mr. Lovelace."

The Powers Below called that ball of light, that bank of misery, *inspiration*. Dante called it something different.

"My melancholia."

Iago still lovingly doted upon the monster beside him. "Precisely. He's caused a lot of trouble—and I don't mean tearing up the Sunday paper or befouling the neighbor's lawn—but he'll be a fine pet," he said. "We'll take him on walks. I'll feed him scraps when you're not looking."

Dante approached the beast with a timid hand. It sniffed with cavernous nostrils. "I had the operation a mere two days after I received the letter stating I would be a catastrophe artist. They took me somewhere. The veil between Hell and Earth was thin there, but I was blindfolded." He finally touched the creature. It warmed to him. "They gave me something, perhaps witch hazel, to calm me, but it did little good."

Dante scratched the beast under the chin and continued, "When I was finished, they took me back to Philadelphia. They would give me orders soon, they said, after I acclimated. For days, I was ill. There was something foul inside of me, but I could not purge myself of it. Eventually, my body accepted its new organ. And then, I saw nothing but destruction. My mind was plagued by thoughts of misery and terror, and all because of their *inspiration*."

He had never told the real Iago every detail of that wretched operation. The real Iago knew not to ask. A catastrophe artist's journey was a profoundly personal one. "Sad," this Iago said. "Consider my heartstrings plucked, my dear. But you learned to control it."

This examination of Dante's psyche stood to become quite tiresome. "I had to. If I did not, it would control me," he answered, and the beast looked at him with animal reverence.

Iago said, "Not here, not anymore. You don't need

to worry about anything ever again. You will stay in here forever, with me."

"You're not Iago."

"But don't I look like Iago?" he said. "And sound like him? And have all of his over-exaggerated hand movements and theatrical bravado?"

Those were Iago's eyes, weren't they? It would be terribly easy. Dante could retreat into his mind for eternity. There was an entire world in here for him to create, perhaps the very world he'd imagined at Beatrice Dickens's breakfast table days ago. It felt like it had been a century since then!

"I know everything we have shared," Iago said.

"But nothing we have not." Dante drew a deep breath. "No. I haven't time for this."

"For Death?" Iago laughed, and his melancholia snorted. "Neither do the thousands you condemn in your work for Hell. It is your duty to kill both innocents and sinners in fiery tragedy. Did they have time for Death? Did Death care? Did Dante Lovelace care?"

"I did care. I *do* care."

"Did you?" Iago asked. "As you sat at the fireplace and collected newspaper clippings and prided yourself on the number of those dead, did you care?"

"Yes! Lucifer knows, I cared. I did not ask to be a catastrophe artist," Dante said. "But there are certain behaviors that are expected. I played the part." He paused. "And it was easier to look at numbers than it was to look at faces and names."

Iago smirked and got to his feet, slipping his hands

into his trouser pockets. "It doesn't matter now. You're *dead*. It gives responsibility a good kick out the door, doesn't it? And if you stay," the faux Iago said, and motioned to the craggy beast, "eventually Rover won't even remember his original purpose."

The gargoyle's nostrils flared in excitement. And was its tail wagging?

Iago pressed a hand to Dante's cheek. "Peace, dear Dante. You will know peace."

From somewhere, far from this facsimile of his Marlowe home, Dante heard screaming again. These were desperate cries, different from those he heard in his mind's Hell.

"I can't stay here," Dante said.

"You have no choice."

"Mr. Lovelace!"

A familiar, jarring voice. Dante stumbled backward, away from Iago. The sound enveloped him, grabbed him by the shoulders to pull him away from this place. The melancholia crept over and perched upon Iago's shoulder. The world began to bleed away, though Iago still beckoned him to stay.

"Awaken, Mr. Lovelace. Come now," the disembodied voice barked. The speaker seemed somewhat annoyed at Dante, as though his death were a hearty inconvenience.

Atchison.

"Mr. Lovelace!"

The world around him faded away into nothing. The faux Iago vanished in a smoky haze. Finally, all he could see was the gleaming gaze of the melancholia before it, too, faded to black.

He opened his eyes and sucked air into his lungs.

Everything spun around Dante as though he'd been dropped on the carousel back in Calamine. He was in a lumpy and unfamiliar bed. His stomach clenched, and he gave a wet, sputtering cough. Viola Atchison brought a hand to his shoulder, and never had he been so relieved to see her.

Another woman offered him water. Sofia, he determined. He tried to sit upright to take it and only somewhat succeeded. He might have poured half of it down his shirt. Still, not bad for a revenant.

A revenant? he thought blearily. Lucifer Below, he'd been dead! The realization made black bile surge within him again, but he maintained his composure.

A grand sigh of relief blew from Beatrice Dickens's lips on the other side of the room. Harry Foster cheered. They were all still watercolor pictures of themselves, his vision blurry, and he wished dearly they wouldn't be so loud. Dante fell back limply on the bed. Movement was not wise.

"Tell me, what is your name?" Viola asked crisply.

"Dante," he muttered.

"Dante...?"

"Dante Lovelace."

"And where are you?" she pressed.

"Bedroom. Not Bessie's. Indiana." He could recall being shot, then only darkness. There were no dreams to remember, just an oppressive absence of anything at all.

However, he also couldn't shake the feeling that he had been somewhere else, somewhere far away.

Sofia Atchison stroked his hair. "He has his senses, and after three days' time. Brava, Mrs. Atchison."

"Yes, *brava*. I have betrayed every demon hunter thrilled by the bounty of the Zero Formula," Viola growled. "I will be ever so popular."

"I was unconscious for three days?" Dante asked.

"Yes," Viola said as she stood. She had returned to wearing trousers, Dante noted, and her hair was swept back. She looked more like Thomas Atchison than she had in two years. "I administered the antidote nearly a day ago. I wish I could have arrived more quickly, but that doesn't matter now. Mr. Wick, you have your antidote to the Zero Formula."

Mr. Wick. Dante looked to the end of the bed, and for the first time since he woke up, his gaze met Iago's. Mr. Wick's jacket and necktie were missing, his shirtsleeves rumpled. Dante had never seen him so disheveled. He leaned against the wall at the foot of the bed as though he needed it to stand upright. "And from the bottom of my heart, I thank you, Mrs. Atchison," Iago said weakly.

A wave of dizziness forced Dante to close his eyes. A moment or two passed in the meantime. Beatrice said something about leaving the room, allowing Mr. Wick to relay all that had happened. When he opened his eyes again, there was only Iago, sitting in the chair beside him.

The skin beneath Iago's eyes was raw. Dante reached to brush his thumb over his cheek, and Iago kissed him softly. He tasted of whatever swill Arrow McClellan had lying about his house—and *a lot* of it, perhaps even enough to tamper with a demon's senses. Iago Wick was utterly pickled. It was clear he had *been through Hell* in Dante's absence, an expression which demons knew was not to be used lightly.

And yet, there was no taste of witch hazel to be had. From the moment Dante threw that bottle from the train, Iago could have conjured another, and he hadn't.

They embraced, and despite the awkward angle, Dante found that familiar space in Iago's arms and the crook of his neck where he just *fit*. "Never do that again," Iago said.

Dante chuckled. "Well, I wasn't planning a repeat performance, my dear." *One Night Only! The Death of Dante Lovelace*. He had woken up to quite an audience, at any rate. Resurrection was a feat better suited to some flamboyant conjurer, convincing rich socialites he'd sorted out all the mysteries of this world and a few of the next.

Dante certainly couldn't claim such knowledge. His mind still felt like cotton.

"I'm afraid I misbehaved in your absence," Iago said, drawing back.

"I don't think an over-indulgence in drink counts as misbehaving, certainly not for a minion of Lucifer."

Iago groaned. "My guts have surely rotted from that poison. A strychnine cocktail might have been more palatable." He paused. "Still, I was not feeling up to my usual glass of scotch. I needed something abrasive."

He continued, "When I say I misbehaved, I mean I killed the man who shot you." His voice was distant but resolute. "I drew upon Hellish power I did not even know I still possessed. Vestigial from my days as a torturer's apprentice in Hell, perhaps. I turned him to dust. I know that under usual circumstances, a tempter is not supposed to kill..."

"But these are far from usual circumstances, Mr. Wick," Dante said.

"Precisely. In addition to that indiscretion," Iago added, "I may have *threatened* your Miss Dickens."

"Threatened her? How?"

"Only a little!" Iago insisted. "I did not lay hands on her... but I *might* have told her that if you did not wake, I would decorate the streets of Boston with her entrails and desecrate the souls of everyone she ever loved." He looked sheepishly to the ground. "You know, typical demonic chatter. I'm afraid I was not in control of myself when you were injured."

Dante shook his head and had never regretted anything more in his seven centuries of existence. He groaned at the throbbing ache behind his eyes and asked, "Where is the Orb?"

"Gone."

"Gone? Bancroft took it?"

Iago leaned forward, arms resting on his knees. His hazel eyes were missing their usual spark. Dante was in for a tale of tragedy, indeed. "I'm afraid so. You, Mr. Foster, and Mr. McClellan were injured. Bancroft insisted he would shoot this woman, Miss Cutter, if Miss Dickens did not give him the Orb. For what it's worth, I am certain he would have. It showed in his eyes."

"And Miss Dickens bowed to his commands to save her friend?" Dante asked.

"Unfortunately, yes," Iago said. "He told this Mr. Hacke to watch the rest of us while he visited the parlor with the ladies, to retrieve the Orb from its hiding place. Hacke's should have been an easy task. We were a pathetic bunch."

"Oh, dear," Dante said. "I assume this was when Mr. Hacke met his fate."

"He was quick. I was quicker. A rather messy affair," Iago admitted shamefacedly. "I'm certain there are still bits of him ground into the rug in the study."

Dante had to admit he was flattered that Iago had defended him so heartily in death. It was good to feel so loved, even if it was from beyond the grave. "And Miss Cutter?" The cogs in Dante's mind turned. He could think clearly now that there was not a gun pointed in his general direction. Miss Cutter had been in love, he sensed, when she was in Marlowe. Was Bancroft the poison apple of her eye? "Lucifer Below. She's known Miss Dickens and Mr. Foster since childhood. She was our letter writer, wasn't she?"

"Yes, but she's also quite the snake in the grass," Iago hissed. "The clever bastard had covered her eyes and mouth. We could not read her intent. Indeed, she was frightened. That was true fear, but she was also complicit. Bancroft did not even stop to consider Hacke's body as he left. He had his bounty. He only looked at me and said, 'Your time is coming.'" Iago gave a bitter bark of laughter. "In that moment, I didn't care if it was. I watched him go with Miss Cutter and the Orb. He had given Miss Dickens a knock on the head."

"What an utter catastrophe," Dante lamented. "I could not have done better myself."

Iago leaned back in his chair, exhausted further merely by retelling the events. "Miss Dickens has been tending to Mr. Foster's wounds. The fire caught his shoulder. Nasty scarring. Slow healing, but it certainly could have been worse. It was a weak attack. He managed to smother the flames."

"And Mr. McClellan?"

"Lives to fight another day, as well, though I imagine he'll conduct routine examinations of his firearms from now on," Iago said. He threw his hands in the air. "And there you have it, my dear. Quite the drama, isn't it? We should contact Ibsen—we have the subject of his next play."

Dante took a moment to fully digest all that had happened in his absence. It felt as though he'd missed centuries, though only three days had passed. He attempted to shake the fog from his head. "Well, we can't just laze about if Bancroft has the Orb." Dante tried to hoist himself from the bed, but a sharp pain bloomed beneath his ribs. He gave an unseemly whimper.

Iago held him still. "You were *shot*, my dear. Need I remind you? And how is your wound? Atchison removed the bullet. I asked Sofia to mend your waistcoat."

Wincing, Dante lifted his bloodstained shirt. An

angry swirl of gray and black bruised his flesh, but it was unbroken. The hole itself had healed, just more slowly than usual.

"It's nearly better. In an hour or two, I'll be fine," Dante said. His body screamed otherwise.

Doctor Wick wasn't having any of it, either, placing a firm hand to Dante's chest. "*Sleep.* You need real rest. I shall lash you to this bed, if I must!"

"Oh, listen to that bedside manner," Dante teased.

Iago gave an oddly bashful smile and uttered those three words demons were not accustomed to saying. Dante returned the favor.

They sat in silence, Iago stroking the back of Dante's hand with his thumb while Dante was forced to fully contend with the fact that he had died. And come back. Few creatures could claim such a thing. How many humans who died in the catastrophes he orchestrated had come back? None of them. How many men and women had surrendered to misery as Iago Wick had in his absence? How many noble quests and humble, happy lives had been cut short? Why should he, this choreographer of death, be given the opportunity to live again?

Dante felt suddenly like the lowliest stain on the bottom of the lowliest creature's shoe. And then, he heard distant voices. They were mere figments of dreams, but he could not silence them. Their words danced through his mind, upon his tongue, until they forced him to speak.

"Iago, there's something I wish to discuss."

"If it's how tiresome witches are, I could write an epic on the subject," Iago muttered.

"No, I... I wish to speak to Lucretia with you."

Iago blinked. "You do? Lucifer Below, you didn't hit your head, did you?"

"No, it's not that," Dante chuckled. "I've only been afraid, Iago. But death has opened my eyes. I shall finish my work with Miss Dickens first, of course." He smiled. "I'm looking forward to this reunion. I've not seen Lucretia in decades!"

"Nor have I. I'm certain she is quite invested in the current ostentatious trends in women's headwear," Iago said before squeezing Dante's hand. "Rest. We'll discuss Bancroft while you sleep. You are certain about this?"

Dante nodded. A strange face flashed through his mind, an angry gargoyle's visage. Perhaps it should have frightened him, but he only felt some delight at its displeasure. "Yes, Iago Wick. I shall follow you into glorious uncertainty."

His proclamation was enough to send Mr. Wick on a long and happy oration of everything they might achieve once they turned their backs on Hell. Dante let him talk. He needed it. "We might even have a dog one day!" Iago exclaimed.

And at the suggestion, that craggy gargoyle's face returned with slobbering jowls and gleaming eyes. Dante put a ginger hand to his forehead and winced. Iago was right. He needed to sleep.

XIV.

It was the stuff of romantic literature, waking up to see one's lover craned over his latest work, the first light of dawn sifting through the window as though God Himself blessed the artistic mind.

Alas, Iago looked like some mad poet, shirtsleeves still crinkled and rolled to his elbows as he chewed on the tip of his pencil. And alas, God would not have taken the time to spit on him if he were on fire. Still, the sight brought a sleepy smile to Dante's face. He managed to sit in bed. "Writing to Lucretia?" he asked.

"No," Iago answered. "It's a funny little story about a nun. People do love naughty nuns. Writing calms my nerves, though I do miss my dearly departed witch hazel."

Dante stretched carefully. "You don't need witch hazel."

"That does not mean I don't want it," Iago said and

then conceded, "However, I was not myself when I was in its grips. It's inhibited me for too long now. It is a foul habit." He paused. "All the same, I am demon, and a demon should have a few foul habits, shouldn't he?"

"You have enough. You don't need any more."

Iago looked puzzled. "Do I? What are they? Out of curiosity, of course."

Dante raised a brow. "In addition to your blatant overindulgence in dessert? Let's see. You frequently forget our engagements, you spend far too long dressing yourself...oh, and when you choose to sleep, you snore."

"I snore?" Iago asked with bald horror in his eyes. Dante might have suggested he was cavorting with angels for the copious offense he took.

"Tremendously," Dante said. He cracked his back and peeked at his wound, which had—thanks to demonic resilience—fully healed while he slept. It was a touch tender, but nothing he couldn't bear. After all, what was a mere bruise to a man who had just come back from the dead? "Bad habits aside, we can't simply sit around. Where is Beatrice?"

"In the study. Miss Dickens wishes to speak to you, presumably alone."

"Send her in."

Iago could not conceal a sneer as he left the room, and Dante was certain he heard him muttering something about 'damned witches' under his breath.

Dante ruffled his hands through his hair. Demons were not accustomed to truly being tired, but he was certain he could have continued sleeping for a century if he remained undisturbed. *Was that a yawn coming on?* he wondered. What a strange sensation. He gave in, though he felt slightly ridiculous with his mouth opened so wide.

The door opened again, and a freckled face appeared. "Dante?" Beatrice entered timidly, smoothing her hair. "How are you feeling?"

"Better," Dante answered, and yawned again. How terribly unseemly. He covered his mouth with one hand. "Tired. That's all."

She nodded and sat at the desk where Iago had been writing a moment before. In his mind, he fumbled for the connection he and Beatrice had cultivated but found nothing. Her lips turned up in a small, nervous smile.

"I should have seen that Charlotte was a part of Bancroft's plan," she said bitterly, looking out the window. Dust particles danced in the sunlight. "I didn't want to believe she could do something like this. I still can't believe it. Charlotte Cutter doesn't eat ginger snaps because they're too flavorful, but here she is, assisting a murderer!"

"Love makes fools of us all," Dante said. "I sensed she was in love when she was in Marlowe, but I couldn't see with whom." He paused. "Really? Ginger snaps?"

"She says they have too much bite," Beatrice said, rolling her eyes. "I never suspected she would have read my diary all those years ago and learned our code. It was all harmless then. Everything happened so quickly. I had played out every single situation we might have encountered in my mind. None of them ended with Bancroft stealing the Orb, removing Lottie's blindfold and giving her that horrid smile. He hit me with the butt of his pistol. I wasn't unconscious, but I couldn't stand, either. Perhaps I am simply not the warrior I thought I was. He's long gone now. I've failed."

Dante sought to interrupt her moping. "We're not defeated yet, Miss Dickens."

Her murky green eyes strayed from his. "I'm certain you've noticed. You can't feel the bond between us." Dante nodded. "Just before Bancroft intruded, I intended to break the spell. Harry makes a passionate argument. He opened my eyes. I was like a headstrong little girl playing with fire. I thought the world was mine to bend and break. I know better now."

"You broke the spell while I was dead," Dante said.

"I did. I had to. You died, and it was my fault."

"You do sound quite beastly when you put it that way."

"You may stay, or you may go. I would not blame you for choosing the latter." She bowed her head.

Dante carefully removed himself from bed. His joints ached and cracked, but he swiftly donned his waistcoat. He buttoned his collar fully before retrieving his necktie from the edge of the bed.

She added, "When I set out to bind a demon, I didn't think he would be so..."

"What?" Dante asked. "Powerful? Complicated?"

"Human," she said softly.

If what doesn't kill a man makes him stronger, then Dante imagined death and resurrection surely made quite the Goliath of a man. *Or perhaps not,* he thought as his head throbbed. And yet, despite his aching and foggy mind, his path seemed clearer than ever before.

"I should leave," Dante said.

"Yes, of course."

"But I will not."

"What?"

"We share a common goal, Miss Dickens," Dante said, and approached her. She smelled of smoke; she had indulged in her own bad habits in his absence. "I will see that we triumph over Zero Bancroft. I require vengeance myself. I'll help you, so long as you promise me two things."

"Anything."

"No more binding, and please, never bring me to Indiana again." He held out his hand. "Deal?"

She smiled. "Deal."

~

Arrow McClellan held in his hand the small wooden figure of a rather well-endowed woman who, unless Dante was mistaken, had misplaced her dress. Perhaps this was Bessie. He stroked the effigy with an unsettlingly affectionate thumb as Dante entered the study.

Harry Foster's shoulder was wrapped in bandages while he read. Arrow McClellan sported twin wrappings on his shoulder. Beatrice fell pathetically into one chair, wringing her hands before reaching for a cigarette. Iago, meanwhile, concealed something of a nervous tremor brought on by a lack of witch hazel.

They were an unapologetically sorry sight.

"Perfect. Mr. Lovelace rejoins the land of the living," Viola Atchison said dryly, and turned to Iago. "Now that I've fully delivered on my promise, you can return to assisting me in matters of the supernatural. I cannot rely on Harriet alone. The poor girl rusts in the rain."

"Is it wise for you to be out of bed, Mr. Lovelace?" Sofia Atchison asked, brow creasing in motherly concern.

"Perhaps it isn't, but I must," Dante said. "Bancroft has the Orb. Where do you think he has taken it?"

Viola gave a sharp bark, rising to her feet to speak. "Easy. Boston. He fancies himself the city's protector, and he craves an audience for the debut of his soul-eating beast."

"All the world's a stage, and all the men and women merely dinner," Iago said morbidly.

Harry winced as he reached for his pipe. "I've pored over my library, Mr. Lovelace. I don't have much information about soul-eaters, but I can say this: if Devorog is released, it will be confused, lost and haphazard at first. Use that confusion to your advantage. The longer it is at large, the more difficult it will be to trap again. I hope it does not come to this."

A massive, discombobulated beast racing through Boston and devouring sinners' souls: what an utter delight. Dante said solemnly, "Miss Dickens has decreed since the beginning that it shall be the two of us who see this matter through to the end."

"It does not have to be so," Beatrice said once more.

"I assure you," Dante said, and placed a hand on her

shoulder, "it does."

"Hah," Arrow grunted. The fuzzy old man nodded heartily in solidarity.

Dante cleared his voice. "Precisely, Mr. McClellan. Thank you. Come, everyone. We've quite a journey back to the train station at Clarkton."

~

"I've a story to tell you, Miss Cutter," Zero Bancroft said warmly.

They had spoken little of Mr. Hacke's demise on their journey back to Boston. Mr. Bancroft was scathingly indifferent. That demon, Iago Wick, had burned Mr. Hacke to dust, but Charlotte couldn't bring herself to see it as much of a loss, either. Perhaps there was someone somewhere who would mourn the death of the foul creature, but Charlotte felt as though she had finally had some unpleasant abscess removed.

Admittedly, Bancroft never told her he would tie her up and use her as leverage. He merely did it without asking. She recalled the press of his pistol to her throat. Surely he wouldn't really have killed her had Bea not complied. A chill seized her heart, and she shuddered now at the recollection.

Charlotte pushed such thoughts from her head. *All for the greater good*, she reminded herself, and smiled to hear Mr. Bancroft's voice as they approached Boston Common. She was equally delighted to be wearing a dress again, a cream walking dress that was, though unseasonable, simply a dream.

"A story, Mr. Bancroft?"

"Perhaps you should call me Zero. Perhaps I should call you Charlotte. We are about to embark on an endeavor so intimate that I feel it requires such familiarity between us," Bancroft said, and Charlotte felt heat rise in her cheeks.

"Zero," she said delicately.

"Charlotte. Many years ago, there was a demon in Boston called Brindle. A clever devil. A tempter, a cruel one, who relished in torturing and manipulating humans. He was a proud beast, but Brindle became too certain of himself, too extravagant in his temptations. He garnered the attention of Frederick Faust.

"Faust was a conqueror of vampires, ghouls, and demons. He set his sights upon Brindle," Bancroft said. They entered the park where children laughed, and prospective lovers tipped their hats and twirled their parasols in ways that constituted flirting. It was a sunny day. "Brindle gladly accepted the challenge. Every demon has his principal sin. His was pride, but his pride was his downfall. It blinded him."

They stopped in the center of the park before a worn stone, lodged in the brick promenade. It looked like a squat mile marker, but it had no inscription. "Faust sent the clever bastard back to Hell on this spot." He motioned broadly to the stone.

"How does someone send a demon back to Hell?" Charlotte asked.

"*Carefully.*"

Bancroft looked stoically at the stone, and for a moment, Charlotte feared he would begin to recite poetry. He had something of a Shakespearean glint in his eye. Fortunately, he did not indulge it. He said, "Frederick Faust's wife gave him three children."

"Oh?"

"Then, she died."

"*Oh.*"

"And his second wife gave him four children," Bancroft continued. "His descendants still hunt the wretched creatures that sully our earth. My mentor was one of his distant descendants." Bancroft reached into his knapsack to retrieve the Orb of Morgana. He smiled as he let it settle in his palm. "Today, we will do more than simply send demons back to Hell. Today, I will surpass every one of Faust's descendants in greatness."

"Where is your teacher now? Will he be proud?"

Bancroft narrowed his gaze upon the Orb. Within, there seemed to be movement, smoke. It gleamed in the sunlight. "No, he won't. I fear I made certain of that myself."

Charlotte looked anxiously to the other people in the park. "Will this hurt?"

Bancroft's jaw set. "For you, I cannot say. Your transgressions are your own, and I don't wish to know them." His body swelled with breath. "For me? Yes. It will."

Without another word, Zero Bancroft hurled the Orb of Morgana to the brick beneath them.

It was quiet at first, pleasantly so. And then, there

was a flash of something like lightning. Charlotte caught only a glimpse of dark fog. It was there, and then, it was not. She might have seen eyes or gleaming teeth, but she couldn't be certain. The hair on the back of her neck stood up.

Then, something unseen knocked her backward, and she tumbled to the ground.

A scream cut through the air.

Charlotte looked to the screeching woman, and then looked to Zero Bancroft.

The authorities would later insist that Zero Bancroft had been struck by lightning, though it had been a clear, beautiful day. His skin was like thick, dark leather stretched unforgivingly over bones, and his eyes turned to a white, oozing jelly. He was drained of all life. Devorog had deemed him unworthy.

And Charlotte Cutter would be judged in kind.

She felt her mind turn to mush before it was pulled apart like the stringy innards of a gourd. No, not just her physical brain, but her thoughts, as well. Its touch sucked the moisture from her skin. Her insides were torn to nothing before the beast sank claws and teeth into the pulp of her soul and ravaged it.

But until the very moment she lost consciousness, she could not draw her gaze from the creature, its bubbling eyes, its many hungry mouths. She had never seen something so terrible and so *sublime*.

The early edition of the newspaper proclaimed, *Man and Wife Killed in Sudden and Tragic Lightning Strike*. Later, the editors corrected that mistaken relationship, but for a fleeting moment, Charlotte Cutter had her wish.

~

Arrow McClellan found it in his heart to forgive his rifle for failing him. He had it at his side, waving it as amicably as a rifle can be waved, as he and Harry bid farewell to their troop of houseguests. He gave a friendly grunt, dropped the gun to his side, and wiped a tear from his gleaming eye.

Dante would not miss Indiana, but he would miss Mr. Foster and even Mr. McClellan. A demon knows, after having lived for so long, when he has made the acquaintance of a reliable ally, and he had a feeling this would not be the last time he saw Harry Foster.

Before they departed, Beatrice gave Harry a small bottle of greenish elixir. "Don't stop taking that. Once a day," she said.

"Of course, doctor," Harry said with a grin.

"Favor that shoulder, Harry," she continued. "Don't strain yourself! No heavy books. Dictionaries and encyclopedias are out of the question! There are many fine pamphlets in publication for you to read."

He clutched her hands. "I'll be fine. Don't worry," Harry said, and kissed the top of her head. "Boston waits for you, Honey Bea. Be careful. I'll see you soon."

~

The train carrying Dante and his crew back to

Massachusetts was a pitiful thing that chased alongside the track of *The Boston-St. Louis Bullet*. It rattled and shook, and there were alarming stains on the seats. And that was not to mention the pungent smell, which might have been the train car itself, or—if the flies were any indication—might have been the seedy slumbering man seated across the aisle. Sofia Atchison held a flowered handkerchief to her nose throughout the journey.

Still, it was good to rest their bones after the long walk back to Clarkton. They waited only two hours for a train to Boston.

Demons learned very swiftly that if something bad can happen, it not only does, but it usually does so with infuriating gusto. And so, Dante humored Viola Atchison and Beatrice Dickens as they discussed how they would find Bancroft, topple him and retrieve the Orb without releasing the wily beast within.

The plan, despite its use of fire power and artfully-set traps, was one of candy floss and rainbows, in Dante's considered opinion. A catastrophe artist could sense true calamitous misery, and it gave off a mighty stench in Boston's direction.

"So, let's imagine," Dante began, "that Bancroft has already..." He looked cautiously to the sleeping man across from them, their only travel companion. They would surely collect more along the way. "He's already let the cat out of the bag, so to speak. How do we capture the beast again? It's been done before."

"There is a way," Beatrice said. "I was hoping this would not be necessary." She retrieved her grimoire from her satchel and leafed through the thick, worn tome until she came to the page she sought. *"A sprig of mugwort and lavender to calm, the meat of one ripe apple smashed within the palm. Ay, 'tis required—a storm within a storm, all flavored with the flesh of one part-demon-born. This alone shall steal the creature from its feast and rightly trap within the monstrous beast."*

Iago laughed derisively. "Of course. This monster is so old that it requires magic written in hackneyed verse to stop it."

"The spell must be performed at the time of capture. Otherwise, it loses efficacy. I know witches in Boston. If necessary, I can easily acquire the initial ingredients," Beatrice said.

"Consider it necessary," Dante said. "The flesh of one part-demon-born. Dear Iago, it occurs to me that we know someone who fits such a description."

Iago smiled a bit too broadly at the suggestion. "Ah, yes. It seems a bit foul to simply toss Mr. Gregor Hawley into a cauldron, but since he is so intent upon serving me, and we must do what we must…"

And at that moment, the train car was assaulted by the most frightening sound Dante had ever heard on Earth or in Hell: Viola Atchison laughed. *Uproariously.*

She managed through her mirth, "Mr. Wick, only you would suggest tossing your own great-grandson into a cauldron of boiling oil and potions. It merely calls for the flesh of someone who is part-demon. A hand will suffice! A foot!"

Iago grumbled under his breath. "A storm within a storm, it says. Is that literal? Metaphorical?"

"In the case of spells, it's frequently a matter of interpretation, I'm afraid," Beatrice said.

"Matters of interpretation," Iago proclaimed, "have caused entire schisms, dear lady."

Viola peaked her pale fingers. "Miss Dickens, could you, through your own power, craft something of a lightning storm?"

"It is of the elements. I'm certain I could."

"Excellent. Then, perhaps I can provide your second storm through more scientific means."

"Scientific?" the witch asked warily.

"I know your kind tends to scoff at science, but perhaps now is the time to rethink your philosophies," Viola said.

Beatrice sniffed haughtily, holding her grimoire over her chest like a shield. "Science has gotten many men in trouble."

"Men, perhaps," Viola said, "but I am not a man."

"Mrs. Atchison, matters of magic should remain as such. If you—!"

"Now is not the time for ideological battles, ladies," Iago interrupted. They fell silent, eyes narrowed in contempt as the train rattled on. "Provided we gather the necessary ingredients, how do we lure the beast into our trap?"

There was a familiar stirring below Dante's heart. He had a feeling he would regret what he suggested next. "Devorog can sense supernatural energy. That is how it finds us. While it devours the souls of the living, what it truly desires are supernatural beings."

"Yes, we're like little bonbons," Iago added.

"Harry said Devorog will be confused if it's released, perhaps desperate. It will latch on to something comforting and highly desirable. I have an intense pocket of supernatural energy lodged within me at all times," Dante said. "If I cease to control my melancholia, I should put out so great an energy that Devorog cannot help but come to me and follow me back to our trap."

"Absolutely not," Iago said. "Devorog will devour you in an instant. I won't let you do that."

"He may not have to," Beatrice said, flipping through the pages of her grimoire. "There is a spell."

Iago groaned bitterly. "Of course, there is."

"It's rather complicated and a little dangerous," Beatrice said, "but it may work."

"Complication and danger have never stopped a catastrophe artist before. What is it?" Dante asked.

Beatrice drummed her fingers upon the desired page. "This spell was originally crafted to rid other magicians of their abilities, but I don't see why it couldn't be altered to fit our needs. It requires no other ingredients, only my power. I could extract your Hellish inspiration."

Extract it? It had been a part of him for over a century and a half, an annoying voice he could never entirely silence, an itch he could never scratch. Dante felt the strange force within him rebel at the idea, pattering frantically. *But we're such a grand team,* it insisted. *You can't live without your inspiration!*

On the contrary, Dante realized with a smile. He found he quite liked the idea.

Iago sneered. "That's madness, as well. You would not reach, bare-handed, into a man's belly to rip out his liver, would you?"

Beatrice paused thoughtfully. "Under most circumstances... no. Besides, I like to think I have a measure more finesse than that. I would replace it with a concentrated dose of my own magic, Dante. This will prevent your human body from being too disturbed or, worse, rejecting you."

Viola stroked her chin. "Such unfettered Hellish energy *would* make marvelous bait. Undeniably tempting. Devorog wouldn't be able to resist the allure. Such a treat would utterly stupefy it. The Powers Below would certainly forgive you, Mr. Lovelace, if it meant stopping the beast. I'm sure they'd furnish you with another operation to get you working again."

In theory, yes, Dante thought, but he *wasn't* ever working again. Viola did not need to know that. Not yet. Dante had a feeling she would not receive the news well. He asked, "Magic, you say? I would have my own source of magical power? A witch's power?"

Beatrice nodded.

Iago threw his hands in the air and yelled, "Am I the only one here who hasn't completely gone mad?"

"If this plan must be enacted, and I have a strong feeling it will, I want to try," Dante said definitively, "when we reach Boston."

"Perfect!" Viola said. "You can perform your little operation in our home."

"What?" Sofia coughed over her handkerchief. "Not

on the nice linens, they won't!"

"We'll make do, my dear," Viola soothed. "It will all be fine."

Iago's gaze narrowed at Beatrice. "If you hurt him—!"

"She won't," Dante said calmly. "She's seen what you're capable of when someone harms me." He leaned to whisper in Iago's ear. "And you know as well as I do that magic—cloaking and banishing spells, in particular—may come in handy in our future. The world can be a frightening place for a defected demon. I will ask her to perform this surgery even if Devorog hasn't been released. It would afford us much."

Their gazes met, and Dante peaked his brows amicably. Iago disintegrated into a miserable groan. "Oh, someone wake me when this nightmare is over."

Their smelly travel companion snorted awake suddenly and surveyed his company. He rubbed his eyes and stroked his chin. Sofia cleared her throat and looked away. The old man nodded. "Hello, folks. Do you have a moment to discuss the end of days?" he asked sleepily. "The end is nigh, you know."

Iago muttered a curse under his breath, but Dante smiled. He said, "It isn't if we can help it, sir."

XV.

The Bostonians in Haymarket Square carried newspapers and clucked about something warranting hushed voices when Dante and his companions arrived. Tragedy, of course. Dante knew these faces well, these muttering lips and only somewhat sympathetic eyes. A part of them, something deep and dark and inherently human, was excited. So long as tragedy was not befalling them, they would revel in the chance to speculate and chatter.

There was a bitter scent in the air. The space below Dante's heart tightened. Devorog was certainly free.

He tried to find a newspaper, but Viola Atchison found one first. "Bancroft's dead." She shook the crinkled paper. "*Man and Wife Killed by Sudden Lightning Strike.*"

"May I?" Dante asked as he took the paper. "*Zero Bancroft, resident, and his wife were killed by lightning strike at*

Boston Common, it says. They do not name his wife, but it can only be Miss Cutter."

Beatrice sighed. "Stupid girl."

Dante couldn't help but feel a little bitter that they couldn't punish Bancroft. He got his way, the bastard. A little revenge might have been nice.

Viola gave her customary grimace of a smile as she read the article. "Skin turned to ashen leather, liquified eyes and tongue." Sofia cringed at her wife's enthusiasm. "That's the calling card of the soul-eater. It's loose. Not a surprise Bancroft was judged negatively. He was hardly a benevolent soul."

"And I always thought Bancroft's death would be a happy occasion," Iago muttered. "I'm feeling less like celebrating and more like running for my life."

There was a strange electricity in the air as they left the depot. A woman of bolts, gears, and dark smoke rattled toward them. Her hat was a bit askew, and her false hair was a mess, but when there was information to be shared, appearances simply had to play second fiddle. Harriet's skirts rustled wildly as she approached.

"Mr. Wick, Mr. Wick," she cried in her music box tones, and came to a grinding halt before them. Her wheels squeaked and squealed like a distraught pig, and her arms waved stiffly.

Viola scolded, "I made you, Harriet. And still, as always, you greet your father before your mother." Harriet bowed her head in what she had been told was apology.

"What do you expect? I'm the more agreeable

parent, *dear*," Iago said with a grin. "What troubles Miss Harriet?"

"There is much," she said, turning back to her patient father with a mechanical creak and *pop!* "There is a monster here in Boston."

"We suspected there was. That's why we've returned, Harriet," Dante said.

Dante's very presence made her bat her eyelashes and coyly cock her head, but she maintained her focus. "Zero Bancroft is among the dead, but this monster has killed over a dozen supernatural creatures. People say there are other human deaths. They found pieces of one gentleman in the trees outside Delrubio's. His feet, however, remained firmly upon the ground."

Iago winced. "You always had an eye for detail, Harriet."

She nodded squeakily. "The beast is a fearful thing. I hear it has a thousand eyes and a hundred mouths. Boston's demons are alarmed. Vampire families are fleeing." She paused. "A matter of lesser importance: Mr. Grimwood is *furious* with you."

Iago said, "Ah, yes. I haven't received a letter from him in a few days. I imagine he's beyond writing letters at this point. He's just stewing in his own enraged juices, like an infuriated Christmas ham."

"He'll be more than infuriated if Devorog finds him. Where have the attacks taken place, Harriet?" Dante asked.

"All over the city, Mr. Lovelace. This monster has been striking quite haphazardly."

Beatrice nodded. "It's confused, as Harry said. Give it a week, and it will find its stride."

"Fortunately, we don't plan to give it even another day," Viola said. "Thank you, Harriet! Come now, Mr. Lovelace. Our plan of attack is required. We must pull that nastiness from you, and soon."

Dante's melancholia spasmed again as Viola Atchison led him toward the elevated line terminal. He placed a delicate hand to his breastbone. It was not going to come out without a fight.

~

The Atchisons' home possessed a bright floral perfume, which could only have been by Sofia's design. The scent assaulted Dante as he followed her back to a small bedroom beyond the staircase.

Sofia dove into action, peeling the colorful quilt from the narrow bed and tucking the pillow under her arm. "If you ask me, this entire business is far too…"

"Messy?" Dante asked as he leaned against the chest of drawers.

"I was going to say dangerous, but messy is entirely appropriate, too," Sofia answered. "I often wonder what my dearly departed mother would say if she knew where I was today."

"What do you think she would say?" Dante asked.

Sofia laughed. "She would be horrified! Monsters and demons and danger… and no handsome husband!" She smiled as she reached under the bed to retrieve a stack of plain white sheets. She patted the dust out of them. "Mamá had no idea that I was never interested in male companionship. It would have broken her heart."

She plainly dressed the bed, and when she was finished, she clapped her hands. "There you are, Mr. Lovelace."

"Thank you, Mrs. Atchison."

She placed her hands on her hips and said softly, "Your Mr. Wick is planning on abandoning his endeavors with my wife, isn't he?"

Dante coughed. "Ah… I can't…"

"Mr. Lovelace, I know the look of one who wants to run away. There was a time when I frequently saw it in the mirror."

Dante nodded. "Yes. He does. He wants to run away from all of it. Defect."

"And you will follow?"

"Yes." He paused. "Sofia, do you enjoy the path your life has taken? Would you continue to follow your wife, even though it's not what your mother expected?"

"Well, I'm not my mother," she said. "Mostly, I enjoy it. There are times, however, when I wish Viola would just… stop. Just for a moment. A moment to stop and breathe." She gave a delicate shrug. "I will make certain that she is not too harsh on Mr. Wick."

She left to retrieve Beatrice, and Dante settled on the bed. He was surrounded by hair wreaths and small, quaint portraits, and he wondered what life Sofia might have lived, had Viola Atchison not come her way.

Moments later, every one of their party traipsed into

the room. Once again, Dante would not be without an audience.

"You'll cut him open?" Viola asked bluntly.

"No need. I'm going to draw it out magically. Which," Beatrice allowed, as she took one more glance at her grimoire, "might actually be more painful than cutting you open, but I do not trust myself with a blade. Using a blade for ritual and performing surgery are two different matters entirely. I apologize in advance. Are you comfortable?" She sat beside him on a small cushioned chair.

Dante nodded, unbuttoning his waistcoat and removing his necktie. "Just hurry."

"You might want to bite down on that tie, Mr. Lovelace," Viola said. Sofia gave her a gentle smack on the arm.

"I can't watch," Iago murmured.

Beatrice placed a firm hand to Dante's chest. She drew it downward, until she settled just below his heart and above the spot where he had been shot days before. They momentarily breathed in time, and she said, "Here."

"Yes, there," Dante answered shakily.

And suddenly, there she was, as though their bond had been rekindled. Though he knew she had not bound him again, her intent flooded him, sweet like honey but strong like vinegar. She muttered under her breath, words he could not decipher. His melancholia stirred, tensing like a cornered animal.

Pain blossomed in Dante's chest. He drew a sharp breath through his teeth and screwed his eyes closed.

Beatrice's fingers clawed against him. There was creaking somewhere. Floorboards. Iago was pacing.

His melancholia rattled in his chest like a second heartbeat, roaring in his ears. His throat seized.

"I have my hand around it," Beatrice said. "Stay fast."

Dante smelled fire and ash and felt heat within. A shrill scream cut through the air, but no one else seemed to hear it. The Cunningham homestead crumbled. The Lady Liberty crashed to the ground with dozens of souls within. Marlowe, Massachusetts burned because of the pride of two stubborn demons.

And then, there was cold water, a crew who did all they could. A row boat capsized. Lungs filled with icy water, and limbs were caught in terrible suspension. A new flock of women in black dabbed their eyes and ushered their children close.

There were shipwrecks and carriage accidents. There was freak tragedy, and there was perfectly plotted doom. And behind all of it, plucking puppet and heart strings, was Dante Lovelace.

He tried to breathe but choked on decades' worth of misery instead. Tears burned his eyes, and after forcing them open, he saw Beatrice's hand in a tight fist over his chest. His melancholia rattled angrily.

"Hold still, Dante," Beatrice insisted.

There came a sound like bones breaking. *CRACK!*

Dante shuddered violently, dizzy and aching and feeling as though every part of him would split off into a thousand pieces and shrivel.

"Almost there," Beatrice said urgently. He heard scuffling on the other side of the room and strained to see the bright light she had removed.

He must have swooned, and there was darkness, the weight of water on his chest. Dante tried to draw breath, but his lungs were uncooperative. His hearing turned to cotton, and the Atchisons' home seemed worlds away. Couldn't he make it through one day without extreme bodily peril? But it was worth it, he told himself weakly. *This will be worth it.*

Beatrice's open palm pressed to his heart. It started small in his chest, so small he barely felt its presence. Then, a sudden warmth, new and invigorating, flourished inside him. It sang of glowing, happy firelight. It was the spice of autumn air and the warmth of a morning spent in bed. He gasped, lungs full and mind spinning with sudden ecstasy.

And again, he might have fainted. He sure was spending a lot of time unconscious these last few days.

When Dante opened his eyes, Iago stood above him, brushing damp hair from his forehead. "You are a stronger demon than I, my dear," he said. Dante's vision strayed to the small chest of drawers. Atop it sat a jar containing a strange glowing globule.

"How do you feel?" Beatrice asked.

Sofia Atchison grimaced at the ball of light, and her wife wondered aloud whether such energy could be harnessed as a power source.

Dante managed, "Never better."

"Good," Beatrice said. "I would not try to use your

new power just yet. You're weak. It could sap all of your energy."

He couldn't imagine being any more drained than he already was, but he limply shook her hand. "Thank you, Miss Dickens."

Iago smiled and gave him a firm squeeze on the shoulder. "I think the Atchisons would like to place your melancholia in a zoo and charge admission. You needn't tend to Mr. Hawley with me, if you do not wish. I know this city well. I'll be careful."

"No," Dante said. "With Devorog out there, it's not safe. I'll join you." He tried to stand, and the room spun violently around him. He groaned and sat again. "Wait a moment. Just… one moment." He breathed deeply, eyes closed. The second time, he managed to stay on his feet. He might have still been a tad muddy-minded, but Devorog wasn't going to wait for him to recover.

Iago led the way, but Dante paused at the bedroom door. The ball of light hovered in the jar like a trapped firefly in the middle of summer, calling to him.

He grinned to himself. He would never heed its call again.

Viola Atchison promised to take excellent care of the jar and its Hellish contents while Dante and Iago went to fetch the necessary flesh for their spell. Dante felt like a parent leaving his child alone with the nanny for the first time. Still a bit wobbly, he left with Iago.

Mr. Hawley lived in a single rented room in a tenement where dozens of children wailed in their mothers' arms and people hacked and coughed and spit and, occasionally, died where they stood. Not every social issue, it seemed, garnered the same attention in Boston as modernization and progress. The room was all Hawley could find upon arriving in the city. It was a fine room, he insisted. He spent much of his time wandering the streets, anyway. Or, Dante thought, trying to win the approval of his demonic ancestor.

In the cramped and somewhat water-logged room, Hawley sat in the only chair, twiddling his thumbs and occasionally conjuring a nervous flame. The bed creaked beneath Dante and Iago as they sat.

"Let me... I just want to clarify," Hawley said, and he reached for a cup of muddy coffee. "You need me, Mr. Wick."

"Yes, Mr. Hawley," Iago said with a warm smile.

"You need... a hand?"

"Or a foot!" Iago said. "Flesh is flesh, Mr. Hawley, and beggars cannot be choosers."

"And... why do you need my flesh again? I'm not opposed! Certainly not if it means serving Iago Wick, but I'm only trying to suss it all out."

"It is for a very good cause," Dante said.

"I'm certain you've read the newspapers. Something is attacking humans and supernatural beings in Boston. This will help us put an end to it," Iago said solemnly. "You could be a hero, Mr. Hawley. Humans and demons will be saved, and are you not the progeny of both? If this creature, Devorog, exhausts its resources here, it will move on to the next city. Then, the next state, the next country. You can stop this before it becomes truly catastrophic. Most of all, you shall receive my blessing." And Iago stood and gave a grand bow.

Dante nodded sagely, his countenance somewhat disturbed by the large drop of water that fell on his nose from the ceiling.

"And you see!" Iago said, and reached into his jacket pocket. "We even brought a bag! It's perfectly hand-sized. Or foot-sized. We'd even take an ear if you were so inclined, a few fingers. That choice is yours, though I recommend you choose something *good*, Mr. Hawley, something you won't necessarily miss. A man can live without an ear, a foot, a hand." Iago winked. "No one wants to give up his balls to save the world."

~

Dante and Iago left the tenement with Mr. Hawley's left ear in a sack. He was dedicated, but not *too* dedicated, to his cause.

"I really believed he would at least give a hand," Iago said, "but what's done is done, and we have our flesh." He peered into the bag once more and shrugged. "And how are you feeling? You were quiet in there."

"Dear Iago, he was yours to persuade, not mine," Dante said with a grin as they walked back to the elevated line terminal. "I am well. It's only a strange quietude. There's nothing to silence, no little voice to scold. That internal battle has ended. I feel whole."

"And the magic?" Iago asked. "You're going to cast spells and protect us in our future endeavors?"

"That is my plan, more or less."

Iago tisked. "My partner, the witch. …You're not going to start dancing naked in the moonlight, are you?"

"Why? Would you prefer it?" Dante asked devilishly.

"*Maybe.*"

Perhaps it was strange to travel with an ear in a bag, but no one stopped to ask them about the grisly parcel. It might as well have been a dozen pastries, for all they knew. Dante imagined Mr. Hawley sitting and looking out his window, his head packed with bandages, and knowing that he had done something worthwhile for his ancestor—indeed, for the world.

"Did you fetch a hand?" Beatrice asked when they arrived at the Atchisons' home.

"An ear," Dante said.

"What a pity. I was hoping your great-grandson would be a bit more giving, Mr. Wick."

"Please don't call him that," Iago said with a shudder.

Viola, meanwhile, had her arm around the jar containing Dante's melancholia as though it were in for a bit of necking on the settee. She tapped upon the lid lovingly. "Mr. Lovelace, it occurs to me that you have not yet met *Ariel.*"

"*Ariel?*" Dante asked.

"Come to the laboratory," Viola said, and gingerly handed the jar to her wife, who did not show it quite the same affection. "I promised Miss Dickens I would contribute to your plan through more scientific means, whether she liked it or not." Beatrice rolled her eyes. "I have your storm… and something else. I think you'll find it very useful."

Viola Atchison's laboratory happened to be her attic, and Dante cautiously followed her up two flights of narrow, noisy stairs until they reached a door that was *passionately* locked.

"Three padlocks?" Dante asked.

"Of course," Viola answered, retrieving a ring of keys. "Thieves abound, Mr. Lovelace."

Dante cleared his throat as she searched for the proper key. "Mrs. Atchison, I should thank you properly and apologize." She arched a brow. "I have never been terribly receptive to the idea of Iago working alongside a hunter, particularly one who tried to exorcise him. I may have been cold to you. But your ingenuity and, indeed, kindness in these matters at present cannot go unnoticed, and I—"

She placed a firm hand on Dante's shoulder and looked like someone had just asked her to undress in a busy thoroughfare rather than tried to apologize to her. "That's enough, Mr. Lovelace." And she unlocked the door.

The workshop was home to a dozen unfinished gadgets, and the entire room smelled of oil and wood. A metal box with a golden label reading *somnioscope* collected dust in the corner. A scaffolding of beakers and tubes decorated one table, and in the center of the room sat a large, motorized bicycle with a thick and hearty body and brass details.

The machine possessed two substantial wheels and two seats. In the back was a large, metal box with a grate over the top. Something gray swirled within. The occasional puff of vapor seethed from inside.

"Mr. Lovelace, meet the *Ariel I*. It is powered by this box upon the back," Viola said. "I call that box The Tempest. It happens to be how I defeated the sirens on the coast earlier this month. Storms at sea befuddle sirens and draw them out of hiding, you see. So, I created a storm in a box to achieve similar effects. At present, it is my pride and joy, and I shall sacrifice it for your cause. The *Ariel I* handles magnificently. You'll do well."

Dante blinked. "Me? You want me to drive it?"

"Of course. You're an able-bodied minion of Lucifer."

"And what would you have me do with it?"

"It's very simple, I assure you," Viola said crisply. "The Tempest is an engine, using an electrical charge and manipulation of air flow and temperature to create a pseudo-storm within. Miss Dickens's spell requires a storm within a storm. She will conjure a small storm using her magic, projecting it into The Tempest. She will then add the flesh of one part-demon-born and all that other hocus-pocus nonsense the spell requires. The last ingredient will be your Hellish inspiration, a tempting little morsel that Devorog will not be able to resist. The beast will charge for it. When The Tempest senses it has trapped a monster, this grate on top will shift and completely close. The Tempest, though I regret it, will serve as Devorog's new prison.

"Of course," Viola continued, "it does occur to me that the process may have an unfortunate side-effect."

Dante paced cautiously around the machine. "Unfortunate? How?"

"Oh, you know. An explosion. Nothing you don't know all about," Viola said. "That's where *Ariel* comes in."

"I see," Dante said.

"You will speed through the city on the *Ariel I*, the enchanted Tempest acting as your motor. Devorog will follow you, itching for a taste of your Hellish inspiration. Drive to the West Boston Bridge. It's north of here, one third of a mile long. Allow Devorog to get just close enough. When you're just shy of the middle of the bridge, have Miss Dickens pull this blue lever and press this red button here. Then, she will push the box from the machine for Devorog to claim. Or rather, the box will claim the beast. Driving to the middle of the bridge will hopefully give you some space, limiting death and destruction." She peaked her brows. "Simple, yes?"

"Simple?" Dante swung his leg over the metal monster. He took the handlebars in his palms and twisted. Despite his nerves, something felt quite *good* about gripping the machine and settling atop it. "Two questions, Mrs. Atchison."

"Ask."

"What do the aforementioned blue lever and red button do?"

"Wouldn't be very responsible of us to let Devorog sit in wait at the bottom of the Charles River, would it? The box is water-resistant and water-ready. The lever releases The Tempest from the machine. The button activates the flotation device, should it take a tumble over the side of the bridge and into the river." She leaned in and prevented him from fiddling with a switch on the machine's body. "Cultivated power from The Tempest will continue to propel the *Ariel I* for a few hundred feet once it is released, allowing you to clear the area."

"I see. Second question." Dante smiled and removed himself from the *Ariel I*. "In what universe did you learn the definition of the word 'simple'?"

"Hmm. You're lucky you're so charming, Mr. Lovelace. Now! As I said, you're an able-bodied minion of Lucifer. Let's take the *Ariel I* to the street. Come now! Lift with your legs."

~

When the sun had finally set, and Boston was lit only by electric street lamps, Viola Atchison wound wire around the top of the jar containing Dante's melancholia, manipulating it until she had made a suitable hook. She proceeded to hang it over the front door, like a worm wriggling from the end of a fishing line.

Dante sat on the home's front stoop and looked up at it. There had been nights when that small blossom of nastiness had overtaken him entirely. It didn't seem so powerful caught in a jar.

"Have you caught any sign of it?"

Dante turned to see Beatrice settling beside him, her skirts rustling. Her red hair was pinned up haphazardly, and she squinted into the night. The street was quiet and unpopulated. "Not yet."

Beatrice viciously rubbed her forehead. "What a disaster. This has turned into a complete catastrophe."

"I've seen worse," Dante said. "Many citizens are used to sloppy, soul-sucking beasts roaming their streets, anyway. Happens every time there's an election." Dante looked down the empty street, but still, the jar above did not draw out the beast. "I must thank you for performing such surgery earlier today."

"Even that was to clean up the mess I've made!" Beatrice moaned. "I knew, however, why the thought of magic appealed to you. You've been talking about it between yourselves from the start. What will you and Mr. Wick do when you abandon your duties?"

Dante chuckled. "You know, I'm not certain. There is an entire world out there we have never explored." He paused. "Really, I would like to... No, it's foolish."

"What?"

Dante looked bashfully to the glowing jar above him again. It would be so disappointed in what he said next. "I want to learn how to bake."

"Why is that so strange?"

"I want to create things that make people happy. Food does that. Mr. Wick will enjoy it, at least, provided I don't do too poorly. And you, Miss Dickens? What will you do when this is all over?"

269

Beatrice leaned back on her hands. "I plan to return to Clarkton. If I am damned—and I am—I should spend this life happily, with the man whose company I most wish to keep," she said. "Tell me. Is Hell frightening?"

"It's Hell," Dante said frankly. "I believe you know the answer. Perhaps, due to your motive, the scales will still smile upon you." He couldn't entirely put faith in his own words.

"Fate already has," she said, and took his hand. "I am very happy to have known you, Mr. Lovelace. I am just sorry that it was under these conditions."

"*You bastard!*" The front door flew open. Viola Atchison stormed onto the stoop and growled, "I never believed you would actually do this, you ignorant—"

"Spare me your name-calling and outrage, Mrs. Atchison. You only wish me to stay so that you can glean whatever information I have to offer about my supernatural brethren," Iago said, close on her heels. "Well, I have nothing left to give. I wash my hands of it."

"A deal," she said. "We had a deal—two years ago!"

"I do regret leaving you, Atchison, but I must."

"I put my own life on the line for you, Wick, my reputation," Viola insisted. "I went behind the backs of my fellow demon hunters, so your precious Mr. Lovelace would walk again. And now, you simply want to leave! I won't allow it. Not after what I've done for you."

Sofia crept onto the porch and gave Dante an apologetic smile. So much for protecting Mr. Wick from her wife's wrath.

"Done for me?" Iago cried. "Everything you have

done for me has been purely in your own self-interest. And I seem to recall a time not so very long ago when you were passionately trying to exorcise me!"

"Oh, surely we have put that behind us."

Sofia placed a gentle hand on her wife's shoulder. "My dear, you always knew Mr. Wick and Mr. Lovelace were... *independent* creatures."

"They're being foolish," Viola said, "running away on a whim."

"A whim?" Iago rounded on her. Their argument was a passionate dance of words and frenetic feet pacing the front stoop. "I am abandoning my work, the very craft to which I have dedicated myself for a millennium. This was not an easy decision to make."

"You are indebted to me," she barked. "And you once told me, a demon always honors a debt. You can't leave."

"I must, Viola," Iago said evenly and then, softly, "I'm sorry. Perhaps I am not so skilled at being a demon anymore."

"And what does Mr. Lovelace think?" A wounded animal's vigor colored her every word, her teeth and claws bared. "Would he follow Iago Wick to the ends of the Earth and then off the edge into oblivion?"

Dante stood and brushed the dirt from his trousers. "Mrs. Atchison, I do not simply follow. I shall *stand by his side* as he has stood by mine. And while I find this conversation to be a crucial one, perhaps now is not the best time to have it."

"Fine," Viola said, "but when this is over, Wick,

make good on your promise and go."

"I shall. You have my word, and—"

"And if I ever see you again, I will exorcise you where you stand," she said firmly.

Iago's jaw set, and disappointment darkened his hazel eyes. He bowed his head. "I see. Then, the natural balance is restored."

"I understand your frustration, Mrs. Atchison," Dante began, "but we mustn't—"

"Look," Beatrice said softly, and pointed down the street.

A dark and rolling fog seethed at the end of the sidewalk, there one instant and gone the next. It flickered like a candle flame in the night. An angry face erupted from the mist, and then it had many faces, all with teeth gnashing and eyes gleaming. One face had square teeth the size of a head of lettuce and curling lips. Another had rows of shining icepicks in its mouth. It looked like a dozen monsters fighting for dominance, each one peeking out from the fog to observe.

"Devorog," Beatrice whispered, her chin quivering. Sofia gasped and shrunk behind her wife.

A long and slack-jawed face protruded suddenly from the fog and sniffed the air. Drool dangled from its chin, then turned to vapor.

Carefully, Viola reached for the iron shepherd's hook beside the door and lowered the jar containing Dante's melancholia. Dante tip-toed down the steps, and from the bushes beside them, he pulled the *Ariel I*. He turned the crank on the back, and The Tempest began to give a low, bumblebee hum.

Beatrice was frozen to the spot, beholding with wide eyes the creature her father had bequeathed her. This monster…was hers. Fear glistened in her gaze, but beneath that was something else: awe. Dante couldn't blame her. In its guts were the remains, still churning, of every soul, every supernatural creature it had ever devoured. Morgana's people, attacked so long ago, resided in the belly of the beast.

"Beatrice, come," Dante hissed. Her trance was broken.

At once, Devorog turned a thousand eyes upon them, all gleaming and bulging. It hovered, faded out of sight, and reappeared ten feet closer than before. Briefly, the creature solidified and slammed into the ground with massive paws. It admittedly made Cerberus look like a French poodle.

"You know how to drive this contraption?" Beatrice asked quietly as she hurried to Dante's side.

"Mostly. I think," Dante answered. He hung his melancholia over one handle of the *Ariel I* for now, a lantern to guide their way.

The *Ariel I* hummed and trembled as Dante sat in the front. Beatrice sat carefully in the second seat, backwards and facing The Tempest. Her satchel was filled with the spell's ingredients, along with those necessary to conjure the storm: bluebells, oils, and a stray cat's whisker, though Dante couldn't say why. Magic was so bloody arbitrary. *Ariel* shuddered in anticipation of the ride to come. This machine was *excited*.

"Remember," Viola said. "West Boston Bridge."

Devorog stopped, opened four different mouths, and gave a piercing screech that sounded as though it had come from centuries past. A primal chill tingled down Dante's spine. Perhaps *this* was the storm in Iago's premonition, but Dante steadied himself and squared his shoulders. He survived death, after all. *Come on, then, you foul pus bag*, he thought.

And then, the beast raced toward them.

"Go," Iago commanded. "And don't forget to come back!" Viola shepherded Sofia and—with some reluctance—Iago inside.

"That's the plan, Mr. Wick," Dante shouted as the *Ariel I* sped away.

XVI.

Dante drove north. Devorog, for all its gnashing, squelching mouths and otherworldly horrors, followed them like an exuberant cat chasing its supper. The air smelled of rotting meat and ancient grave dust.

"I'm going to start concocting the storm," Beatrice said, her back to Dante's as she faced The Tempest. The electrical storm within the makeshift cauldron simmered in wait.

"Perfect," Dante said, gripping the handlebars of the *Ariel I* tighter. "I'm going to do my best to make certain we aren't killed."

They traveled swiftly over cobblestones, past darkened storefronts. Behind them, the beast gave a bone-chilling roar. This was the sort of creature that made Lucifer Himself uneasy. It had no personality, no human faults to manipulate or exploit. The interests of such monsters didn't go beyond growling, eating, and—their favorite—slavering menacingly. Devorog exhibited the last one flawlessly behind them, and Dante shuddered. It was hungry, and at that moment, he thought queasily, it had set every single one of its bubbling eyes upon his melancholia.

He threw a quick glance over his shoulder. Devorog screeched again, and a handful of those bulging eyes glared from within the charging fog. Bestial legs jutted from the churning, rolling mass and pounded the streets in a gallop. It was gloom personified, its very presence turning Dante's thoughts sour. What if he crashed the *Ariel I*? What if he threw himself at the beast just to end its terrible wailing?

Dante shook the foul thoughts from his head and accelerated. Decades with his melancholia had made him quite adept at silencing such nastiness.

"I call upon the spirits of the earth, the keepers of storm. I call upon you now," Beatrice muttered over and over, as she reached into her satchel for bluebells and whiskers. Eventually, Dante felt a chill behind him, tickling the back of his neck. It was a welcome change from the monster's steaming breath.

With a loud crack, three electric streetlamps shattered in the beast's presence. The machine trembled beneath Dante as he negotiated a tight corner, and excitement mingled with the fear fluttering inside him. Doom itself nipped at his heels. Carefully, he passed an automated carriage filled with unsuspecting humans. Devorog ignored them, opting for the better cut of meat ahead of it.

The streets were sparsely populated with humans who had not gone home yet or had no home to go to. Some of them seemed to see Devorog, shouting about a fog, the smoke trailing the velocipede. Others were oblivious. Dante would later wonder if that had anything to do with the quality of their souls (though he certainly wasn't one to judge).

"We have our storm within a storm!" Beatrice called moments later. "Now, if Mr. Hawley can lend us an ear."

The flesh popped loudly when she tossed it into the brew. Next came a sachet filled with the other ingredients: lavender and mashed apple, a somewhat appetizing combination when not added to fillet of ear.

"Your melancholia, please!" she said.

Carefully, Dante plucked the makeshift lantern from the front of the machine and passed it to Beatrice. He gave the glowing globule one last look. This strange light had poisoned him for over a century and a half, and here he was now, tossing it unceremoniously into a witch's brew conjured on the back of a motorized velocipede.

Dante could say with the utmost certainty that he could never have foreseen this fate. To Hell with it!—and into the brew it went.

Devorog clamored behind them, squealing and groaning in delight. At least, Dante interpreted it as delight. If ancient, slavering beasts had a language, he was nowhere near fluent.

Beatrice said, "We can't be too far from the bridge now. Slow down a bit. Let it get closer."

"Do you know where we're going?"

"What? I thought you knew how to get there."

"I have a vague idea. Go north," Dante admitted. "If we charge headfirst into the Charles River, then at least we'll know we missed the bridge."

"Oh, marvelous!"

They flew past a gaggle of people, stumbling and apparently so inebriated that the sight of a motorized bicycle and a ravenous fog beast charging through the streets warranted only an insipid, "Well, I'll be—!" as they passed.

"Too close! Speed up," Beatrice warned.

"Make up your mind!"

In a great whoosh of wind and fog, they rushed around the corner again—to the left, to the right! The tires squealed, and Devorog bellowed in kind.

"I can see it!" Dante called. "The bridge is ahead!" Rather, *a* bridge was ahead. Dante couldn't be certain if it was, indeed, the West Boston Bridge, but in a situation as harrowing as this, wasn't one bridge just as good as another? He might have taken one made of matchsticks just to get it all over with!

The dull scent of the Charles River wafted toward them. "You know what to do when we're on the bridge, correct?" Dante asked.

"Blue lever, red button," she said dutifully.

"And then, push The Tempest from the back of the machine," Dante said. *Bon Appétit.*

"And if there's an explosion? If the bridge is destroyed?"

It wouldn't be the first time, he thought. *Ariel* would have completely used the power stored from The Tempest at that point. The machine would offer them no good. "Just... *run*."

"Run? Is that all? Oh, if Harry could see me now."

The bridge was upon them. Devorog snapped and gnashed, and Dante gritted his own teeth as the *Ariel I* swayed under the force of the beast's breath. It roared again. It was growing impatient.

The world wobbled around them suddenly. The wind erupting from the monster's mouths was enough to make the *Ariel I* lean sharply to one side. The wheels screeched. The machine grunted as it righted itself again. Beatrice gave a sharp cry, and the vehicle felt lighter. Dante turned back in alarm.

"Beatrice? Beatrice!"

He could see her lying on the ground as the *Ariel I* crossed onto the West Boston Bridge. Devorog's smoke clouded his vision, and the machine wavered again. But Beatrice was mere vittles to Devorog. It ignored her, hungry for the delicacy it had been trailing for blocks.

Blindly, Dante reached behind, fumbling for the lever and button Atchison told him to activate. He threw a glance over his shoulder, latched onto the lever.

He pulled.

It did not budge an inch.

He tried again, and if anything, it seemed even more obstinate than the first time. Dante cursed. Devorog roared. Was that a note of triumph Dante detected in its barbaric holler?

Out of habit, perhaps, Dante reached to where his melancholia once sat. In its place, the burst of warmth he felt after his surgery pulsed in his chest again. This was a new power, one Beatrice had cultivated for years before giving it to him. It tingled in his fingertips. He removed his hand from the lever, focused, and made a quick fist.

Cantrips, utilitarian spells, were the easiest, she had told him back in Marlowe. The lever clicked into place.

"Thank you, Beatrice," he muttered under his breath.

The button to activate the flotation device, fortunately, was not so stubborn. Two bullet-shaped floaters erupted from the sides.

The center of the bridge approached. Bending his arm backwards, so that his palm could meet the side of The Tempest, he tried to push. It was heavy, and driving a motorized velocipede with one hand while a monster chased behind was not something Dante would ever recommend. He shoved again, and this time, the box went sliding backwards. It fell from the *Ariel I*. Dante coasted onward.

Devorog gave the unholiest of screeches and launched itself at The Tempest.

Bright light engulfed the entire bridge, and the beast wailed to the Heavens. Dante brought the machine to a halt, turning back to look while still straddling it. He shielded his eyes and squinted. So far, the bridge was not collapsing, a detail which might have once perturbed his melancholia. Too bad it was playing the role of the main course that night.

Devorog clawed at the air as it was drawn down into

The Tempest. Faces twisted in horror, clusters of eyes bulged, and mouths gaped as though they would swallow the sky. The stench of rotting flesh intensified. It tried to drag itself out again, gaining some ground with two long, seizing hands like naked branches. With a final burst of energy, the monster howled and fought against the spell. But the magic was stronger. It sank into The Tempest as if it were consumed by quicksand.

The beast gave a rather pathetic whimper at the very end. Dante was not moved to pity.

And then, like a shooting star, it was gone.

Spots danced in Dante's vision. The night grew quiet, and all he could hear was his own ragged breathing. He looked to the sky. Boston's smoky haze covered the stars, and he wished he could see even one. Instead, he looked upon a sky of smog as thick as Devorog's nebulous form. He caught his breath.

"Beatrice," he said softly, then louder, "Beatrice!" He abandoned the *Ariel I*, feet pounding the bridge as he passed The Tempest. He would collect it as soon as he found Beatrice and made certain she was all right.

He managed one, but not the other.

Her eyes were wide open when he found her, but she saw nothing, not even a second of Devorog's capture. She was limp and awkward on the ground. Her blood stained the railing behind her, where a sharp metal nub protruded. Her satchel lay open, her grimoire exposed. No magic, no heart, no fire—a woman reduced to mere flesh.

The world was silent and still. Demons did not

escort the damned to Hell. It was a lonely journey, one Dante knew her soul now made.

Few deaths have any real pomp or circumstance, and it was not usually someone dragging himself across the stage, clutching his heart and gasping just percussively enough to garner the critics' approval. True death came in all guises. It didn't care about your cause, your narrative. It took what it wanted and moved on swiftly.

Dante waited for the bitterness in his chest to sing at such tragedy, but it was no longer there. Instead, he felt an icy sickness in his stomach. His breath caught in his throat, and he settled next to her on the cold ground. He closed her eyes for a more suitable, peaceful death mask. Humans liked to imagine death was peaceful. He took her hand, still warm, in his.

Death draped a friendly arm around Dante's shoulder, for they knew each other well.

"We shall finish it from here, Miss Dickens," Dante said softly, and threaded his fingers through hers. "I promise."

He did not think of her home or her father. He was not reminded of her cause or her naïveté. Rather, Dante thought of Harry Foster, living in Indiana, oblivious to the tragedy that had already befallen him. He thought of Belle, of Ellie Malark, their inevitable sorrow.

The living do not truly mourn the dead. They mourn the plight of those left behind. The real victims of tragedy are the survivors. Every catastrophe artist knew that well. It was the weight and detriment thrust upon the souls of the living which Hell desired, and there were no small tragedies.

Dante looked out across the dark river. Above, the indifferent and empty night sky covered the Earth.

~

When the sun was beginning to rise on a new and wonderful and terrifying day, two demons sat in silence in a study on Beacon Street.

The night had been a blur to Dante, a strange nightmare. When he closed his eyes, he could still see the white light of Devorog's capture, the whites of Beatrice's eyes. In his mind, he tried to word the letter he would send to Harry Foster, but it all seemed wrong. He knew death so well, but he'd never had to speak of it in such a way.

Assuming the name of Benedick Hurley, Dante had given the police all they wanted to know: a story about a man and a woman on a motorized velocipede and how the sudden white light in the sky had distracted him, blinded him, causing the accident that took the woman's life.

Demons can be quite persuasive. The police had believed every word, and after he'd given them the name of her brother, Nathaniel Dickens, they'd sent him on his way.

It felt as though she should still be following Dante. But perhaps, he thought as the tender and comforting knot in his chest flourished, she was.

Dante had heaved The Tempest onto the front seat

of the *Ariel I*, released the brakes, and walked it back to the Atchisons' home.

Viola Atchison. There was a name, Dante thought as he took a sip of scotch, that Iago would likely not let him utter for a while.

She'd offered her stilted condolences for Beatrice's death, agreed to find a suitable curator for The Tempest, and let her demon go without another word. Her eyes had been steely, and her lips were thin and pale. Dante couldn't say what conversation had transpired in his absence, but judging by the exhaustion in Iago's eyes, he imagined it wasn't a pleasant chat.

Dante knew now, in the familiar study at Beacon Street, that Mr. Wick turned every moment of the last two years over and around and inside out in his mind. He was an expert at stewing when given the opportunity, and Dante couldn't blame him.

"You don't think she'll betray us, do you? Tell Grimwood of our plans?" Dante asked, shattering an hour's worth of silence.

"No. Viola Atchison only worked with one demon." Iago paused, then conceded, "Or two, if she was feeling particularly adventurous." He exhaled. "She understands why we must do this. She said so. And I think that's what makes her angriest of all."

Dante supposed they were heroes... or something like that. The role of *hero* was a strange one for a minion of Lucifer. But here they were like two soldiers at the end of battle, licking their wounds and mourning their losses.

And yet, the sun was rising.

"Do you need anything?" Dante asked, though he did not intend to move. His body hurt too much for that. He met Iago's warm hazel eyes. His partner's grim countenance cracked in something of a smile.

"Dante Lovelace," he said, and took Dante's hand in his, "I have abandoned Hell and every one of my affairs in Boston to wander into the world with only you at my side. I have all I need."

~

Boston remained mostly ignorant of the evil that had stalked its streets just two days prior. Of course, they were still atwitter about the tragic lightning strikes and the calamity at West Boston Bridge—whatever could that white light have been?—but they certainly didn't entertain the notion of an ancient, soul-eating beast roaming their streets.

It's a sign of the end of days! said one woman atop a soapbox. It very well might have been, had Devorog not been secured. Some humans said they saw the fog that night, shooting through the city, and many more claimed to see the light over West Boston Bridge. More meteorological anomalies, officials said, and the sensible citizens of Boston believed them. Most humans tended to believe anything, no matter how outlandish, if it meant they did not have to acknowledge the unknown.

And of course, the people of Boston talked about the young woman who perished at the bridge. It was a dreadful accident, they chirped to one another, and of course, they recounted every detail the newspaper provided in gossipy glee.

"If I never see another train, it will be too soon," Iago proclaimed at Haymarket Station, suitcase in hand. It had been such a to-do, determining what clothes he would bring with him, and Dante was shocked that he managed to squeeze it all into one case. It was likely, Iago told Dante, that he would never return to his home at Beacon Street.

Dante found it difficult to grasp the reality of defecting just yet. His mind was still on the West Boston Bridge.

Harriet and Osgood Quinn saw Dante and Iago to the train station after Richard Grimwood, somewhat pleased that Iago Wick had played a part in stopping the soul-eater plaguing Boston, grumbled an apology for his bitter letters.

"It was all in jest, Wick," Grimwood had grunted when they met earlier that morning, before adding, "Just never do it again, or I'll remove your spine through your left nostril."

He was not aware that Mr. Wick had killed a human... but what Mr. Grimwood didn't know couldn't hurt him. And so he allowed the troublemaking Mr. Wick one more *short* journey to Marlowe to tie loose ends. He expected Mr. Wick to be back in Boston in three days' time.

Life is full of disappointments.

"Where is Mrs. Atchison?" Harriet asked, her long lashes fluttering in alarm. "Oh, I'm certain she wishes to say good bye."

Iago cleared his throat. "She already has, my dear Harriet. Now," he said, and took her mechanical hands in his, "you will do as she says. Listen to your mother in my absence. Help her."

"Will I ever see you again, Mr. Wick?" Harriet asked.

"Oh, perhaps, Harriet. Who is to say?" Iago said gently.

"And Mr. Lovelace," she said with a shade of mechanical lust in her voice. "Will I see you again?"

Dante smiled. "I hope, Harriet."

"How sentimental," grumbled Mr. Quinn, and he shoved his hands into his pockets. "Stories, Wick. You'll send them?"

"Indeed. As soon as matters settle down, Virgil Alighieri shall write again," he answered dramatically, clutching one hand into a determined fist.

Quinn grunted. "Charming."

They said their final farewells, and Dante looked over the station before meeting the gaze of a gentleman across the way, tall and thin and dour. His blond hair was neatly combed, and his wife, a petite woman with her dark hair tucked beneath a delicate hat, stood at his side.

They watched but made no move to approach.

"Iago," Dante said, and motioned to them.

Iago Wick looked and frowned sadly before ushering Dante onto the train.

Thomas Atchison had returned.

~

Marlowe greeted Dante and Iago like a bitter, old friend.

Somehow the city seemed to know they could not stay there, where they'd met and worked and fallen terribly in love. This city, which had collected a thousand scars from Dante's time as a catastrophe artist, was about to say farewell to its demons. The wind was cold, and the streets were quiet, and the usually warm scent of autumn seemed stale.

Dante and Iago walked the short distance from the train depot to Beatrice's home. Belle waited at the door, a somber look in her green eyes. She already knew, Dante thought, and something made him bow to the crotchety feline. After all, he had come to pay his respects.

He sadly penned a letter to Harry Foster in Beatrice's study, to be sent by Hellish post.

Demons were not accustomed to doling out condolences, and he knew his words could barely soften the blow Harry Foster would feel, but still, Dante chose his words delicately. He read the letter four or five times when he finished. It left him feeling cold, gloomy, and a bit awkward.

It left him feeling *human*.

Iago looked skeptically to the cat. "She wants your attention," he said.

"Or yours. Cats tend to find the person in the room who most dislikes their species," Dante said as he sealed the envelope. He thought intently of Harry Foster and conjured the proper flame from his thumb to send the letter across the country. Fire licked up the envelope, and then it was gone. Dante resolved to visit Mr. Foster again, when the time was right.

A shrill meow interrupted his thoughts.

"What is it?" Dante asked Belle.

She trotted to the bookcase on the far wall of the study before pawing at one book on the lowest shelf. Dante followed the cat, and at her feline insistence, bent to retrieve a tome not unlike every other dusty book of herbs and potions kept there. She trilled and walked in circles at his feet, looking up at him intensely.

He opened the book to find definitions of different plants, the beneficial properties of each and how to boil them properly. Ornately-decorated pages stained with watercolor showcased spells about the moon, the elements. There were pages of sigils, notes about which spells were successful and, more importantly, which were not. "This is her first grimoire." He looked to Belle. "You want me to have this. You can sense the magic she left behind in me."

Belle cocked her head to one side and hurried from the room, tail swishing.

There was such promise on these pages, and he observed the dates. Beatrice had been barely more than a child when she had written the first entries. Dante thought of the magic, however puny, he had used to release the lever upon the *Ariel I*. This was a skill to be well-cultivated. He welcomed the challenge.

"At least the cat was good for something," Iago said. "We should go. Miss Dickens's brother may be arriving soon."

Dante enjoyed the weight of the book in his grasp. There was *good* in these pages.

Before their séance, Beatrice had said, "The greatest tribute to the dead is to continue living. You might not understand that, my dear immortal, but it is true."

He did understand.

"You're right. I feel 13 Darke Street is calling to me," Dante said. "And I believe Lucretia Black will be visiting."

Dante walked once more through Beatrice's home. The smoky smell of spice and potions lingered. Perhaps it would never fade. Lionel Dickens stared at him from above the fireplace, bitter as ever as he waited for his son's arrival. Dante wondered what Mr. Dickens would think of his daughter's final adventure. Probably not much. He looked as though he disapproved of everything but hearty scowling. Dante bowed shallowly and left the parlor.

They encountered Belle at the front door again. She gave a melancholy meow and looked expectantly at Dante. He nodded, bowed once more, and released her.

She shot into the street, and in moments, Dante could not spot her anymore. And he knew she would never return. The affairs of a familiar were strange, secret. They were not to be shared, certainly not with some tailless, whiskerless biped.

And so, the witch's house was empty.

~

Iago's hypothesis had been correct; Lucretia Black was utterly smitten with large hats.

Iago greeted her warmly when she arrived at 13 Darke Street. She wore an enormous chapeau not only because it was fashionable, but because it hid her face. Feathers fell across her countenance, and she looked like an actress or an opera singer or some other woman few respectable people would want anything to do with. She was as full-bodied as a good wine, and she clothed and cradled every curve with care.

Lucretia took Iago's hands in hers and smiled her sunny smile. "My dearest Mr. Wick. Clever, naughty Mr. Wick. It has been an age since I last saw you."

"Indeed, it has been too long," Iago said, "but until now I could not afford to be seen with wanted criminals."

"Oh, yes. I am a regular Robin Hood," Lucretia laughed. "And Mr. Lovelace, as beautiful as ever."

"I am nothing compared to you, dear lady," Dante said.

"That is true. You're skin and bones," she said. "Mr. Wick, you need to fatten him up. He'd blow away in a stiff wind."

She walked into the parlor and observed each of the stuffed beasts, the post-mortem photographs on the wall. She consumed the intricate details of each of them before speaking. "I love death, don't you? There is something truly beautiful about it."

"Spoken like a true catastrophe artist," Dante said, but couldn't bring himself to agree.

"I have not worked in such a capacity for nearly a century now, thank you," Lucretia said, utterly transfixed by Montgomery, "which is precisely why I'm here."

Dante offered to fetch Lucretia a cup of tea. She opted, instead, for bourbon.

"Before I say another word," she said as she sat, drink in hand, "I must know that you have made your decision. Abandoning one's ties to Hell is terribly invigorating, but incredibly dangerous."

"We know," Iago said, and looked to Dante for assurance. "And we are certain."

She placed a gloved finger to her lips, chewing coyly upon the tip. "How romantic."

Lucretia Black spent the next hour telling them of the life of Mama Florentina, a matchmaker in a small town in Italy. She spoke of Grizelda, a fortune teller in England. Then, there was a figure known only to humans as The Woman in the Wood.

They were all Lucretia, lives she had led since defecting.

"It is important that you move and move often. Go to places lacking local demons. It is much easier to hide from a demon who wanders from town to town than one who is in residence. Have a story prepared for any demons you encounter. Most will not think of betraying you even if they do discover you have defected. However, it is Hell's watchmen of whom you must beware."

"The watchmen," Iago muttered. "Are they prevalent?"

"Not overly, but if they suspect you have defected,

they will hunt you until they can drag you back to the pit. They are relentless and very difficult to lose," Lucretia said, and she finished her bourbon. "I've encountered a few."

She continued, "You may want to search for vast, empty places to stay, though you could make a case that it is easiest to hide amongst other people."

And as she spoke, Dante's skin began to crawl. He gave a long breath through pursed lips, and Lucretia noticed his anxiety.

"You are nervous. You should be, Mr. Lovelace. But it is so very rewarding, to live for yourself alone," Lucretia insisted. "No responsibility to Hell. You will be free."

"Of course," Dante said weakly.

"I know a man in New York. If you truly wish to pursue this adventure—and it is an adventure—then I can put you in contact with him. He is wise in all things relating to these matters. He will assist you with travel, tell you which regions are safer than others. Yes, Mr. Harker will be invaluable to you," she gushed, "a tremendous help. And he's so cute, too."

Dante nodded dully, dumbly, and wished he could think of anything to say. He was suddenly forced to recount in his mind every happy memory he had made in Marlowe. It was not all death and catastrophe.

"Mr. Lovelace?"

Lucretia and Iago looked at him with worried eyes. Dante realized then that he was sinking his nails into the upholstery of his chair.

"Yes?" he squeaked.

Iago cleared his throat. "Dear Lucretia, will you excuse us for one moment?"

They left Lucretia with a fresh glass of bourbon and walked into the dining room just off the parlor. Iago shut the door behind them. "Nervous? Second thoughts?" he asked.

"What gave it away?" Dante said. He found himself looking to every little detail of the room: the table where they had shared meals, the rug with a treacherous corner that wouldn't stay down.

"Dante, you needn't do this if you do not want to."

"But, Iago, you—"

"I would continue in Boston. Perhaps it isn't as dreadful as I make it seem," Iago said, and he placed a hand to Dante's cheek. "I have been known to exaggerate."

Dante breathed in the home's familiar perfume. "I want to defect. But it would mean leaving this town, this house. Someone very dear to me bought me this house."

Iago chuckled. "Indeed."

"And then, he was very perturbed when I filled it with dead things."

"Well, the murder of crows outside the bedroom is a bit much, don't you think? And all the bones and the pelts and the..." Iago cringed. "That is not the point. I bought you this house so that you would have a place all your own in this world. You had always drifted from place to place. I wanted you to have a home. But we have grown. And now, I believe we could have that home anywhere in the world, if we wanted. But if you do not feel similarly, then I shall thank Lucretia for her time and send her on her merry way."

There was no melancholia to comment bitterly within Dante now, and he listened intently to that silence, a silence which, in its vast emptiness, beckoned him toward freedom. Marlowe had been his home by Hell's choosing. 13 Darke Street, though he loved it so, was a museum and monument to his tenure as catastrophe artist. Every glassy-eyed beast and decoration of bone were to be relics now. If he stayed, pretended as though nothing had happened, his melancholia would be restored. He would work for Hell once more. And that, he decided, certainly wouldn't do.

Yes, Dante thought. A change of scenery would do him wonders, but still, those old familiar ghosts of Darke Street embraced him.

"You would abandon your chance at freedom, all because I am a silly, sentimental fool?" Dante asked.

Iago shrugged. "More or less, my dear."

Before Dante could say another word, there was the sound of crackling fire, the smell of burning paper. A parchment bearing the seal of Brutus Eldritch appeared upon the dining room table. Word traveled fast. Hell knew Dante was rid of his little witch problem, and they had work for him.

He looked blankly to Iago.

Iago's eyes softened, and he reached to pick up the letter.

"Wait." Dante furrowed his brow and focused on the letter, hand outstretched. He dipped into the power he could now call his. He focused on its invigorating warmth, his intent. What, after all, did Dante Lovelace most desire? And after trembling for a moment, the letter hovered. Iago stared as Dante drew the parchment through the air... and dropped it happily into the small fireplace. It burned away, and Dante smiled. "It no longer concerns us, anyway."

"You're certain?" Iago asked.

"I will join you under one condition," Dante said slyly.

"Yes? And what is it?"

"We must take the vulture with us."

"What?" Iago croaked. "Montgomery? He's enormous!"

"I think he'll be a fine addition to whatever house, hut, cabin, or apartment we find ourselves occupying!"

"I don't know about that," Iago laughed. "We can't keep Lucretia waiting. She likes to remind everyone of how busy she always is." He paused before opening the door. "You are certain, Dante? I couldn't live with myself if I knew your heart was not wholly committed to this endeavor."

Dante smiled. "Yes," he said firmly. "Let us see the world, Iago Wick."

ABOUT THE AUTHOR

Jennifer Rainey is a sometimes-writer, sometimes-folk singer from beautiful Central Ohio. When she's not busy writing, you can probably find her perusing antique malls or watching classic horror films.

You can learn more about Ms. Rainey's writing at www.jenniferraineyauthor.com